Lies

BASED ON TRUE STORIES

Courtney Soling Smith

quarrier
press

Charleston, West Virginia

Quarrier Press
Charleston, WV

10 9 8 7 6 5 4 3 2 1

Library of Congress Control Number: 2016957213

ISBN 13: 978-1-942294-09-2
ISBN 10: 1-942294-09-3

Book and cover design: Mark S. Phillips

Printed in USA

Distributed by:

West Virginia Book Company
1125 Central Avenue
Charleston, WV 25302

www.wvbookco.com

ACKNOWLEDGMENTS

With special appreciation to all of my friends in Greenbrier County who supported me throughout this project but especially to my readers: Lori Evans, Elyse Gerard, and Jim Talbert as well as the original cast of my play, *The Incident at Elmhurst*. Their voices and personalities helped me develop the characters: Danny Boone, Donna LaValle, Mitch Scott, Bob Fisk, Andrew Vass, and my daughter Brennan, the inspiration behind Sally and reason I began writing plays. Nine year-olds can, indeed, speak like Sally. Additional thanks are due to my husband, Roger, who for so many years listened to me as I read passages and talked about the story.

TABLE OF CONTENTS

Lies: Based on True Stories
Anderson Family Tree
May 1863

Charles Anderson (1790-1846) --m-- Grace Weikle (b.1798)

Margaret (b.1820)
--m——Henry Arbuckle

John (b.1822)
--m——Dreama Woods (1828-1861)

Samuel (b.1848)   Sarah "Sally" (b.1854)
--m——Caroline Feamster (b.1844)

Orpha (b.1819)
--m——William McClung

Lyman (b.1840) Solomon (b.1842) Rebecca "Becky" (b.1851)

CHRONOLOGY OF EVENTS

1792 – Theodore McNeil is born a slave. After the McNeils die, he is emancipated and changes his name to **Hartwell** Finney.

1798 – **Grace** Weikle is born in Lewisburg, WV.

1816 – Charles Anderson moves to Lewisburg and marries Grace. The couple live in a home in downtown Lewisburg.

1819 – **Orpha** is born to Grace and Charles Anderson.

1820 – **Margaret** is born to Grace and Charles Anderson.

1822 – **John** is born to Grace and Charles Anderson. No other children survive to adulthood.

1824 – Elmhurst is built.

1838 – Orpha marries William McClung.

1842 – The Anderson family moves to Elmhurst.

1844 – **Caroline** Feamster is born.

1845 - Margaret marries Henry Arbuckle.

1847 – John Anderson marries Dreama Woods of Richmond.

1848 – **Samuel** is born to Dreama and John Anderson.

1854 – Sara "**Sally**" is born to Dreama and John Anderson.

1856 – Caroline comes to Elmhurst.

1861 – Dreama dies of diphtheria. John marries Caroline.

1862 – After the Battle of Lewisburg, John joins the Confederate Army.

1863 – Union scouts under the leadership of **Sergeant Ephraim Richter** invade Elmhurst and take the Anderson family hostage. They are accompanied by **Captain James Tobin.**

PROLOGUE:
A Letter From the Editor

April 16, 1890

Honorable Mrs. Wheelock G. Veazey[1]
1731 P Street NW
District of Columbia

Dear Madam,

A week ago, I had the privilege of meeting your husband at the Grand Army of the Republic's[2] commemoration of the twenty-fifth anniversary of General Lee's surrender. I introduced myself to the Colonel as a fellow Rutlander who had served under his command in the Sixteenth Regiment. His graciousness in this brief encounter emboldened me to visit him at his office yesterday afternoon. My aim was to present him with a token of my appreciation for both his fortitude and his acuity that saved not only the lives of many soldiers, but also the integrity of our great nation.

The gift I offered was a bottle of 1863 Taylor Vintage Port. Your husband insisted that I share a glass with him. One glass became two, and two soon became three as I related the circumstances of how I came into possession of such a fine bottle of pre-phylloxera wine[3]. When he left my company, late for his evening meal and slightly inebriated, he asked me to write to you as an affidavit for his whereabouts that afternoon. Although this initial entreaty was made in jest, he then requested in earnest that I correspond with you to recount my interesting tale. He explained to me that in your work with the Women's Relief Corps, you have been collecting personal accounts from the War Between the States in regard to the affects upon women and home life. Accordingly, you would find the story of interest.

Please note, I was not a participant in the events that I shall relate to you. I am merely the chronicler. The following is what transpired:

In July 1863, I mustered out of the "Valiant Vermont Sixteenth;"[4] yet, rather than return to my boyhood home or re-enlist as so many of my patriotic comrades did, my desire to continue to serve my country impelled me to seek employment in our nation's capital. Drawing on my secretarial skills, I began working as a clerk for the United States Department of State. Two years later, I received an unusual directive from Ambassador Franklin G. Tobin, recently returned from a three-year posting overseas. My charge was to investigate an incident that occurred on May 22, 1863, at Elmhurst, a property in Greenbrier County, Virginia, now the state of West Virginia. The request was made by the Ambassador at the behest of his brother, Captain James E. Tobin soon to retire his commission.

Since this investigation was not an official matter of state but rather of a personal nature, I was provided by Captain Tobin with a generous allowance of seventy-five dollars, took a week's vacation at month's end for my initial enquiries, and ventured south. Upon arriving at the property in question, I discovered that the estate had, as I suspected, been a casualty of the War. The land was now a field of dust where only the most noxious of weeds survived. Trees that had once encircled the homestead had been cut. Their stumps reminded me of tombstones. The house itself was boarded up—whether to protect it from further damage or to conceal its violation, I could not be certain.

Behind the house were mounds of debris, the charred remains of outbuildings. The most predominant of these ruins had presumably been a barn. One tattered wall stood amid a pile of rubble and ash. Next to the destroyed barn, there appeared to be a grave. I walked near to verify my conjecture. The size and shape of the disturbed ground gave every indication that this spot was indeed some person's final resting place. As the grave was unmarked and a great distance away from the family burial plot located at the southeast corner of the property, I assumed that it was not the grave of a family member, but of a soldier, buried hastily and unceremoniously. I knew of many men who had met the same fate.

Although these images were all too common in areas directly affected by the fighting, what I witnessed next was not. As I perused the ruins of the barn, a metallic object caught my eye: a CSA buckle. It had somehow survived the conflagration that had incinerated the barn. Upon closer inspection, I saw a most gruesome sight: the burnt remains of the soldier wearing the buckle.

Who was this man? How had he come to such a fate? Why had he been left among the wreckage and not been afforded the decency of a burial? And who was buried in the unmarked grave nearby?

With these pressing questions, I traveled to Lewisburg, a small town some three miles west of the Elmhurst property, where four of the eight known surviving witnesses to the incident resided. I was only able to speak with two, Mrs. Orpha McClung and Mr. Hartwell Finney. The aged Reverend John McElhenney declined to speak with me, insisting that he could have nothing to add to Mrs. McClung's most lengthy testimony, and a Mrs. Margaret Arbuckle refused to talk with me on the grounds that I was a "Thieving Yankee."

I then journeyed to Richmond, Virginia to visit with Miss Sally Anderson who was boarding at a female seminary operated by Mrs. James W. Pegram[5] and her stately yet affable daughter, Miss Mary Pegram[6]. These two intrepid educators were endeavoring to bring some refinement to their plucky, eleven year-old charge. Although only a child at the time of the incident, and not much more at the time of my interview, Miss Sally remembered the events of the day in astonishing detail and added, as you will discover, an interesting flourish to the tale.

My vacation time exhausted, I returned to the District of Columbia and corresponded with Sergeant Ephraim Richter of New Albany, Indiana. Although he provided me with a written account of the incident that explained his position in copious detail, he also expressed in no uncertain terms that he was averse to our meeting in person.

My next course of action was to locate Mrs. Caroline Anderson. The instructions I had received from my employer insisted that her testimony was essential. Finding the elusive woman proved quite difficult. Mrs. Anderson had left Greenbrier County directly after the incident, leaving no trace of her whereabouts. My only clue was a common reference by three of the witnesses to Mrs. Anderson's skill as a dressmaker. Through dogged determination and a bit of good luck, I was eventually able to locate her in Annapolis, Maryland where she was employed as a seamstress. I traveled there in late November.

We met in her home, a cozy, little row house that she shared with two war widows and their many children. One of the women, a Mrs. Abigail Mundy, confided in me that all of these denizens would have been destitute were it not for Mrs. Anderson's beneficence. Yet, no hint of financial or emotional strain was evident in the furnishings, food, attire or countenance of any of the residents. All were lively and cheery and the scene reminded me of the idyllic prints on family life one sees these days in popular magazines. Every family member appeared engaged with an industrious occupation, be it school lessons or chores.

Mrs. Anderson's hospitality was exceptional. I arrived in the early morning and did not depart until late in the evening. She invited me to join her and her housemates for the most exquisite meal I ever experienced. It was truly a sensory delight. Every last detail was attended to from the elegant arrangement of table settings to the splendid presentations, aromas, and tastes of the dishes, (the perch served with an apple butter bourbon sauce was outstanding!).

Mrs. Anderson herself was markedly different than I had expected. From the references made about her by the other witnesses, I had assumed that she would be plain, of advanced years, and lacking social graces. Imagine my surprise when I was greeted merrily by an attractive and genial young woman of only one and twenty years! Because she was an unassuming woman, slender with soft brown hair and bespectacled eyes, I could easily understand how one might overlook her beauty (her most remarkable features were her full lips and her soothing, melodic voice). I quickly began to suspect that my mission had more to do with amorous affairs than the two dead soldiers I had discovered, and especially not in regard to compensation for improper loss of property, as I had been led to believe by Ambassador Tobin.

After dinner, we retired to her parlor and chatted by the fireside. I was enchanted. With the warmth of the fire, my full stomach, and Mrs. Anderson's genuine attentiveness, I enjoyed such a sense of comfort and contentment that I found myself rambling on all manner of topics. I am certain that during our visit, I told her more about myself than I learned of her.

Accordingly, I greatly regretted leaving her company that evening and journeying back north to my own sparse bachelor's abode.

The final witness to the incident was none other than Captain James Tobin himself. In late December 1865, Captain Tobin arrived here in the District, and I met with him in his rooms at the Ebbitt House[7]. The hardships of war had clearly effected a detrimental change to his personage, for he was no longer immaculately groomed, as the other witnesses had described, and he appeared to be suffering from melancholia. As we shared a bottle of that divine, aforementioned port, I presented him with my findings, and he then provided me with his account of the events.

Enclosed is a transcript of the oral testimony that I documented from these six witnesses. As I was unaware of the purpose and nature of my assignment, I originally applied my knowledge of shorthand and chronicled their words verbatim, as would a court recorder. Several years ago, with an aim to creating an historical record, I spliced the accounts together to construct a cohesive narrative that conveyed what in my opinion was the true story. I also attempted to make the account easier to read by adding chapter titles to each section as one sees in contemporary fiction. However, please be advised that although I did edit the narrative slightly to avoid redundancies, improve the flow, and accentuate the richness of the speakers' accents and diction, I did not alter it to suit feminine sensibilities. Consequently, several components remain that are inappropriate for polite society. I hope you will pardon me for including these elements. Your husband insisted that you would be neither shocked nor offended.

I look forward to meeting you at the Decoration Day[8] cycle races next month. Colonel Veazey informed me that you will be awarding ribbons. As a member of the Columbia Athletic Club[9], I am entered in two of the races (the ones reserved for men of advanced age). I would be doubly honored to secure a prize from you.

Yours most sincerely,
Geo. L. Scarborough[10]

Chapter One:
In Which a Battle is Fought, a Husband is Lost, and a Bridge is Burned
As Told by Caroline Anderson

If you want to know the truth about what happened, then I will need to tell you some lies. Otherwise, you will not be able to puzzle it all out. What I mean to say is: the information you are after cannot be told in one simple story since it is actually many tales stitched up with each other. Years and years of happenings all came together in those hours to make us all act the way we did. You cannot separate the one from the others. It is just like making a quilt. All of the squares sewn together make one big picture; but, each individual square is a picture of its own, and the pieces of fabric in each square are also pictures because they are filled with the memories of what the scraps of cloth had been before they were worn out and cut up into bits.

Now, when you hear the word "lies," you probably think of falsehoods and dishonesty. But, where I was raised up, "lies" are just what folks call stories, and you should know that the people in the hills and hollers of western Virginia are the best liars you ever heard. Most of the tales these folks tell are based on true happenings, gussied up to sound better. They are typically about silly people and strange critters that are half animal and half man and very often the stories are about ghosts. Mountainfolk sure do love a good ghost story! But, the fibbers do not talk much about the War. Not yet, anyways. Some of the war stories are too sorrowful to speak of so soon; others just do not seem to make no never-mind.

The incident you asked me to tell you about falls into both of these categories and more. Parts of what happened are painful to remember, while other parts were all too common and seem trifling to recall. You see, there were always soldiers about in Greenbrier County during the War: one month there were Confederate troops, the next there were Union. For those of us just trying to get on in our lives, we never concerned ourselves with the color of their coats. What truly mattered were their empty bellies and the meanness of their spirit that came along with their fight to survive.

And then, some of what happened is of an intimate nature and not the sort of information a woman should share with anyone let alone a stranger. You have asked me to take my gloves off and tell you all that happened on those two days. A proper woman would never do so; but, as I suspect you already know, I am no proper woman.

So, I will tell you what happened. I am not certain why you believe it signifies, but I would like to be helpful to you. Perhaps it is because you have gone to such considerable trouble to find me here, and also because after spending this day with you and hearing your stories, I have come to trust you. More likely, it is because my sister-in-law has a tongue a mile long that wags at both ends. I am for sure that everyone from Richmond to Charleston has heard her version of the incident and I would finally like to tell my rendering to set the record straight. I cannot say I am proud of everything I did; but I am not ashamed neither.

To tell you rightly about that incident at Elmhurst that you asked after, I will have to begin exactly a year before it happened, in May of 1862, for that is when I lost my husband, and none of this ever would have happened if he had still been with us. You see, there was a battle in the streets of Lewisburg. I cannot tell you much about the battle itself, because, thankfully, I was not witness to the fighting and never did become familiar with all of the bloody details. However, I do know that Union troops were occupying the town, and a Confederate force decided to run them out. Only trouble was, the Rebels were green and the Yanks were seasoned. I also heard tell that the Confederate leader had got hisself liquored up the night before. People said he was so dizzy that morning that he had to hold onto the grass just to lie down on the ground.

The actual battle lasted only an hour or so. At daybreak, the anxious Confederates, who were occupying the high ground on the east side of Lewisburg, began firing on the Union encampment on the hill that marks the west end of town. When the Union soldiers heard the cannon fire, they threw aside their morning meal, grabbed their jackets and guns, and charged down one hill and up the other toward their foe. As was to be expected, several cannon balls went astray during the bombardment. One went through the wall of the Methodist Church and another came right down the chimney of the Carey mansion. Poor Widow Carey and her three young daughters had to work franticly to keep their home from burning down.

If I had been living in town, the experience would have terrified me. As I heard tell, bullets flew past houses and across the fields. Cabinet doors blew open and everything rattled inside and out. The noise must have been deafening. Even as far away as we lived, I could still hear the cannons boom and I was frightened for the safety of my family and our home. Yet, most of the folks that I heard talk of the day seemed to take the matter in stride. At that time, they were still acting like the war was merely a sporting event. A few more years of fighting was needed before people had enough sense to hide in their cellars when battles were being fought on their property.

In the end, thirty-eight Confederate soldiers lay dead, sixty-six were wounded, and nearly one hundred were captured. Thirteen were lost on the Union side, including at least one who was shot by a bushwhacker from inside a home as the Union troops headed back to their camp. The identity of the bushwhacker was never discovered. Rumors quickly spread that the town of Lewisburg[11] would be burned to the ground if the man responsible for the cowardly killing were not surrendered. Troops searched every home looking for the culprit. I do not know what they were exactly looking for. I cannot believe they expected to find the triggerman hiding in a house behind a curtain or something of the sort. More likely I suppose, they thought that the presence of armed soldiers rummaging through private homes would distress someone enough to spill the beans as to bushwhacker's name. It did not.

Directly after the battle ended, the defeated Southern troops withdrew to the East and walked right past Elmhurst, kicking up a storm of dust as they went. They were a sorry lot, but still much better off than they were to be in a year's time. At this point, they were only wounded by bullets and lost pride. They had not yet been entirely devastated by the carnage, starvation, and disease as they would come to be by the end of the war.

My stepson Samuel sat on the bench at the upstairs hall window that faced the road, watching intently as the soldiers passed on by, his face full of longing and frustration. I knew that when he looked out, his eyes could not see the bedraggled march of defeat but only glory in the bravery of military service. He wanted nothing more than to be with them. Samuel was just fourteen years at the time and, as typical of his age, he had the body of a man but the face and mind of a boy. He was desperate to prove his manhood. I joined him at the window and rested my hand on his shoulder in an effort to console him. He shrugged it off. At his time in life, he wanted the men's company and not comfort from a woman.

Following his gaze, I was horrified to see Sally, standing cheerfully on the bottom brace of the fence[12] with her head peeping through the pickets. She was hanging on with one hand and waving at the soldiers with the other. "Oh dear God," I gasped. Gathering up my skirts, I ran like there was no tomorrow to get her out of harm's way. My heart was beating wildly. What if the Union troops were in pursuit? She could find herself smack in the middle of a skirmish and be hit by a stray bullet. I was going so fast that I do not remember my feet touching a single stair tread; still, it seemed like forever till I was out the front door and had her in my arms.

Sally was only eight years old at that time. But she was not like any eight year-old you have ever met. Everyone was convinced that she was a changeling. One reason for this belief was on account that she was an uncommon reader for her age: gobbled up books most adults could only nibble at. But, for all the knowledge she gained through reading, Sally was like every other young child in the sense that she was short on real life experiences. Like her brother, she could not see that the troops had been beat. She acted as though this retreat were just another grand parade, same as she had seen when the men of Edgar's Battalion[13] first headed off for service.

I gathered up my skirts and ran as fast as I could to get her out of harm's way. But, Sally was so intent on staying right where she was, I had to hook one of my arms around her waist and use my other to pry her hands off the fence, finger by finger. Then, I lifted her up and folded her in half to contain her squirming. Her nose was practically touching her knees. Still, she wriggled like a fairy diddle[14] caught by the tail, shouting all the while, "No, please, Caroline, no! I cannot miss the procession. They need me." I was lucky that she was such a bitty thing or else I would never have made it to the front door without dropping her.

Once we were safely inside the house, I sent her to her bedroom. Not in the least bit resigned to her fate, she climbed the stairs slowly, dragging her legs like they weighed one hundred pounds apiece. She kept glancing down at me to see if I would take pity on her and change my mind. I watched her carefully to be certain she did not try to sneak on back outside. When she reached the landing, she stopped and looked down at me with the most mournful expression, her lower lip quivering. I smiled and blew her a kiss. She pretended to catch it in her hand, grinned back at me, and then ran the rest of the way up the stairs.

When I heard her bedroom door BLAM shut, and was assured that she and Samuel were out of danger, I turned, only to see my husband John Anderson standing in front of me. At forty-two, he was in the prime of his life and was one of the most respected men in the county. People would often say that Mr. Anderson was, "The very picture of a man," meaning they thought that every man should look like him. He was tall and broad-shouldered with dark hair, dark eyes, and a full, dark beard. All of the Andersons had especially dark hair and eyes excepting Sally. She was towheaded and fair-skinned which only added to the rumors that she was not of human making. Even though I was Mr. Anderson's wife and I looked upon him every day for seven years, I always avoided his gaze and never really got a good look at him. Sad to say, I cannot describe to you any other characteristics about his face or form that distinguished him. As I recall, he looked like all the other Confederate leaders whose portraits appeared in the newspapers.

I do remember well, though, that Mr. Anderson was a measured man: never did any more or less than what was expected. His father had been a lawyer, so he became one too. They worked mostly with wills and the like. As I understood, Mr. Anderson earned most of his social standing from a particular court case that involved a burial spot, property lines, and a dispute between the Tuckwillers, one of the most affluent families in the area, and the Honakers[15] who were poorly off. I do not know the specifics of the case, but I do know that afterwards Mr. Anderson was invited to fancy gatherings and became a member of the Freemasons. He also made quite an enemy of the Honaker family; but that didn't make no never mind to him.

As he took a step closer to me that morning, my mouth went dry. Mr. Anderson was wearing the uniform of a Confederate lieutenant. "I am leaving," he announced. I was stunned. Ever since the trouble began he had made it clear that he wanted no part of the argument, did not believe in the Cause. When they passed the conscription law, he had been pleased that men over the age of thirty-five would not be drafted and said that if they lowered the age limit, he would pay for a substitute. I wondered when he had begun to think differently, and who had sewn this smart, new uniform for him without my awareness.

I knew better than to question him about his change of heart, but he could see that I was dumbfounded. "Do not look so surprised," he said. "Every able-bodied man is fighting. It is not about a cause anymore. It is about honor. I am not a coward, and I will not be made a prisoner just to save my home. I have crossed the Rubicon." With that pronouncement, he threw his pack and his gun over his shoulder and headed out the front door. Perhaps I should have broken down and cried, grabbed on to that man and begged him not to leave. That is what the loving wives do in books I have read. I suppose at the very least, I should have said something of comfort to him like, "Take care," "God bless," or "come home to us." But, at that time speaking up was not in my nature, rearing, or training. Why, I was so meek I would not even have said, "Boo" to keep a rattler from striking me!

So, I just stood at the door and watched him join the fray. Oddly, no one greeted him or made any sign to recognize his joining up with them. They just marched on like a procession of ants, doing what they were designed to do without any thought to the matter. Mr. Anderson's bright, new uniform marked him from the others and allowed me to follow him for a bit. It was like watching a breadcrumb that the ants were carrying. Mr. Anderson never looked back at me or toward his homeplace, and after he took that first turn in the road, I lost sight of him forever.

Before I had time to worry about what Mr. Anderson's leaving would signify, my attention was turned in the opposite direction by the strong smell of smoke. The last of the Confederate men had crossed the bridge[16] over the Greenbrier River, so they set it afire to keep the Union forces from pursuing them. The bridge belonged to Mr. Hunter. The most recent time he raised the toll on that bridge, people joked that someone was likely to be so angry as to burn it down. And now it was ablaze, set by someone whose concern was to live another day and not whether he could afford the six and one quarter cent toll.

My first thought was to run and grab a bucket, but then I came to my senses. It was useless for me to try to put out the fire. The blaze was already too great for a lone woman to combat, and I would receive little useful assistance in fighting the fire from my remaining family members: two young children and a mother-in-law who only exerted herself in the giving of orders. Besides, I was certain that the three of them were all shut up in their bedrooms, lost in their own fantasy worlds. Samuel would be reading his newspaper articles about the war heroes, Sally would be playing some odd game with her dolls, and my mother-in-law would be fixing her hair or applying a face cream, unaware that her baby boy had just left her home. None had any care for a bridge. I comforted myself with the thought that now that Mr. Anderson had left, there was nothing in Lewisburg that any of us needed in the near future. We could certainly cross down at Hoke's Landing until a new bridge was built.

I was in no hurry to go inside and tell my mother-in-law the bad news about her son's leaving. I knew that she would become hysterical. So, once again, instead of doing anything helpful, I just stood by and watched the bridge burn. It was a sorry sight. The bridge, poor thing, seemed to moan in pain as pieces dropped from its sides. They landed in the rushing water with loud sizzles. The flames grew higher and higher and soon the roof fell in. Then, with one final groan, the bridge buckled and fell into the river. When there was nothing more to watch, I braced myself for the troubles to come and went back on inside the house.

Like everyone else, we carried on at Elmhurst as best we could without a man in charge. New routines were established, and soon again we had a sense of normal. There were deprivations, and fear was always hanging over our heads like mosquito netting, but we made do. That is, until the following May, a year to the day Mr. Anderson left home, when the Union soldiers arrived ... and our lives changed forever.

CHAPTER TWO:
Wherein the Heroine is Forewarned of the Coming Danger
As Told by Hartwell Finney[18]

How old am I? Don't rightly know. But my memory's still strong. I remember that day at Elmhurst you aksed about. I remember it well. It were a day I could never forget—for some bad reasons and some good.

Back then, I was handyman to the Andersons; did odd jobs, bits of carpentry and the like. Missus Anderson done hire me some years back. Her son Mista John Anderson was a big man, but no good a'tall at fixin' things. He couldn't even hammer a straight nail. Then, after he, Mista Anderson that is, joined up, there was more chores to do. Missus Anderson liked to keep up appearances. If you'd've looked around at the other places in the county you'd've seen hard times, but the roadway into their place was as smooth as water—no potholes nowheres, and that lawn of hers was as neatly mowed as it had ever been, and you would've had to look real close to see that things wasn't as they had been. But not no more. No, Sir. What a difference a day can make!

No one ever aksed me about my age before. I'm 'bout seventy I suppose. You could go down to the courthouse and find out. They keep records down there on all the free men of color[17] 'cause before the war, we had to register down at the courthouse if we

10

wanted to live in Greenbrier County. Otherwise, we had to go—had to leave the county. They gave you papers to prove you was free. Them papers told your age, how tall you was, and if you had any scars or marks and the like. You had to carry them papers about y'self every time you left your house. But, they wouldn't give them papers to you if you didn't have a job. You had to have a job or you had to leave. That is why I had to keep on workin' and workin' even though I was rightly too old for work. I kept on workin' 'til I learned about the E-man-cipation. Then, I figured it was right for me to enjoy a rest.

Was I always free? No, Sir. I was born into slavery. Didn't never know who was my mama or who was my daddy. Like the little baby Moses, I was left in a basket on the doorstep of the McNeil place. Now as I understand it, there weren't hardly no free men of color in the county way back then; so, Mista McNeil supposed that I had come from one of the slaves who worked on a neighbor farm. He aksed around to see who I belonged to. Nobody claimed me. So, Mista and Missus McNeil decided to keep me and raise me on up.

Bein' that they had never had no chillen, they raised me up almost as their own—notice, I says almost. I had a room of my own, ate at the table with them, had family-type chores to do, and every night Missus McNeil would see to it that I said my prayers the way I should. Missus McNeil was a very religious woman, a Methodist. In the South, you understand, there is two Methodist churches for white people: the Southern Methodist Church and the Methodist Episcopal Church. They split over the issue of slavery, the one believin' in it and the other not. Missus and Mista McNeil went to the Southern Methodist Church that do believe, do believe in slavery. Only, unlike many other folks, the McNeils also believed that we should all bear Christian good will t'ward each other no matter if you was white or colored.

They always treated everybody kindly, all the time, 'specially me. Mista McNeil, he never took the switch to me unless I had done something to deserve it. But it weren't no whippin' like slaves got, it were like the type of lickin' a child of your own would get for doin' somthin' naughty or ornery. He'd send me up the hill to cut a water branch off one of the apple trees. Now the whole time I'd be walkin' over to get that branch I'd be thinkin' on what was to come and I'd be frettin'. A course, Mista McNeil never did hit me hard a'tall. The dread of what was a comin' was always worse than the switchin'.

I lived almost like any white child did back then. 'Cept if ever we had visitors, I had to make myself scarce. I used to think that the McNeils didn't want me 'round at those times because I was only a child and they wanted to do a-dult business. I didn't know it was 'cause they were afraid of what other folks would think if they saw how familiar we all was. You understand, I didn't know I was diff'rent when I was a child. I didn't never leave the farm, so I didn't know about slavery. I knew my hide was brown and theirs was white but I didn't know that was important. We raised brown cows and white cows, brown chickens and white chickens, and no one treated them any diff'rently based on the color of their hides and feathers.

As I got on up, though, like ten or eleven years, I kept aksin' how come I couldn't go huntin' with Mista McNeil or go to town with the two of 'em, 'specially when they went on in for church. They kept on sayin' it was on account of that I was too young. But, a course, I thought I was a man a'ready. I didn't like their explanation. So I kept after 'em—tryin' to prove that I was an a-dult. Fine'ly, Missus McNeil sat me down and she explained to me 'bout slavery. She said she was mighty sorry, but it was the way of the world, and there was nothin' she could do about it. Once the cat was out of the bag, they no longer tried to keep me away from the truth. I went to town with them; but, when we were out in the public, I had to act like their "boy" instead of their son.

After that time, the McNeil's didn't really treat me no diff'rently, but I sho' felt diff'rently about them. Since they was my mastas now instead of my daddy and my mama, I knew that I didn't have to obey them anymore. It were my choice. The Bible says in the Commandments that we's got to honor and obey our father and our mother, but not our mastas. No, Sir, we don't. That Moses he done rise up against the slave mastas and set his people free. That's what the Bible tells us. Now believe you me, I wasn't in a mind to have no uprising—I am no prophet like Mista Moses. But, I made up my mind at that time, that I was always gonna' keep myself free in spirit, and that I was gonna help other people to feel the same way whether their hides be white, brown or red. Can't nobody make no one a slave if his soul is free.

Now, Mista and Missus McNeil were old folks when I came on into their lives. He died right as I was truly becomin' a man and Missus McNeil, she died when I was a young man. Bein' that she had always treated me almost like a son, she set me free in her will and gave me one half of her prop'aty. She left the other half to her church. They used the money to fancy up the church and pay the pastor a higher salary.

First thing I did when I was free by the law was to get me my own name. Even though the McNeils was kind to me in most ways, I didn't want to be Theodore McNeil no longer. Couldn't stop but 'sociating that name with slavery. So, for my Christian name I chose "Hartwell" which is what my friends always called me anyways. Then, I aksed my girl Nellie what family name she'd like to have when we was married in the church, and she chose "Finney." She wouldn't never say why. Took that secret to her grave, but it was fine by me.

After all the years I'd worked for the McNeil's, I figured I was genuinely en-titled to some a that money they gave me and I accepted the rest of the money as a gift of kindness. Don't really know where the money woulda gone had I refused it. Prob'ly woulda been a big fight and the lawyers would have got most of it. I used a portion of the money to buy a home and get myself started in life. I bought me a four-acre plot of ground and built a fine wooden house on it, right here in Lewisburg. I live just up beyond the courthouse where the other colored folk live. Kept the rest of my money hidden safe. Couldn't use it to free no other slaves, no I couldn't. Missus McNeil wrote that into her will too.

Couldn't put it in the bank. No, Sir. Couldn't trust the bank workers. I do believe most bank workers are Sunday Christians which is to say that they break all of the Commandments Monday through Sat'aday. Why, I had a colored friend who put one hundred and twenty-five dolla's in the bank. When he tried to get his money out, they insisted that it was only one dolla' and twenty-five cents! Nothin' he could do about it.

Yessir, my memory is strong. I remember that mornin' you's aksin' about I came to work early 'cause I needed to see Miz Caroline right off and tell her some important news. We colored folks always knew the happenin's befo' most a the white folk did—'cause most a the white folk thought we was so dumb that they could talk right in front of us 'bout anythin'. Like we didn't speak the language or somethin'. So, a course, whenever there were danger, we would spread the word to each other. Since I had news of a danger to Miz Caroline, I hurried to get to work that mornin'.

Usually, took me 'round an hour to walk to work, maybe more when the weather was mean. Only way to get to Elmhurst is down the Kanawha Pike. Now, at that time there still weren't no bridge 'crost the river cause the Southern soldiers had burned it down. Mista Henry B. Hunter[19] was op'rating a ferry instead. He was the o'rignal owner of Elmhurst, you see, but lived in another house 'crost the west side of the river. I did some work once for Mista Hunter and he took kindly to me, so he let me 'crost without payin' the toll each day. I said I was goin' to help him build a new bridge, covered just like the old one, but he said that 'til the war was over, he didn't want to chance havin' someone burn it down agin, and that the ferry would be just fine.

But the ferry weren't fine a'tall. Last year ago in the spring, when the river was real angry with flood, a cable broke and his son, Mista Henry F. Hunter, he was drownded. It were such a shame too with all the boys who were dyin' in the war to have another young 'un die.

Now the river she were swollen that day too, but she weren't angry and I was in a happy mood 'cause the day was startin' out nice and warm—so warm I didn't have to make no fires in the house. That was a big relief to me because that ol' house had eleven fireplaces and Missus Anderson didn't like the cold none so she kept most of 'em goin'—from the beginnin' of October to the end of May. That made for a heap a work for me, choppin' and stackin' all the wood.

And it were dry out too that day. Norm'ly, the fog would be so thick on the river that time of year that you'd be soakin' wet for walkin' through, just as if it were pourin' down the rain. So I was very happy that mornin' indeed. I was a whistlin' as I walked. I'm a fair good whistler too. I make up my own tunes.

When I got to the Anderson place, I slipped through the side fence rails, past t'ward the kitchen. I never bothered with the front gate, it being locked and all. As I came down the path that day, I remember I saw Mista Samuel a workin' in the garden. He didn't like the garden work—thought he was too much a man for it. Thought men were supposed to be the hunters and the money makers and that gardening and home chores were for the women and chillen. But, mosta the men I knowed would be right proud

to be workin' a beautiful garden like that one. It was filled full
up with beans and corns and taters and melons and pumpkins.
Even that year with all the snow and cold weather we'd had, the
Anderson garden was startin' off just right.

"Mornin', Mista Samuel," I said. He nodded at me kinda sour
and kept on workin'.

So, I went on in to the kitchen and I was surprised 'cause
the room was empty. Norm'ly, Miz Caroline would be in there
workin' hard. But she weren't, and that meant the day was a'ready
turnin' crooked. I was worried. I called "Miz Caroline?" She didn't
answer. So, I started to search for her.

I looked in the dinin' room and the parlor and the lie-bry and
fine'ly I got to the room downstairs that the Andersons used to
keep for guests. Used to be a right many people would stay with
them, but no one had visited since the war began. Miz Caroline
had turned the room in to a sewin' room. She was makin' dresses
for other ladies so she could help earn money for the family. The
room was always filled now with black cloth and dresses in all
stages and sorts.

The door was closed as it always was. So I rapped on it. No
one answered. I rapped again. Still no answer. So, I slowly and
carefully opened the door. The curtains were still drawn shut and
it were dark in that room. It took my eyes a moment to ad-just, but
then I sees Miz Caroline.

She was lyin' on the bed with her day clothes on. That wasn't
like her a'tall. She was the busiest person I ever seen. I wasn't sho'
if she was dead or alive or sick or what. "Miz Caroline?" I said.
She didn't answer. So very carefully I moved closer to the bed.
"Miz Caroline?" I said agin. She still didn't move. I crept up closer
and saw that she was a' breathin.' So that meant, a course, that she
was sleepin'. Didn't know why she was sleepin' in the day!

Now norm'ly I wouldn't bother with anybody sleepin,'

'specially a white woman. I would just go right on my way. Some folks say it is bad luck to wake a person sleepin'. I don't believe it one bit, though, 'cause I am not a superstitious man. You prob'ly have heard that colored folks are superstitious, but I don't believe that coloreds are any more superstitious than are white people. I believe it comes down to learning, 'specially learning of the Good Lord's ways. Ignorant people are apt to believe in charms and the like and educated people are not. Now, I cain't read, but I've gone to church faithfully since I was a young man and I listen carefully to what my pastor says. Ain't nothin' in the Bible about good luck or bad luck or charms a'tall.

As I said, normly, I'd have turned myself right around and marched out a the room, but not with Miz Caroline. She was almost like a daughter to me. She was always kind and respectful and thoughtful to me. She made me special foods I liked to eat when I was at the Elmhurst house and sent me home with food for the weekends when I wasn't. I did whatever I could to ease her burden and she was most appreciative. Also, she liked to listen and I like to talk, so we made good company for each other. Miz Caroline always aksed after my health and about my friends in the neighborhood and at church.

I was married for forty-fo' years 'til the Good Lord took my Nellie on up to Heaven. Never had no daughter b'fore. My Nellie and I had five sons to survive on up to manhood. The only one who is still livin' now is livin' up North, in Ohio. I haven't seen him in forever and that's a sorrow for me.

Now, as I was sayin', I was worried 'bout Miz Caroline sleepin' in the day. Thought maybe she was sick. So, I gently nudged her arm a bit and that woke her. She sat up real startled. "Everythin' all right, Miz Caroline?" I aksed all worriedsome. A course, Miz Caroline weren't angry with me for wakin' her as most folks would be, just the other way round.

She said to me in her sweet, singy voice, "Oh, yes, everything is fine. Thank you for asking. I was up late sewing is all." Then she thanked me for wakin' her 'cause she knew Missus Anderson would pitch a fit if there weren't fresh flowers in all the vases before she came on down for her breakfast. Miz Caroline got up, excused herself, and went to get busy. She looked all right to me so I didn't worry no more about that.

Just then, the clock at the end of the hall struck seven times, and that made me remember that I had somethin' to tell her. So, I followed her and I told her, "I have news, Miz Caroline; bad news. The Northern army's on its way here agin. And they be burnin' and lootin' all the homes 'long the Kanawha road." She sighed real deep but didn't stop her workin'. I kept on. "Be here in about fo' or five days they 'spect."

"Well, there is not much left for them to take," she said, but she was wrong.

"There's always more," says I. "It's dangerous times, Miz Caroline. You need to git out a here."

Then she stopped her neatenin' and sighed agin. "You are right, Hartwell. Of course you are. How long before they arrive?"

"'Bout fo' or five days is all."

"That gives us a little time at least to get packed up. Do you suppose it will be any safer in town?"

I shrugged my shoulders. "At least they'd be others around to protect you some from the danger I'm talkin' about. Round here, you are too far away from your neighbors. Wouldn't no one hear your screams."

Miz Caroline bit her lip and nodded her head as she thought hard on the matter. Fine'ly she says, "You are right, Hartwell. I will speak to Orpha and Margaret about the situation to see if we can stay in town with them for a while." Missus Orpha and Missus Margaret are Missus Anderson's daughters, you see,

Miz Caroline's sisters-in-law, that is. Then she says, "But, I do not want to frighten anyone, especially Mrs. Anderson. If she were to hear tell of it, she would be so scared she might do a great harm to herself with worry. I will start packing up the clothes and other necessities tonight after dinner when no one will be paying me any mind. I should have everything ready by the day after tomorrow. Then, I will let on to Mrs. Anderson and we can leave without too much commotion."

This sounded like a fair enough plan. So, I let it be. But it didn't stop me from frettin'. I knew those soldiers were comin' soon and that they would be real trouble for that girl and her fam'ly when they got there.

CHAPTER THREE:
Which Includes a Surprising Premonition, the Truth of Which Will Be Later Revealed
As Told by Sally Anderson

I am delighted that you have asked me to recall the events of that day. You should know that I have already written all this down in my memoirs. They are entitled *The Life of Sarah Anderson, a Precocious Child Whose Wisdoms and Gifts Were Appreciated by Neither Her Family nor the Citizens of Greenbrier County*. Thus far, I have one hundred and ninety-four chapters written. It is a fascinating story.

I am also writing a history of the United States of America. In it, I explain many things, like why the Pilgrims really left England, and what really happened to George Washington after he cut down the cherry tree. You do not actually believe that little George escaped punishment after he cut down his father's favorite English cherry tree just because he told the truth, do you? I can certainly attest that an experience like that has never happened to me. I always get punished even if I tell the truth—which is not that often—but I am most definitely telling you the truth now!

The morning of May 22, 1863 began like any other. I was on my way to begin my daily chores when… I discovered that not even my own little bedroom was safe from the terrible violence of the War. You see, poor Emmeline Brewster had gotten herself into trouble the night before and that morning she had come to me for help. Emmeline was a spy for the Confederacy and had been relaying valuable information to a certain dashing Captain named William Walsh. Unfortunately, the jealous socialite Prudence Meeks had ratted her out and Emmeline had to flee for her life. She mounted her faithful steed and was galloping away when a Yankee fired at her. The shot hit her in the arm and she was terribly wounded—the ball had gone right through her, leaving a gaping hole. If it were not for all the blood gushing out, you could have seen straight through. Fortunately, Emmeline was able to escape and arrive to the safety of our home. But, she was living on borrowed time. Her wounds needed to be dressed; she might even have required an amputation. Also, she had to gather supplies and go into hiding, for the Yankees would certainly be in pursuit and there was no telling what they might do to her. I began to bandage her arm.

That was when Caroline entered my room. Like most adults, Caroline thought that Emmeline was just a ragdoll and started to chastise me for "playing" rather than doing my chores. I tried to explain to her how serious Emmeline's condition was and that she was a very important spy for the Cause. But Caroline said that the only cause I needed to concern myself with was making sure my family had enough to eat.

I was going to stick out my lip and give her my sad puppy dog face—it always made her take pity on me, but found that I could not. Poor Caroline was trying ever so hard to make things right. Instead, I shrugged and skipped on out of the room. Just as I was leaving, I saw Grandmother entering the hall. I raced down the stairs as fast as I could.

Chapter Four:
In Which Despite the Danger, An Elegant Dinner Party is Planned
As Told by Caroline Anderson

When I saw my mother-in-law standing at her bedroom door
I stood at attention and lowered my eyes as I had been instructed
to do when I first came to Elmhurst. Even after all the years I had
spent with Grace Anderson, I was still as jumpy as a long-tailed
cat in a room full of rockers whenever she came around.

Mrs. Grace Anderson was somewhere between sixty and
seventy years old. Although she insisted on a grand celebration of
her birthday each year, she never divulged her age. Years of careful
grooming had made that woman look much younger than she
was, a fact she delighted in. She kept a copy of *The Arts of Beauty
or Secrets of a Lady's Toilet*, by Madame Lola Montez[20] on her
dressing table and followed its commandments much more closely
than she followed the Bible. Her other source of information
and inspiration was *Godey's Lady's Book.*[21] She bragged that she
had every copy of that monthly since they began publishing it in
1830. As a result, she had two armoires in her room: one for her
extensive collection of clothes and accessories, the other stacked
full with nothing but *Godey's*.

Grace Anderson never missed an opportunity to relate to us all
a compliment she had been given. She was tall and slim and had

an air about her that could convince you of her beauty. She refused to allow anyone to call her by her surname—said it made her sound like her mother-in-law who she openly despised. Her friends and relations all addressed her by her Christian name. Since I was not permitted that intimacy, I continued to call her "Ma'am" when she was in hearing—and Mrs. Anderson when she was not.

That morning, she was wearing an elegant nightgown and had her hair styled as if she were dressing for a grand party. "Caroline? I thought it was you making all that noise," she barked at me.

"Good morning, Ma'am," I replied courteously.

"Good morning? Hardly. You would not say so if you had a night like I had. I could not get a minute of sleep."

"I am sorry to hear that."

"And do you know why I could not sleep? You should. Do you know what day it is today?"

"Friday?"

"Not the day of the week, you ninny, the date. Tomorrow will be exactly one year since Johnny left... and the day I shall die."

"You are feeling poorly?"

"Yes, I am feeling poorly. As you well know, I have been sick to death every day since Johnny left. You do not know what it is like for me. You have never lost I child. I have lost five... and six grandchildren. And I am certain that I shall never see my only son again. No word from him, or about him, in a year. He must be dead."

Mrs. Anderson had a tendency to make a mountain out of a molehill, but in this instance, she was being truthful. From the moment my husband, John Anderson, had walked round that turn in the road, no one had seen or heard a thing about him. Mr. Anderson's law partner had worked feverishly at our family's behest to uncover any information on my husband's whereabouts. He was not listed among those serving and he was not recorded among the heroic dead. Only thing I could figure was that something terrible had happened, the Confederate army did not want to account for it, and someone had the power to keep it all hushed up. Maybe one of the Honaker boys in his battalion had finally made good on their threats to do him a harm. It would not do much for the morale back home to admit to lawlessness among the ranks.

I never did discuss this speculation of mine with anyone, and I wondered if Mrs. Anderson thought the same. If she did, she never let on.

Mrs. Anderson walked over to the window and stared at the empty road. With a dramatic sigh, she sat down on the bench and continued her harangue. "No husband, no son, and no hope of ever having a man in my life again. I may as well die. I have nothing to look forward to now. All of the men who have not gone off to fight are decrepit."

I tried to soothe her. "What about your daughters and your friends?"

"What about them? They are all widows. There is nothing for us."

I started to protest. She stopped me in my tracks. "Do not argue with me. What has gotten into you today? You are never this sassy."

"Yes, Ma'am," I replied in deference.

She stared out the window again and thought for a moment as I waited patiently. Finally, she stood and faced me. "Send for my brother, Doctor Simpkins, not that it will do any good; and Reverend McElhenney. And fetch Margaret and Orpha while you are at it. Their bickering will not do much for my health; but, they should be by their mother's side in her time of need." With that command, she turned her back to me and went into her bedroom, locking the door behind her.

The clock was striking eight as I went outside to do Mrs. Anderson's bidding.

I should tell you a little about that clock, for it was quite a beautiful piece of workmanship and central to life at Elmhurst. It was a long case clock and stood over seven feet tall if you included the decoration on top: a golden eagle perched with his wings outspread on top of a golden ball. The cabinet was a fine mahogany and there were two fancy columns alongside the hood. The dial said it was made by Slade of Trowbridge, England. It was an eight-day clock, but Mrs. Anderson used to wind it every Sunday night, right before she went to bed. She lived by the clock. Things happened at precise times in her house. Every member of that household knew what time it was every waking hour and probably in their sleep as well.

Before coming to Elmhurst, I had never really seen a clock. Country folk like us did not own them. We got up in the morning and got busy with our daily routines and I suppose everything happened at near the same time each day. The necessity of keeping to Mrs. Anderson's schedule was a big change in my life and it put a great amount of pressure on me until I got the knack of it. At first, the ticking was like a scold telling me to "hurry up, hurry up," and it made me awful nervous. Later, as I grew accustomed to it, the sound became more like a drum, helping me keep to the beat of my life's rhythm.

Before I could leave for town that day, I wanted to apprise Hartwell of the situation. At one time, Elmhurst was maintained by six servants; but at that time, Hartwell was the only one being called a servant on the place. He was a tremendous help to me and, until then, he was the only man who I had come upon who did not act like I was their inferior. I called him my guardian angel because not only was he willing to be of assistance in any manner, including some women's work around the house, but also he had a full head of bright white hair that looked like a halo when the sun shined down on it. He was as old as the hills. Even though years of hard work had taken their toll on his body in regard to his appearance, he still had the strength of a lion and the skill of a master carpenter.

I found Hartwell repairing the roof on the hen house. Sally was with him, throwing breadcrumbs to our few remaining chickens. They were still laying eggs, but at their ages, they would soon be done with that and in the cooker. I explained to Hartwell and Sally that Mrs. Anderson was feeling poorly and that I was going to town to fetch Dr. Simpkins, Reverend McElhenney, and my sisters-in-law. Sally became excited.

"Will Becky be coming?" she asked.

"I expect so," I answered. Then I realized that I would have to figure out something to feed everyone.

"Oh, Miz Caroline, we don't have much," Hartwell fretted. "And we are clear outta apple brandy. Won't be able to make no panada.[22] An' the Good Reverend he sho' do like that panada. Looks forward to it every time."

I told them not to worry, that I already had the starter going for the salt-risen bread, and that I had just finished sewing some dresses. The money the dresses brought would be enough to buy a few treats.

"Huzzah, a party!" Sally cried.

"Mo' like a last supper," Hartwell reminded me, thinking about those advancing troops.

Sally did not understand Hartwell's remark. "What do you mean?" she asked.

Hartwell knew better than to frighten her. "It is troublesome times is all," he said.

"But there is no danger just yet," I added to reassure her. "So tonight, we are going to have a wonderful dinner, a family dinner, just like we used to have before your daddy went away."

"Are you sho' that's what you want to do?"

"Absolutely. This may be our last chance to be together as a family in good spirits before things get worse."

"Well then, what can I do to help, Miz Caroline?"

I thought about all the preparations, what little I had in the pantry, and what I would need. Thank goodness it was spring. "If it is not too much trouble, could you look for some mustard greens and morels?"

"No trouble a'tall. The mustards will take a little huntin' but I saw a patch a' them mushrooms just yesterday."

"Thank you, Hartwell. And Sally, I would like you to go and wait upon your grandmother. Please, please, stay in her room and do not leave until I return."

She pouted. "Oh my, this is surely the worst punishment anyone ever gave me!"

Chapter Five:
Wherein We Learn of the Dangers that Plagued the Community
As Told by Orpha McClung

I was not the first born, but I was the eldest surviving child of Grace and Charles Anderson.[23] Father was an attorney and Mother was the daughter of the clerk of the courts. He moved to Lewisburg from Richmond in 1816. One day, he caught sight of Mother as she was delivering a dinner basket to her father at the courthouse. He was instantly smitten. They were married three months later and built a fine brick house in town on the corner of Lafayette and German streets. This is the home in which my siblings and I were raised. Mother and Father did not move to Elmhurst until 1842, four years after I was married. My betrothal was not as romantic as Mother and Father's, but I was married at the most appropriate age of nineteen. My sister Margaret resided at Elmhurst for three years, as she was not to marry until 1845 when she was twenty-five years of age and at serious risk of being an old maid.

My wedding, naturally, was a most elegant affair and very traditional. I wore my favorite blue evening dress. Blue, you should know, is the proper color to wear for weddings being that it is the color of purity like the Blessed Virgin. For the celebration of my nuptials, the women of our family prepared a genteel and tasty dinner that was enjoyed by everyone. Everything was done in perfect moderation and no one left the party feeling tipsy or full as a tick or anything of the sort.

Margaret's wedding was another story altogether. It was fashionable. When she finally married, she married "Money," plain and simple. Following the example that Queen Victoria[24] had set at her wedding to Prince Albert, Margaret wore a white lace-covered, satin gown. She had it made especially for the wedding. Her father-in-law hired servants to help prepare and serve the wedding feast, including four of the Stantons' slaves. I thought the entire affair a bit profligate; but, Margaret has always had those tendencies, and since she married into wealth, it was expected of her to have a grand affair.

My sister's full name? It is Margaret Hazel Anderson Arbuckle. My full name is Orpha Ruth Anderson McClung. Margaret is my younger sister but only by a year—almost to the day! You have not met her yet? Well, aside from our statuesque height, raven-colored hair, and a family resemblance to each other in the face, we two could not be any more different if we tried. I, as you can see, am healthful, full-figured and womanly, while she is thin as a rail. I am serious and frugal while she is flighty and extravagant. My brother, John Emanuel Anderson, is, or rather was, I suppose, a year and a half younger than Margaret, two and one half years younger than I.

You should know that when we children were growing, our father and mother had many social obligations. They were always busy with extremely important society matters. As the eldest, it befell me, when I was of an age, to watch over my siblings. This task I undertook with solemn purpose. You see, Mother had three more babies after John. My two youngest brothers died before their fourth birthdays and another little sister died as an infant. Although I was only a mere child at the point of their untimely demises, I was mature for my age and felt an oppressing sense of helplessness. Their deaths affected me so deeply that I resolved to protect my surviving sister and brother from all harm.

Naturally then, I never had time for dolls and the other trifles of childhood. The needs of real life babies occupied my playtime. I was always the practical one, the one exposed to the uglier details of life. This sacrifice allowed my surviving sister and brother to enjoy a blissful childhood. Be assured, I do not regret my position and I do not resent either of my siblings for their fortunate circumstances. You do what you have to do for the ones you love. That is all there is to it.

At first, my concern was for their physical and spiritual well-being. I made certain that they ate and slept well, kept themselves tidy, and said their prayers. But as we matured, I became equally concerned for their social well-being. I have known a few people who became social outcasts due to their ugly behavior and it was a sorry life for them, I will tell you that. I would not wish it upon anyone, let alone someone I cared for. Can you imagine the horror of never being invited to parties or dinners, having people whisper about you when you walk down the street, or worst of all, that no one will sit beside you in church? Why, it is too much to bear!

That is why, even after we were grown and had families of our own, I continued to look after my sister's and my brother's concerns. They often had their heads in the clouds and needed the assistance of someone with two feet firmly planted on the ground. Many of my friends in the community are the same and they have come to rely on me in a similar manner. That is the reason I keep track of all the comings and goings in town. Having full knowledge of a situation is the best method of avoiding harm to yourself and others. For example, I would never commit the grievous error of complimenting Mary Perrine on her hair because I have learned that she had a high fever, went completely bald, and must wear wig. If I had not been apprised of this situation by my dear friend Mrs. Bell, I might have said something hurtful to her in the way of being kind because she truly looks much better with the wig than she did before with her God-given hair that was stringy and could not hold a curl. Naturally, it was my duty to warn others before they, in their ignorance, said something gravely wounding both to poor Mary and their own social standing—the Perrine's throw the most wonderful soirees; it would be tragic indeed to be left off the guest list.

Also, and perhaps more importantly, had I but known that my brother John was planning on joining up, I could have told Mother about his plans and she would have found a way to keep him safe at home. But no one in this town knew his mind—no one. That is for certain.

So you see, I have always kept my eyes and ears open at all times. My careful observations are the reason why I saw Caroline ride into town that day you are asking after. I was sitting at my bedroom window when I saw her in the cart. You would be amazed at what I have seen from that window! I live right on Washington Street, the main street that passes through the town. It is a fine wooden house with well-appointed rooms. Everyone says so. Margaret's house is, naturally, a large and showy brick house located on Jefferson Street, the other main thoroughfare.

Well anyway, I knew if Caroline was coming to town, it concerned me. Consequently, I got my hat and my shawl, and I went after her.

Lewisburg, I am proud to say, is the county seat. The town itself is situated on the low ground between two hills flanking its east and west sides. Some call it the "saucer village" but I do not think that is a very refined name and I wish that it would not be repeated so often. I have a sister-in-law who lives in Charleston. She acts like Charleston is London or Paris or something wonderful and she looks down her long, pointy nose at us. But anybody with an ounce of common sense who has been to both towns knows that Lewisburg is much nicer than Charleston or any other town in this new state for that matter. The only reason Lewisburg was not chosen to be the capital is because we preferred to stay with Virginia and the South. We did not even send delegates to the convention in Wheeling that created the state: West Virginia, what an uninspired name! I would have chosen something more profound, if they had asked me, which they certainly did not.

Anyway, in our lovely town, we have six stores, three churches, the courthouse and its library, the newspaper, three taverns—but they are genteel taverns, and, of course, there is the Academy. The Academy was founded by one of our most prominent citizens, Reverend John McElhenney, the pastor of the Presbyterian Church. He has been our pastor ever since he arrived in Greenbrier County near over fifty-five years ago, and, at the time of that ghastly incident we are discussing; he had recently celebrated his eighty-second birthday. He was with us that horrible night at Elmhurst.

Reverend McElhenney started the Academy shortly after arriving in the area. It was the first brick building in Lewisburg, the Reverend's home being the second, and the academy stood in a grove of walnut trees across from the Presbyterian Church. Most of the students were from the area, but others came from the surrounding counties and from Pennsylvania. For a few years there were even five French boys who came all the way from Lou-i-si-ana. But, the Academy suffered from the changing times. When the War began the teachers were left with no option but to close the school. Then, during our military occupations, both sides utilized that fine building, either as a barracks for their soldiers or as hospitals for the wounded.

But, I do digress. Now where was I? Oh yes, I was telling you about the morning of that dreadful incident. Well, when I got to town, Caroline was in Mr. Creigh's dry goods store. That is spelled "C-r-e-*i*-g-h" but pronounced "C-r-e-e," and refers to Mr. Thomas Creigh[25] and is not to be confused with his son, the martyr David Creigh, who was arrested by the Yankees just a short time after our incident. You see, a vile marauding Yankee soldier had come into Creigh's home and was stealing from him, and that dastard might have even done some insults to his wife Emily if Mr. Creigh had not happened along the scene. Entering his home, he heard an altercation between his wife and the villain during which the scoundrel used some of the most unsavory words you have ever heard that I shall most certainly not repeat. Naturally, Mr. Creigh charged up the stairs to confront the desperado. The two struggled with each other, and as they tumbled down the stairs, the soldier's gun accidentally discharged. It was an accident for certain, but the rogue was seriously wounded. Mr. Creigh knew, of course, that he would never ever get a fair trial in a Yankee courtroom so he decided to hide the body and hope that no one would miss that despicable man. Mr. Creigh took an axe and made certain that the marauder would never threaten anyone ever again. Then, he put the soldier's body down a dry well with the help of one of his slaves.

Unfortunately, that slave told the story to his cronies, and, some months later, when some Yankee troops arrived in Lewisburg, those other slaves told an exaggerated tale to the Yankees. Naturally, Mr. Creigh was arrested. They held a trial for him, but in a military court. Now how was that poor man to get justice like that? Also, it violated his Constitutional rights, it did, to try a civilian in a military court. But, as you most likely have not been told, this practice was common during the War. President Lincoln did not care a whit for Constitutional rights.

He suspended habeas corpus and other such atrocities. Yes, even though I am a woman, I know all about habeas corpus and the Sixth Amendment. I always liked learning about the law. I do not mind saying that I could have been a lawyer just like father and my brother, if I had been a boy.

Well then, the Yankees hung that poor martyred man who was just protecting his home and doing what anybody else would have done. I tell you this story to help you understand how horrible those Yankee soldiers were to us and how much danger we were in that day. You just never knew what a Yankee might do to you. They were also going to burn Mr. Creigh's home, Montescena, but for some unknown reason, it was spared. However, the Yankees did burn the glorious hotel at Blue Sulphur. All that remains of that fine establishment is the springhouse. Burn, burn, burn, alas! There was so much senseless burning during the War.

But, where was I? Oh, yes, Caroline had gone into Mr. Thomas Creigh's store to sell some dresses. At this time, the establishment was being operated as "Bell and Montgomery," but those of who had been in the community long enough, still referred to it as "Creigh's." Many was the newcomer who found himself befuddled by our references to names of yore! Creigh's store, Bell and Montgomery that is, sold ready-mades as well as fabric. (I do not believe they had a store in Charleston at that time selling ready-mades). Before the War, it used to be that Caroline sewed the wedding dresses and Mrs. Feamster, Mrs. Elizabeth Feamster that is and certainly not Mrs. Wanda Feamster, she sewed the grooms' suits. At that time during the War, though, Mrs. F. was sewing uniforms and Caroline was sewing the mourning[26] clothes. Now, for all her other faults, Caroline was, and I suppose still is, quite the artist with a needle and thread. People would pay a pretty penny for one of her dresses.

I arrived at Creigh's just as Caroline was exiting the store.

Her arms were filled with bundles including two bottles of apple brandy. "Why hello, Caroline," says I, "looks like you are planning for a party."

"Your mother is feeling poorly."

"And that is reason for a celebration?"

"She would like for the family to come over this evening."

"I hope you are planning a better meal than you made the last time she was ill. There was barely enough for anyone to eat, and nothing at all to drink. If mother had known how little you were serving us, the idea of it might have made her sick for real."

Just then, I saw the Fry sisters, Miss Rebecca and Miss Rose, walking down the street and I wondered what they were up to. They were the town's darlings. Not only were they the granddaughters of Reverend John McElhenney, but also, at that time, Rebecca was engaged to marry none other than the hero George Edgar, Lieutenant Colonel of the Twenty-sixth Battalion, Virginia Infantry. Why only a few weeks earlier, we had word that the Yankees were on their way to burn our lovely town and Edgar's ingenuity saved us from disaster. He and his brave men took a position just west of town on Tuckwiller's Hill. It was night when the blue coats arrived. Edgar knew that he was outnumbered, but when the first shots were fired, he started shouting out orders to imaginary troops to position imaginary artillery and other weapons. The silly Yankees who knew that they had the poorer position at the bottom of the hill, thought for sure that they were out manned and out gunned so they retreated back toward Charleston.

Thinking upon his ingenuity caused me to reflect how fortunate we were that times were quiet again. As Miss Rebecca and Miss Rose passed by me, I commented to them of the same. They both agreed, naturally, and I added, "Makes you believe the War could be over by Christmas."

When the Fry sisters were out of earshot, I turned my attention back to Caroline. She asked if I had heard anything about Northern raiding parties. "Heavens no!" I declared. "Edgar and his men have a good hold on the valley. Mrs. Bell told me so herself, so it has to be true. Who told you otherwise?"

Then she said it was Hartwell that had provided her with the misinformation and that he claimed a large group of Yankees was expected any day now. I told her, "You put too much stock in that man. You know how colored folks are: always exaggerating. Everything will be fine. The dirty, lowdown Yankees are nowhere near us."

With that issue resolved, I accompanied Caroline in the short walk to my sister Margaret's house. Margaret was surprised to see us at first. Then she saw that Caroline had a new dress for her. She snatched it up with excitement and said, "You finally finished—how wonderful!" She held it up to her shoulders and twirled around. "A bunch of us are gathering tonight to make bandages at Virginia Alderson's[27] home. It will be ever so nice to wear something new, even if it is black."

Margaret's husband had been dead for eight years already. He died before the War. Margaret was well beyond the two and a half years of mourning expected of a widow, and she had actually been wearing patterns and bright colors for approximately five years; but, when the War began and nearly everyone else started wearing black, she thought it best to join in. My husband had died the year before we are discussing, but considering the circumstances behind the manner in which he died, I did not see a reason to be quite so grief-stricken. I was only in heavy mourning for two months, dispatched with the veil and full mourning after six months, and I have been in half mourning since. No one has judged, believe you me.

Unlike my sister and myself, Virginia Alderson could not

have been wearing black that evening. She was not a widow. Poor Virginia was still unmarried when the war began and still with no prospects in sight. Given the circumstances and the number of widows, it would have been considered right uppity of her to wear black. Why with all the eligible men off fighting, everyone was convinced that there was no chance of her being anything but an old maid. But, as fortune would have it, she came upon a wounded Confederate soldier in the apple orchard. He had been shot through, three times, and had been left for dead. Despite his nasty wounds, Virginia could see that he was a handsome man of the most genteel form and she had him taken to her home. There, she nursed him, day after day, night after night, week after week. During that time everyone was saying how "noble-hearted" Virginia was and that she was "a ministering angel," but they only said that because they thought the wounds were mortal and that the soldier would most certainly die. Also, when a woman is as unfortunate looking as Virginia, they use terms like that to compensate.

To everyone's surprise, the soldier recovered. His name was, well is, Alexander Robinson. He was twenty-five at the time and he was a private in the Eighth Virginia Cavalry. Not a month ago, Virginia Alderson became Mrs. Alexander Robinson. Since she had saved his life, he naturally felt indebted to her and promised to marry her after the war was over.

But, back to my story, Margaret was twirling around in delight over her new dress. "You will not be going to Virginia's tonight," I told her. "Mother is feeling poorly." Margaret feigned surprise. "She says she is dying and would like us to be at her side," I continued with a most serious expression and then I started to giggle some because this was at least the third time in the past five months she had said the same. Margaret, however, did not find the situation funny and started to throw a fit. "Not again," she complained. "Well, I am not coming. The girls and I are planning a gay evening. Tell her to take some of her tonics and I will be over tomorrow. The Lord and everyone else knows that she has enough medicines to supply a battalion."

Devoted daughter that I was, I knew that I would be by my mother's side regardless, but I understood Margaret's feelings on the matter. Why only last week I had made that same exact point in the same words to Mrs. Bell. I said, "Mrs. B, why you would not believe the medicines my mother has accumulated. I would say she has enough to supply a battalion."

There seemed no reason to belabor the issue with Margaret, so I said "Very well," and turned to leave. Caroline, however, did not. "What shall I tell your mother?" she asked softly and most respectfully.

"Tell her I am ill."

"You are asking me to lie?" Caroline said, looking mighty scared at the thought of lying to Mother and rightfully so. No one ever lied to Mother. She had the uncanny ability of knowing when someone was not telling her the truth, combined with the uncanny ability to make said person who was not telling the truth feel absolutely horrible about him or herself. No one who knew better ever lied to Mother.

"It is not a lie," Margaret declared. "I am sick, sick of waiting on her all the time." Margaret and I both laughed at her remark. But Caroline remained steadfast. "I will not lie," she said quietly, but defiantly which was surprising and out of character for her. It should have been a warning to me of what was to come later, but at the time, I foolishly did not pay it any mind.

Margaret said, "Do not be so self-righteous, Caroline, I am only teasing. Lord knows, you will not have to lie; I will come and wait on Mother. Of course I will. I always do. But, I am telling you, this is the last time—the last time!"

How sad and prophetic those words were.

Chapter Six:
In Which the Remaining Guests Are Invited to the Ill Fated Dinner
As Told by Caroline Anderson

After finding my two sisters-in-law and requesting that they call upon their mother, I went to see Reverend McElhenney. His house was on the other side of town near the Presbyterian Church where he preached.

I was raised up in the Baptist Church. My mama used to bring me into town for church every Sunday without fail. I have learned that in cities like Annapolis, where people live close to the churches they attend, the services are shorter and held sometimes in the evening and on Wednesdays as well as on the Sabbath. But, in a country town like Lewisburg, the custom was to hold two services on Sunday, one in the forenoon, and after a short break, one in the afternoon. Folks like us who lived outside of town would bring along dinner-baskets. Generally, the entire family would come along for the day, but my daddy and my brothers never went with us to church. They stayed at home and did Lord knows what.

The walk to town took about two hours if the weather was fine. Mama never said a word when we walked. It was her quiet time. After church was over, we went straight on back home, silent all the way. She never talked about the sermon with me at home neither, never checked to see if I understood the lesson. I am not for sure why she wanted me to go with her each week. I used to believe her intent was for me to see more of the world than just our homeplace. Maybe then I would have some aspirations. But perhaps she was trying to give me a small break from the unending chores that we womenfolk had to do. Or maybe she was hoping that someone would see me and take me off her hands. After all, that is what happened in the end.

Going to church did give me aspirations. It made me desperately want to learn to read and write. Every week, I would stare at the Bible and pray that the squiggles and lines would start to mean something to me. Neither of my parents could teach me and they certainly did not have the money to pay for me to have lessons. So, I selfishly prayed to God every night before bed for some miracle to happen that would magically allow me to learn.

I used to hope that one day in church, a kindly woman would recognize me as her long lost daughter—that a mistake had been made somehow, and I belonged to her in truth. I would go on back to live with her in her beautiful home and she would teach me to read and write and to have fine manners. Of course, that situation never came to pass. I did move to a beautiful house when I was twelve, and I was finally taught to read when I was seventeen, but it certainly was not a miracle that brought it about. It was, like everything else, from hard work and personal sacrifice.

When I married, I joined the Anderson family at the Presbyterian Church. It was a lovely building. Even though it was only a simple, square building, it was made of stone and was the pride of the neighborhood. The inside walls were all whitewashed and looked as clean and pure as Heaven itself. There were no decorations of any kind on the walls or windows. Down in front, the pulpit was raised on high. Reverend McElhenney would stand up there and bellow out his sermons. I hardly ever could puzzle out the exact meaning of his words, but I knew they were powerful important, and that I ought to pay close attention because it seemed as though he was speaking directly to me.

Reverend McElhenney truly cared about his parishioners and took great delight in visiting with them in their homes. He traveled all around the county and even over to Monroe County when he was younger. He was always invited and present when the Anderson family entertained, and he made it a rule to go around the parlor and talk to every guest. When I asked the Reverend for his help in caring for Mrs. Anderson that day, he said that he was delighted to be of assistance—and asked with a wink what I was serving for dinner. After I told him what I had planned to fix, he smiled and said that he had some business to attend to, but would be along shortly.

Next, I went to find Mrs. Anderson's brother, Dr. William Simpkins. He was a kindly gentleman, beloved by all. He never married, but lived in a large house in town with his young colored servant named Dick, after Dick Pointer,[28] the hero slave who had saved the people of the valley from a Shawnee attack when the area was being settled. Dr. Simpkins was an elegant dresser and his house was furnished more attractively than any other that I knew of. Folks in Lewisburg esteemed his decorating and would often say admiringly, "He has an eye for color." At one time during the early days of the war, two men who worked as illustrators for the magazines came through town. Dr. Simpkins put them up in his home for a spell. In gratitude for his hospitality, they painted a scenic mural on the wall of his back parlor.

When Dr. Simpkins saw me at his door, he knew my mission. A simple nod of his head told me to wait as he retrieved his jacket and bag. Having no horse since the first time the Union men came on through and confiscated his mare; Dr. Simpkins came directly with me in the cart. In as much as she was ill, Mrs. Anderson was fortunate to have a brother who was a doctor. If Mrs. Anderson had been required to pay for all the medical services she received, she would have needed to take up residence on the poor farm instead of living in a fine place like Elmhurst. As we rode out of town, Dr. Simpkins confessed, "I almost did not bring my medical bag, but Grace likes a good show. It reassures her. A warm compress and some patience should be all I really need." Then he added, "She usually feels better after supper. I will ride home with Margaret and Orpha later in the evening."

That was the entirety of our conversation. The day had turned especially fine in regard to the weather. Most traveling companions would have felt inclined to discuss the beautiful conditions, but Dr. Simpkins certainly had no need to converse with me, and I would not have presumed to begin a conversation with him.

When we arrived at Elmhurst, Dr. Simpkins went immediately inside to call upon his sister while I unhitched our horse, Big Red, from the cart. Hartwell came running over and took Big Red into the barn. It was then that I saw Samuel fishing in the river and I was reminded of days past when the Anderson family used to have parties out on that patio that overlooks the river. Mr. Anderson would make a big show out of counting up the guests and then grab four or five poles. Little Samuel, being the only boy, would toddle along next to his father carrying the basket. It was Samuel's job to remove the fish from the lines as fast as he could because just as soon as Mr. Anderson would put a pole in the water, there would be a big ole fish on the line. Mr. Anderson would just pull them out of the water, one after another after another. Within a few minutes time he would have enough fish to feed the entire group. Then, I would clean them and fry them up for everyone.[29]

I walked on over to Samuel. He stood up tall and puffed out his chest like he always did when I drew near. As I got close up to him, I looked down and saw that his basket was empty. His face reddened with shame and frustration. Then, he kicked over the basket angrily and complained, "Nothing good comes out of this river anymore." I nodded in agreement, but he had already turned his back to me and was headed toward the house. Before I could get inside myself, he busted out through the door with his hunting rifle and stormed off toward the woods. I heard some shots go off and hoped that they were coming from him and not at him—you just couldn't be sure back then.

CHAPTER SEVEN:
Questions Asked and Answers Given
As Told by Sally Anderson

I was sitting on the floor of my grandmother's bedroom playing with my brother Samuel's toy soldiers that he had allowed me to borrow without actually knowing he had done so. The soldiers were made of wood. My parents had bought them in Richmond. They were all dressed in Continental or English lobster-back uniforms except for one that was lead and was dressed like a Prussian Hussar. It was Samuel's favorite. I am not certain where it came from. I believe it might have belonged to my father.

Samuel used to play with his soldiers all the time. He even let me play with him a few times until a bayonet broke during the siege of Savannah. (It was not completely my fault—General Ashe was a terrible commander and his troops tried to flee across a swamp. Casualties were to be expected). When the real war began, though, Samuel said that he was too old for toys and put the soldiers away in a box that he hid under a floorboard in his room and thought that no one knew about.

While I was fighting the Battle of Clover Lick (there never actually was a real battle in Clover Lick, but I thought there should have been. Believe me, that town could use some excitement), Grandmother was asleep in her bed. Someone knocked lightly on the door. Excited to be freed from my grandmother-watching duty,

44

I quickly rose and unlocked the door. It was my great uncle. For some strange reason, he preferred to be addressed as "Dr. Simpkins" rather than "Uncle William" or even simply "uncle." Grandmother told me that I should not ask him about it. I never did. It was not high on my priority list of the things I wanted to know.

I opened the door for him and exclaimed, "Oh, Dr. Simpkins, I am so glad you are here!"

The feeling did not appear to be mutual. Rather, he reprimanded me, saying, "Shush, Sally, keep your voice down."

"Why? Grandmother is hard of hearing. Not that she would admit it. She is always complaining about the noise we make; but she can sleep through anything. Why the Yankees have been firing their cannons all day and she has slept right through it." Dr. Simpkins looked confused. I pointed to my soldiers. He looked closely at the battlefield I had constructed.

"Who is winning?" he asked.

"It is a stalemate, Sir."

He shook his head in pity and then looked back at Grandmother. "How long has your grandmother been asleep?"

"She took her sleeping draught and fell asleep right after she ate her breakfast, which she had no appetite for."

Dr. Simpkins walked over to the side of Grandmother's bed. On her nightstand were many bottles of half-filled medicinal tonics. "Do you know which one she took?"

"I did not notice, Sir." He looked again at the bottles and then at Grandmother who was sleeping peacefully.

"No need to wake her just yet" he whispered to me and then added with a roll of his eyes, "we have all evening to learn of her ailments." He removed a book from his medical bag and sat in the armchair by her bed. "You can run along now, Sally."

"Oh no, Sir; Caroline made me promise to stay with Grandmother and not leave."

"You tell her that I sent you away."

"Actually, I would like to stay."

"You would?"

"Yes, because I have something very important to ask you, Sir. Something no one else will talk to me about."

"What is it?"

I walked over to him and looked at him with my most serious and sweet expression trying ever so hard to endear myself to him. "It is that skeleton that hangs in your office," I said with my most innocent voice.

"That is what you want to know about?"

"Yes, Sir, I have been completely beside myself ever since I first saw it. No one will tell me a thing about it and I simply must know how you got it and who he was." Dr. Simpkins' skeleton had been the subject of much discussion in the county. No one had ever seen one before and I would not be surprised if it was the only privately owned skeleton in the entire state. Creepy Jim Glover had skeletons of cats and dogs and rats in his shed, but no one had a real human skeleton… at least, not that I knew of. Seeing the skeleton made Dr. Simpkins patients uncomfortable, though, because they feared that they might wind up that way too.

"It is not a pleasant story," Dr. Simpkins warned me.

"I should hope not."

"As you wish."

He indicated that I should sit on the floor at his feet while he told me the story. I did as he suggested. I included the story in my memoirs, but I will tell it to you now because it is most fascinating. The story was this: there was a man named Joseph Newton[30] who owned a slave called Tom. He was as hard-working and polite a Negro as anyone had ever met. To reward Tom for his good behavior, Newton promised that when he, Newton that is, died, Tom could have his freedom. But, after a few years, Tom got tired of waiting for Newton to die and decided to take matters into his own hands. He took a wooden board, attached a horseshoe to the end of it, and hid in a stall in the barn. When Newton entered the barn, Tom jumped up, hit Newton in the forehead with the board, and killed him with that one blow. Tom must have been an especially strong man. Then, Tom dragged the body over to a stall to make it look like a horse had kicked Newton.

Tom had everyone fooled... except Reverend McElhenney. He knew that Newton was too good of a horseman to get kicked. Reverend McElhenney went to the courthouse, asked for money to investigate, and it was granted. I am not exactly certain what the Reverend did, but somehow he got Tom to confess. While Tom was awaiting his hanging, he promised that Dr. Simpkins could have his body to examine after he was dead. That was evidently what happened. The skeleton was Tom.

"Poor Tom," I said.

But Dr. Simpkins said, "Poor Tom? He was a murderer, a premeditative murderer. Poor Mr. Newton. He was the one murdered."

"Did you ask for his body to examine too?"

"Of course not."

"Doctor Simpkins," I asked, "is there a difference between a white man's body and a colored man's?"

Chapter Eight:
Wherein Preparations for the Dinner are Commenced
As Told by Hartwell Finney

Now Miz Caroline started getting ready for the big fam'ly dinner. First she started with the cookin'. It were too early for most of the veg'tables to be ready but there were some asparagus and some greens a'ready and I knew she'd be using them. There were also still some taters left from last summer, so she got the shovel and dug up the barrel where they was stored under the ground just outside the kitchen. She scraped 'em up good and set 'em to boil whilst she began to work on the salt-risin' bread. That's about when I came back on in to the house. Not only did I find the mustards and a big handful of mushrooms, but I also caught her two wild turkeys in the traps I'd set. Turkeys make for some good eatin' but those birds are none too smart. To catch one, all you gotta do is set out a barrel upside down with some corn on the top. After a few days, you turn the barrel right side up and the silly birds will fall right into it, not realizin' that you done turned it over. Then they cannot spread their wings and they's trapped.

Miz Caroline was real excited 'bout them turkeys, 'specially since Mista Samuel's fishin' hadn't turned out so well. He had given up on the fishin' and had grabbed his gun and gone off a' huntin'. He was lookin' for deer but he wasn't gonna find none. It

48

was too early in the spring. They'd be deep in the woods at that time, to have their babies, and, b'sides, we hadn't seen deer on the prop'aty in long days. They knew enough to hide themselves from all the soldiers.

Mista Samuel was very handy with a gun. I, a course, had never shot nothin'. Colored folks wasn't allowed to have no guns back then. They's afraid we'd use 'em to kill white folks. They say there was almost a slave revolt[31] in Lewisburg the year the Northern army first came on through. They found a whole store of guns and such in a barn and one of Masta Sam Tuckwiller's slaves told how they was gonna kill their mastas. In the end, they blamed the whole thing on Old Uncle Reuben, one of Masta John Withrow's slaves. They had a trial at the courthouse and they hung him. Most of us is sure it weren't Old Uncle Reuben that got everyone fired up to kill 'cause he was real quiet and slow and nice and very, very old. But killin' an old slave who cain't do much work is a lot cheaper than killin' a young buck, and it still sends a message to the whole herd that they better watch on out.

Miz Caroline gave me a big thanks for the turkeys. She told me how beautiful they was and that I had saved the day and that now they was going to have a wonderful meal and that she would cook the turkeys and have some for her fam'ly and some for me to take on home with me. I was mighty pleased. Then, I went out to pluck them turkeys and I heard her a singin' as she worked. Miz Caroline had a real pretty voice that sounded like she was singin' even when she was only talkin', but most of the songs she sang were terrible sad. They was all about girls like Barbree Allen[32], Fair Ellender, and Pretty Polly who all ended up dead and gone, mostly cause some sweet-talking man had done them wrongways. I don't know why white folks make up so many songs about pretty young girls a' die'n. Colored folks didn't sing about that sub'ject—no, Sir! Most of colored folks' songs that I ever heard is about gettin' freedom and not about the bad things you can do once you got it.

CHAPTER NINE:
In Which the Dinner Preparations are Completed
As Told by Caroline Anderson

I spent the remainder of the day fixing for our last family dinner at Elmhurst.[33] I knew that I should be packing as I cooked and cleaned, but it was such a fine day and I was in such a joyful mood that I just could not believe that the danger was as close at hand as it turned out to be. I kept on repeating to myself that I had at least three more days before trouble arrived. Also, I did not actually know where to begin with the packing. I had never packed before. For most of my life, I did not have any belongings to pack. When I came to Elmhurst, all I had were the clothes on my back. Even though my wardrobe increased to four dresses after I was married: two for working days and two different Sunday dresses, I never needed to pack them up. My husband did not enjoy travel and preferred to stay at home.

There were two old traveling trunks in the attic that his parents had used. Grace Anderson and her husband Charles Anderson had traveled quite a bit together and filled their home with souvenirs. The trunks were dirty now from disuse. I figured that I would wait until after the dinner to get them out of the attic and clean them up.

However did one decide what to take and what to leave behind? I supposed that I should just pack the necessities for getting by until the war was over, but I could not imagine leaving behind so many wonderful things for the soldiers to steal or destroy: the beautiful china tea set that had belonged to Mrs. Anderson's mother, the family christening gown, and, of course, all of the books in the library. I was for sure that the soldiers would use them as kindling, or worse, for... personal business. I believe that thought horrified me the most.

Rather than fret about the soldiers and what they might do, I kept my mind on dinner. We had been scrimping and making do for the past year, so I was excited to prepare something nice for a change. We all needed a break from the horrors of the War and a good meal certainly would help to take our minds off all of the suffering. As I did not return home from town until a little after ten o'clock, I got busy as soon as I walked through the door. I had food to cook, a table to set, and in the public rooms there was furniture to dust, window glass to clean, and floors to sweep and scrub. I wanted to bring the sunshine right into that old place.

Before I tell you anything else about what happened that day, I must tell you about Elmhurst. Since you have seen the ruin that Elmhurst is today, you should know that it was a magnificent place before the War. The property was located in a gap where three mountains met. It began at the foot of a steep ridge and stretched for fifty acres along the waters of the Greenbrier River. Because the river flooded each spring, the buildings on the property had to be placed a good distance back from the riverbank for protection. I heard tell that back in 1847, it poured down the rain for three full days and the river water came right on in the house—about waist high. When the water started coming up, Grace Anderson had the slaves carry every piece of furniture up the stairs to safety. The family and the slaves all camped out upstairs, in whatever space they could find between the tables, desks, and couches—for six whole days until the water receded and the slaves could get the ground floor cleaned on up. What a mess that would have been!

Fortunately though, flooding was the only trouble that Mother Nature every stirred up. Other than this concern, she had provided the area with four glorious seasons as well as plenty of fish, game, and edible wild plants. Therefore, it only made sense that, with the exception of a few acres that had been cleared for the house, kitchen garden, and pasture, the remainder of Elmhurst's land had been left to her design.

Even though the land was blessed with fertile ground and rich woodlands perfect for farming and hunting, the site had actually been settled for other reasons. Being situated right in the fork where the James River and Kanawha Turnpike met the Salt Sulphur Springs Turnpike, it made an excellent stopping place for travelers to rest and take in a meal. As such, the house was originally built to serve as an inn. It welcomed guests of all means with accommodations that varied according to the size of their purses. The highest paying customers were given a large room facing the road; those with a little less to spend were placed in the rear with the windows opening out to the barn, sheds, necessary, and other structures less pleasant to look at or, if the windows were open, to smell. Those with still less could sleep in the kitchen wing with the servants, while those unfortunate souls with barely two nickels to rub together were put up in the barn.

To increase the likelihood that a traveler might stop and partake of some of the hospitality Elmhurst offered (at a fair price), the house was set only fifty yards or so from the road with the water well tucked in safely around back of the house beside the kitchen. I expect that when many weary travelers stopped with the intention only to water their horses, they were tempted by the smells from the kitchen to purchase a meal for themselves as well.

The house itself must have been especially inviting at that time. It was a two-story brick with tall white columns and two porches in front, all shaded by elm trees. The columns supported an unusual wooden front piece also painted white that was cut out in such a way as to resemble steps. I liked to call it the stairway to Heaven because it looked like someone could climb them right up into the clouds.

It had several other interesting design features as well, like, rather than have two doors leading out to the porches, one above the other, with two windows on either side of them as most houses did, the second floor had five windows across the front and provided no access to the upper porch. Perhaps the builders thought this design was attractive, but it certainly made cleaning the leaves and snow off of the porch a great difficulty. Oddly enough, an additional entry was located instead on the first floor directly beside the main entrance. It provided access to a bedroom of all things. I have absolutely no idea what the builder's intention was in this matter.

Being only one step above the ground, the grand front porch was never used much that I know of. Instead, people in that time preferred to sit out in the grass. Sometimes during those early days, Elmhurst's lawn was used for large picnic parties. Important guests at the Old White hotel like Senator Henry Clay[34] would journey west some six miles from White Sulphur Springs to rest under the crape myrtle trees, drink wine or champagne, and enjoy fine meals.

When President Martin Van Buren[35] came to take the waters at the Old White, he had a picnic at Elmhurst that lasted from two in the afternoon until seven at night. It was a bachelors-only affair. Around one hundred men were in the party—the most eligible in our nation's capital. As I heard tell, the belles were left behind at the hotel, pining away over the lost opportunity for securing a wealthy and powerful husband. The picnickers, however, enjoyed themselves mightily. They were served dish after dish of venison, chicken, beef pies, and every sort of fruit and vegetable grown in the Greenbrier Valley. I have never cooked for more than thirty. I can only imagine the work required to provide five hours worth of food for such a crowd.

The Anderson family purchased the property about four years after this famous visit; but they no longer operated the house as an inn. Instead, they kept it as a private residence, open only to extended family and special guests. Before they moved in, my mother-in-law, Grace Anderson, made many changes to the place that she called "improvements" because they removed any sense that the place had ever been open to the public. The workmen spent six months at it. First, Mrs. Anderson had them enclose the area directly surrounding the house with a high picket fence. It was so tall that the points of the pickets were level with my chin. It made me feel as though I lived in a pioneer fort like they had in this area when they were afraid of Indian attacks.

Where the picket fence ended, split rail began, surrounding the remainder of the cleared land. On the eastern side of the property, along the road, a large gate allowed people, horses, carts, and carriages to enter the domains. Once inside this gate, a wide path brought you alongside the kitchen garden to the back of the house where, like I said before, the well, poultry shed, pigsty, and other outbuildings were located. It also took you around to the main entrance to the barn. This passage was the family's means of entrance and egress. They would put the horses directly in the barn or out to pasture and come into the house through the back door.

Visitors, however, could disembark earlier, back where the only gate in the picket fence offered an entry toward the front door. Mrs. Anderson kept this gate padlocked as if somehow she could keep out trouble.

Oddly, Mrs. Anderson never removed that extra door in the front; but, she did add a small patio and English-styled garden to the western side of the house. She had boxwoods planted and paths marked off in patterns just like she saw in the book *Cottage Residences*[36], by Mr. Andrew Jackson Downing. She took great pride in showing everyone that book and how her garden looked like it had jumped off of one of the pages. It certainly was a beautiful spot. When the weather was fine and I had a minute or two to spare, nothing delighted me more than to sit outside on this patio overlooking the river. With the brilliant colors that unfolded each season, the sounds of the river water rushing away and the feel of the warm sun and the crisp air against your skin, why it was like Paradise!

I have been living in Annapolis for two years. It is a charming city. I could talk on forever about all the different buildings and the beauty of the Chesapeake Bay. I have friends and opportunities now the likes of which I never had before. For example, I attend diction and elocution classes every Monday and Wednesday night at the First Presbyterian Church just down the street. I have been trying to improve myself and to sound more cultured. Most people believe I sound common and do not find my backwoods sayings as charming as you appear to. Still, as much as I am better off now than I ever was before, I must say that when the weather here is the kind of cold, gray, damp, and dreary that chills you to the bone or the air is thick and hot and suffocating with smoke and city stink, I cannot help but wish to be back in western Virginia in the fresh, mountain air.

When I first arrived at Elmhurst, Mrs. Anderson went to considerable trouble to train me up. She was very particular as to how I should dress and speak and in the ways of housekeeping. At that time, she had a copy of Catharine Beecher's[37] *Domestic Receipt Book*. It explained everything that a proper woman needed to know to run a superior household. It told how to select meats at the market, how to cook food not only for the best taste but also for nourishment and good digestion, as well as how to prepare for daily family dinners and small entertainments. Miss Beecher thoroughly covered every topic. Why the book even had diagrams showing you where on the table you should place each item of the meal!

I took special delight in cooking. After I learned all of Miss Beecher's receipts, I began to make up receipts of my own. I liked to use ingredients that we had in these parts that Miss Beecher was not familiar with, like ramps and Poke. My mama taught me how to hunt in the woods for the edible plants. With some, like Poke or dandelions, you could dig up the roots and keep them indoors in a basket away from the sunlight. With water, new shoots would grow and you could enjoy fresh greens all winter long.

I never let on to Mrs. Anderson that any of the receipts were mine, and she would continually praise Miss Beecher for her "Refined and exacting taste." But, after Miss Beecher's sister wrote that anti-slavery book, the women of Greenbrier County shunned them both. Instead, the ladies all turned back to Mrs. Mary Randolph and her book, *The Virginia House-Wife*.[38] But, it was just a book of receipts and did not tell anything more.

Mrs. Anderson never asked me to change my ways of housekeeping, but she did tell me that I was never to mention Miss Beecher by name again. She acted like she had been betrayed by a good friend and threw her copy of Miss Beecher's *Domestic Receipt Book* into the fireplace and burned it up. It didn't make no never-mind to me. By that time, I knew Miss Beecher's book by heart, so I continued to follow her rules: my tablecloths were always white, I never sliced my bread more than a quarter of an inch thick, I wiped all soiled spots from the outside of articles used on the table, and I always garnished my dishes in order to give, what Miss Beecher called, an "Air of ease and refinement that pleases the eye." Mrs. Anderson never again complimented my work.

I took extra care that day in the dining room since I knew it was where we would spend the most time. First, I rolled up the drugget[39] that we kept in place for everyday dining. Then, I took down the draperies, gave them a good shake, and let them air out in the sunshine for most of the day. I had stitched those curtains up in 1859 from some beautiful gold brocade fabric that Mrs. Anderson had purchased at the same time she bought our sewing machine. Funny to think on it now: she bought that machine and that expensive fabric and never once had thought that I would not be able to manage it, tassels and all. She simply gave me a copy of *The Workwoman's Guide*[40] by a Lady, and pointed at the picture she wanted them to look like. Mrs. Anderson was so pleased with the result that she also bought some white, grey, and tourmaline damask for the parlor curtains and pointed at another picture in the book. The rest of the draperies, though, remained the old moreen[41] ones from her first overhaul of the house.

I also set out some beeswax tapers that I had made. The rule on table candles was to use half as many candles as the number of guests, to place them on the table symmetrically, and never to allow the flames to get below eighteen inches from the table. I cannot remember the exact source of that rule, though, but I know I saw it in a book. Before I came to Elmhurst, the family had purchased all of their candles. When Mrs. Anderson learned that I could make them, she decided to save the family some money, and it became another of my duties. Of course, the candles were only decorative. Since it was May, we would be dining in the daylight. Even if it had been dark at that hour, town folk like the Andersons had been using coal oil lamps for years. Western Virginia was a great source of the cannel coal that was used to make the oil. I heard my husband say once that there were near forty-six companies mining cannel coal and a plant to make the oil from it in every western county.

In spite of all this work in the dining room, I still spent most of that day cooking in the kitchen. To protect the main house from fire and also to keep the cooking grease and smells out of the finer rooms, the kitchen was in its own building attached to the back of the house. Because Elmhurst had been built for commercial enterprises, the kitchen was grand. It was larger than the home I grew up in. Although it was not as tall as the main house, the kitchen building still had an upstairs and a downstairs. The upstairs was for storage and where the slaves or servants had slept. The downstairs was one large room with cabinets to store dishes and cooking pans and all the other needs. There was a large table to prepare the food on in the middle of the room and a large fireplace on the end. It had a fancy black stove in it and two Dutch ovens on each side. Mrs. Anderson even kept a supply of those Swedish safety matches[42] to help light the ovens.

I fixed quite a few dishes that day: turkey, asparagus, black-eyed peas, mashed turnips, a rhubarb and potato pie, panada, and cherry pie for dessert. Yes, I still remember the entire menu for that night although I would have a time of it remembering what I made last week Thursday. You remember what you fixed for important nights and it was certainly an important night. Also, as we were missing so many flavorings and ingredients that we used to have about the house before the War, I had to be very creative with the receipts and that helps me remember as well because I was rather proud of the way the dishes turned out.

Getting such a late start, I am not for sure how I was able to get all of my work done, but I did. The only task I left off was scrubbing the walls. Whenever we had dinner at Elmhurst with company beyond the immediate family, Mrs. Anderson liked for me to wash the downstairs walls with whiting in order to remove any grime from the fireplaces and to be certain that the paint colors looked as bright as possible. She claimed that she wanted a cheery, clean house; yet, in a low mood one day, she once confided her true reason for the wall washing: she associated the faded wall colors with being past her prime in beauty and wealth. You see, to Mrs. Anderson's kind, the amount of pigment you could afford to put in your paint was a sign of your wealth. That is why all of the public rooms in Elmhurst were painted such strong colors while the private rooms were left white, and also why Mrs. Anderson had not used any wallpaper as was most common. Wallpaper could not be scrubbed clean of all the fireplace smoke that left grease on the walls, and wallpaper faded with the sunlight and years.

The house had been painted back when Mrs. Anderson had done all of her improvements. Here, she relied on advice from *Godey's Lady's Book* and favored reds and yellows. The halls were painted Golden Beryl, the dining room was Vermillion, the parlor was Tourmaline, and the library was dark Amber. For some reason unknown to me, Mrs. Anderson had chosen not to re-paint the downstairs bedroom, the one with the strange door that opened to the outside. It remained its original shade of Jungle Green.

She had also allowed the original furnishings, bed cover, and draperies to remain. These had been abandoned by Elmhurst's original owner. The linens were only cotton gingham: quilted for the coverlet and simple pleats for the curtains, but they still looked fresh and clean even after all those years. They did, however, have an unusual pattern on them of jungle green vines with salmon pink and maize yellow flowers on them. They made the room look like a hothouse, the kind they use for growing plants that is. Perhaps it had been used as the other kind of hothouse and that was the reason for the extra door. Or, perhaps the Andersons believed the room was haunted. Either way, the door to that bedroom always remained shut and no one ever went in there except me.

The furnishings in that room were simple: a bed, nightstand, armchair, and dressing table with mirror. They were a matching set all made of rosewood. I added the sewing machine and placed it below the window that faced the road. It had a wonderful southern exposure and provided excellent light to sew by. Mrs. Anderson insisted that the door remain closed, though, even when I was inside.

With all the cooking and house cleaning done, the last task of the day was to get myself ready for our company. After a hard day of work, I looked as if I had been drug up the chimney. Because it was only a little after three o'clock and I was in a festive mood, I decided to spend some extra time I saved by not scrubbing the walls to take a tub bath and wash out my hair. Although I have never been concerned with making myself pretty or stylish, I must confess that I have always liked to make myself neat and clean. That preference actually started when I was a little girl and it got me in a heap of trouble one time. I still have the scars on my back from the whupping I got that day.

You see, my daddy was a true mountaineer. The most important thing in life to him was his independence. He did not want to be beholden to anyone for anything. We owned a small plot of land that was part of a parcel given to his granddaddy for service in the Revolutionary War. My daddy built our house and its furniture all by himself from trees in our woods. The food on our table was always the meat he and my brothers hunted and the vegetables that were grown in our garden.

The few necessities that we could not produce on our own, like flour and cloth, were purchased using money he earned by selling the soap that my mama and I would make from goats' milk, lye, corn oil, and lavender. The soap smelled like Heaven to me; but it was deemed too precious for anyone in our family to use. We needed every bit earned by that soap and could not afford to lose even a quarter of a cent. Besides, any bathing beyond getting the dirt off of your hands and face was seen by my family as the folly of the rich. We were a healthy lot and did not need baths to prevent or treat sicknesses. Also, there was always so much wood smoke about the place that you could not smell anything else indoors or out. No one could see much point in a bath… except me. For some reason, I just did not like the feeling of dirt and sweat and grime on my skin.

One day, when I was nine years of age, I snuck off, went down to the creek with a bar of our soap, and cleaned myself from head to toe. As I luxuriated in the smell and feel of clean, one of my brothers happened along. When he saw me, he grinned like a mule eating briars and ran off to tell our parents of my crime. They made certain I repented for my wickedness. My daddy beat me for being a thief and my mama beat me harder for being vain. I did not have a true bath again until I came to Elmhurst where I was actually required to bathe.

Since Lola Montez recommended frequent tub baths and sponge washings in tepid water as a way to brighten the skin and improve the complexion, Mrs. Anderson bathed often—twice a week! She insisted that I do the same. She did not understand why her son had chosen to marry me excepting that he thought I was attractive; therefore, she insisted that I had a duty to him and the family to remain that way, especially in public. As filthy as I got with my daily work, I was more than happy to oblige.

Because Mrs. Anderson washed up so often, she had turned one of the bedrooms in the quarters above the kitchen into a special bathing room. She had a large wooden tub frame built out of pine with a sheet lead basin inside. I must confess that it reminded me a little of a coffin. Mrs. Anderson and I bathed on Tuesdays and Saturdays. Everyone else bathed just on Saturdays. I would bring buckets of water up from outside and heat them up in the fireplace. Then, after each bath, I would have to scoop the water right out of the tub and carry it back outdoors.

In regard to creams for her skin and hair, Mrs. Anderson most likely had as many tonics as Cleopatra, Queen Elizabeth, and Marie Antoinette combined. Somehow, she managed to get her hands on many of the fancy ingredients needed for Madame Montez's beauty tonics like gum benzoin and ambergris. When she discovered that my mama and I were the ones who made the soap she purchased at Creigh's, she went out and bought two nanny goats, had a fragrant herb garden planted, and set me to work making soap. Even though she locked up her tonics and creams in a large cabinet, everyone, myself included, was permitted to use the soap.

After washing up well, I put on all of my Sunday finest and then some[43]. Back at that time, I actually owned a beautiful silk corset and a pair of silk stockings. They had belonged to Mr. Anderson's first wife and she had worn them on her wedding day. I had never before worn them. It just never seemed right for me to wear something so personal that had belonged to another. But, at least fifteen years had passed since she had worn them, and who knew what would happen to them once we vacated the house, so I decided that the time had come for me to finally put them on. I must confess that wearing those pretty undergarments made me feel real fine-looking.

Of course, I could not put my lovely silk stockings into my lace-up boots; so, I wore the first Mrs. John Anderson's wedding shoes as well. They were brown kid leather slippers with a black silk ribbon bow on them. Also, I decided to wear a hoop that day. Because I was always working at something, I never did bother with a hoop around the house, even when we had company. I only ever wore one to church and then off it came as soon as we were back at Elmhurst. But, that day was special.

As I was putting the final pins in my hair, I heard the clock strike four. The guests would be arriving at any moment and I was looking forward to a pleasant evening. Everything was finished just as I had hoped.

Then, I heard some noises coming from the kitchen.

I figured it was just a member of the family—perhaps Dr. Simpkins had come looking for a snack. So, I walked gaily into the kitchen. But my mood instantly went to black when instead of Dr. Simpkins, I saw a soldier. He was in his dirty, grey, Rebel uniform, eating food right from the platters with his grubby fingers.

"No! Stop!" I yelled.

He turned his ugly face to me, smiled real big, and kept on eating.

"Stop it now," I insisted.

"What are you going to do?" he taunted.

I rushed at him and tried to slap him, but he grabbed my wrist, spun me around, and pinned my arms behind my back. He laughed as I struggled. "Let me go," I insisted.

"You never were much of a fighter," he said with a snicker. I could smell whiskey on his hot breath.

"Let me go," I repeated.

"If you swing at me, I'll slap you bald-headed."

"Let me go, Frank."

"All right, but I warned ya'."

He released me with a hard shove that sent me to the floor and sent my spectacles flying off my face. I glared at him but he just laughed and said, "Such an ugly way to treat your own flesh and blood. You got all this and you cain't even share a little with your big brother?"

I stood up and stared him down. Frank was the meanest and laziest of my brothers, responsible for most of my childhood bruises and tears. I am not for sure what my mama was doing when she was carrying him, but it must have been something wrong because he was just plain out blinked.

Being a poor family, all four of my older brothers had been drafted. We did not own slaves and we certainly did not have the money to pay for substitutes—three hundred dollars! That may be more money than my daddy earned in his entire life. Two of my brothers died straight away from diseases they had never been exposed to living so far away from town. I thought perhaps Frank had come to tell me that the other had died.

"What are you doing here?" I asked with true concern.

He wiped his mouth on his sleeve and said, "There was a skirmish over at Second Creek and somehow I got separated from my squad."

"You deserted?"

"I'll find my way back. I always disappear when the fightin' begins. They never seem to miss me neither. I have no mind to get myself killed in some rich man's war. They started it but we're fightin' it. Don't really make no difference to us which side wins. We'll be the same in the end. Only thing that does matter is that I got me something proper to drink. So now I'd like to get me a good meal and a place to sleep for a few hours till I join back up with whatever is left of my company."

"I will fix you a plate. But you cannot sleep here."

I started to look around for where my spectacles had got to. Frank grabbed my wrist and twisted it violently. "Hurry on up, Sissy. I'm starved." With that warning, he let go of my wrist. I did not waste another second. I got a rough plate out of a cabinet, put some food on it from a pile of scraps, and handed it to him.

"Only the best for your true family," he sneered.

But he was so hungry that he stopped complaining and began to eat greedily.

Seeing how hungry and skinny he was, I felt a little sorry for him and embarrassed by my behavior. I started to explain that this might be the last meal we had in the house and I wanted it to be special. He laughed at me. "Won't make no difference," he said with his mouth full and bits flying out. "They'll never treat you like one of their own. When you gonna learn? You done been with this family for seven years and they don't like you any more today than they did then. You gotta stop your dreamin', Sissy."

I wanted to say something in reply but there was nothing much to say. He was right and I knew it, even if I tried to pretend that it was not so. Fortunately, I heard horses approaching and that ended our conversation. "Eat fast and go before anyone sees you," was all I said as I hurried to greet my guests.

As I walked through the dining room toward the front door, I could heard him laughing and bragging, "Don't worry; nobody will see me. Nobody ever does."

CHAPTER TEN:
Wherein the True but Unexpected Danger Arrives
As Told by Orpha McClung

My daughter Becky and I rode to Mother's house with Margaret. She had a carriage, or barouche, as she liked to call it. If I have not said so before, Margaret married well. When her husband died, he left her with a comfortable sum and nothing to spend it on but herself, and that she certainly did.

We had a grand time traveling to Elmhurst, chatting and catching up on each other's news. But the dust was awful on the drive, which was quite surprising considering all the rain we had been having. Why it absolutely poured down the rain the night before. I remember this because, well... I just remember things is all.

By the time we arrived, we were parched. Caroline met us in the entryway hall. We gave her our coats and requested that she bring us something immediately to quench our awful thirst. Then, I noticed that my skirts were a mess of dirt. Consequently, I wiped them down—and Becky's too. Got the dirt off of us and onto the ground where it belonged.

Margaret did the same and remarked that she was glad that she had saved her new dress and had only worn "some old thing" that afternoon. "Some old thing" was actually a lovely dress that Caroline had sewed for her, not six months before, which

Margaret had decided to embellish. The original design was a copy of a dress by Charles Frederick Worth[44] that the French Empress Eugenie[45] had worn. Margaret saw a picture of it in the *Daily Richmond Examiner* and went and bought some dark green silk satin at Creigh's before the prices had gone out the roof. Caroline had sewn it beautifully without a pattern or anything. It looked just like the picture. Margaret, however, was not entirely satisfied and overlaid the dress some with black lace flounces to make it look more expensive. But, anyone could clearly see which stitches were hers and that factor actually cheapened it a bit.

My dress was a black taffeta. I reconstructed it myself from a gown that I had worn years before. Naturally, I was not quite as full-figured back then, so I had to let it out some to allow for my more womanly form. The alterations included the addition of a flounce at the bottom. Fortunately, when I first made the skirt—I made it myself you see, having more skill with a needle than my sister—I had lined it with the same material. This clever foresight permitted me plenty of extra fabric with which to work. Now that I was in half mourning, and since we were only having a family dinner and I was not truly in public, I added lilac-colored trimming to brighten it up a tad.

Caroline returned with a tray of apple water. It was a sorry substitute for lemonade. Back then, you could not find a Mediterranean lemon in any of the stores. Did you know that General Stonewall Jackson relished lemons?[46] He was known to suck on them to help ease his dyspepsia. My husband's cousin Paul McClung who lived in Lexington knew General Jackson when the General was an instructor at the Virginia Military Institute, although Paul never mentioned lemons in connection with General Jackson. I believe the General had not developed his dyspepsia at that time. Come to think of it now, that great man died only a few days before that terrible incident we are talking about, though word had not reached us yet. Paul died four months ago.

But back to my story, Caroline informed us that Mother was up in her room. As much as we were devoted to our mother, Margaret and I were in no hurry to deal with her just yet. When Mother was in a mood, she was most trying. Consequently, I said, "We will take our drinks in the parlor and check on her later."

"You mean the library, do you not, Sister Dear?" Margaret slyly corrected and winked at me.

Catching her meaning, I said, "Oh yes, of course, how foolish of me," and winked right back at her. Then I sent Becky to run along and find her cousin Sally, and Margaret and I took ourselves to the library.

The library, with its stunning walnut bookcases, had always been my brother's pride and joy. Father started the collection of books, but John must have tripled its size. The walls were covered from floor to ceiling with books. John would spend hours on end in that room and no one was to disturb him. It was his sanctuary. It was a decidedly masculine room and not the type of atmosphere that Margaret and I normally would have chosen to pass the time in together. In fact, Margaret was never one for reading and always shunned the room.

However, when I was younger, I was quite the reader. As such, I spent many an hour among my father's collection only to discover a very special book hidden amidst the others. Why, it was not a book at all! It simply looked like a book, but when you opened it up, it contained two small glasses and a bottle of whiskey. Naturally, as a young woman, I never disturbed the contents. But, in my maturity, with John gone who-knows-where, and Mother having so many near death experiences, Margaret and I had taken a few sips from the bottle during our visits to nurse Mother. If you had ever had to suffer through one of those experiences with Mother, you certainly would not blame us for our small indulgence.

Margaret sat herself down on the loveseat as I walked over to the bookshelves and found that special book. I poured just a smidge in Margaret's glass and only a slightly larger portion in my own, being that I am a fuller woman than she. As I joined my sister on the loveseat I said, and how prophetic a statement it was! I said, "I have a feeling it is going to be a long evening."

"If only we had some male companions," Margaret added. "Why, I do not know what I would do just to be in the company of a decent-looking man."

"Alas! It is desperate times, sister."

To illustrate just how desperate we had become, why only a month or two before that day, Mother had sold one of her prize possessions to help pay for the necessities of life. They were andiron[47] figurines that had graced the fireplace since Mother and Father had first been married. Father was in Richmond for a short time and he wrote to Mother to say that he was bringing home a present to her of two Negro boys. Naturally, Mother thought that he was speaking of slaves and began making all the necessary preparations.

We used to keep slaves when I was a child, though never more than three or four. My father, as I may have mentioned previously, was a lawyer. However, in addition to his legal practice, Father grew a small amount of feed corn on the property and needed the slaves to work the farm. After Father died, Mother decided that she'd had enough of farming, and sold off all the slaves. Mind you, she was never opposed to slavery on moral grounds. Quite the opposite: she simply was afraid that all the Northern agitators might lead the slaves to do something violent. Mother had a deep fear of dying in a violent manner.

Anyway, Mother was absolutely astonished when the

"Negros" Father spoke of in his letter turned out to be twelve inches high and made of solid iron. Father delighted in telling that story, and the fireplace was always so cheery and welcoming when it was flanked by those two handsome little boys. It certainly looked sad and empty without them. And, of course, Mother did not get nearly what they were worth either. At that time, people of means, such as we were, could barter with shopkeepers. They actually preferred to be paid in gold rings and such as opposed to the Confederate currency, which lost about ten percent of its value each month.

As hard as it was for us, I must admit that life was worse for our relatives in Richmond. We had a kitchen garden, rivers and streams to fish in, and woods to hunt in, so we always had food on the table. Not so in the cities. Why only a month before our incident, in April of 1863, there were bread riots[48] in that city. The women and children marched through the streets and emptied the stores of their contents. Governor Letcher sent the mayor to read the Riot Act but the crowd would not disperse. Even the exhortations of President Jefferson Davis had no effect. He was actually hissed at by some of the boys—imagine!

The authorities were at the point of calling out troops when the situation was resolved. Shortly after that horrible occurrence, the government began handing out rations of rice and a friend of ours in Richmond, Mr. G. W. Gary, published *The Confederate Receipt Book*. It contained over one hundred receipts to help women adapt to the shortages like using acorns with a little bacon for coffee and thorns for pins.

Well, before we knew what was what, our time in the library was concluded. The clock struck five and Mother came directly downstairs. Dinner at Elmhurst was always served punctually at five. Growing up, we children knew to drop everything and get to the dining room when we heard that clock chime or there

would be H-E-double L to pay. We quickly hid all evidence of
our dalliance with the whiskey and went across to the dining
room. Once there, we took our places around the table. Reverend
McElhenney[49] and Dr. Simpkins both escorted Mother to the head
of the table and sat in the two seats on either side of her, left and
right. I sat next to the reverend, and Margaret sat opposite, next to
Dr. Simpkins.

The foot of the table was left empty. That was John's seat. It
had been Father's place before him.

Mother took one look at all of the food on the table and said,
"We have been living like paupers for months. Where have you
been hiding all this, Caroline?"

Naturally, since I knew the answer, I said, "She was not hiding
food, Mother. She bought it at Creigh's today."

Margaret chimed on in and said, "My goodness you should see
the prices that man is charging: two dollars for calico. Seventy-five
cents is all it should be."[50]

So I said, "Mrs. Bell said they are charging four dollars for
calico in Charleston and one dollar and ten cents for a pound of
soap."

"Oh my! It was three cents when we were there last year,"
Margaret fretted, but quickly added, "not that I would have any
difficulty affording it, but I do worry so about others."

Reverend McElhenney cleared his throat to let us know that
it was time for him to give the blessing. It was a very proper and
genteel blessing about freedom and how the only way to truly
be free was through God's grace. I thought the subject was very
apropos.

Our esteemed pastor, Reverend McElhenney, is a most solemn
man with a true reverence for God. I do not believe that I have
told you much about him thus far. You should know that he is an
especially tall, spare man, yet even at his advanced age, he stands

as erect as an Indian. His frame has been hardened by years and years of vigorous exercise, much of which was done on horseback, traveling between the two churches that he ministered to, and visiting with his congregants at their homes. There is not an ounce of extra flesh to be found on him. Also, because he has always spent a good portion of his days in the open air, his complexion is a most healthy color, and, although I am sure I do not know why, he prefers his face clean-shaven.

The Reverend is known for his plain, practical ways: up at six o'clock every morning and in bed by nine at night. His preaching is never sentimental and he never discusses politics or business in his sermons. No matter what absurdities are going on in town or in the wide world, he keeps his mind and everyone else's in the church on the world to come. Outside of church, he was, of course, a son of the South. Although he has never spoken one way or the other about slavery, he did own slaves and, naturally, he deeply resented the trampling of our Virginia soil by the foe. Still, he never advocated for the violence that ensued and always prayed for the return of peace. I once heard him say that he was greatly saddened by the young people who were rushing into the calamity of the War with too much enthusiasm and too little sense of what tribulations would come to pass.

The only indulgence, if you can even call it that, Reverend McElhenney ever allowed himself was to ride fast and hard about the counties. Mrs. Ophelia McLaughlin once chided him for working his horse too roughly and he retorted that it was a greater kindness to ride fast and get his horse home to pasture then to have the poor creature work his whole day moving slowly along the road and never get home to graze. Another time, he was galloping across Mr. Hunter's bridge, the one that abuts the Elmhurst property, and Mr. Hunter reminded the pastor that the law forbade going faster than a walk across a bridge. The fine was five whole dollars. Reverend McElhenney proffered ten dollars and when Mr. Hunter began to search for change, Reverend McElhenney replied, "Never mind, I'll run out the other five as I go back," and galloped on off.

Well, after Reverend McElhenney blessed the food, we began passing the dishes and trying to enjoy the simple food Caroline prepared. Dr. Simpkins asked the Reverend about his new horse. The Reverend said it was a gift from the Hutsenpillers. He said that she was a fine horse, but that he missed old Donum. The Reverend's faithful horse Donum had been stolen by the Yankees the year before. He loved that horse and used to brag that a watch was misleading but old Donum would always bring him to an appointment in good season.

The town so adored and admired the Reverend, and still does, that a delegation was sent to talk with that horrid Colonel George Crook who was occupying Lewisburg to ask him to return the horse. Colonel Crook refused, but now what would you expect from a Yankee named Crook? Afterward, the Reverend said, "I don't wish the person who stole Donum any harm, but I wouldn't object if Donum should stumble, and the man would break his neck." Is that not just too funny? As I said, the Reverend has a quick wit.

What happened after the Battle of Lewisburg was not funny at all. When the Yankee troops were marching back on through town, a bushwhacker, who was not even a citizen of our town, started firing on the Yankees from inside a house. That cowardly man killed at least one of the wounded men and then he ran away leaving us to incur Colonel Crook's wrath. Well, naturally, Colonel Crook was irate and he vetted his anger on the whole town although we were in no way responsible. He would not let us bury the dead. The bodies had to just lie in the vestibule of Reverend McElhenney's Church, day after day. You cannot even imagine how the abominable situation mortified us all. Finally, Colonel Crook and his horrid Yankees left town. By then, there was nothing else to be done but to bury all those heroic souls in a mass grave. Such a travesty!

Well, anyway, we were having a most polite and jovial conversation at dinner that night when of a sudden, Mother blurted out, "You are hiding something from me. You all know something about Johnny, something terrible, and you will not tell me. I am tired of this nonsense, tell me what you know!"

We were not hiding anything. None of us knew a thing and, believe you me, if anybody was going to know what happened, it would be me. Why often times I would learn of news even before Mrs. Bell had heard tale! The truth of the matter was that John had joined up with General Henry Heth's men on the day of the Battle of Lewisburg; but there was such disarray in that retreat that no one seems to have noticed him. And, even though, according to Caroline, he marched off in a lieutenant's uniform, he was never ever listed as having been commissioned.

Della Cutlip's cousin's husband Charles was with the Forty-fifth Virginia Infantry and she had written to him about John several times. Charles Cutlip wrote to his wife regularly yet never answered her questions about John—not ever! Della had shown me the letters so I knew it to be true. Not that I had any reason to doubt Della. Despite her many other faults, she was honest as the day is long.

Well anyway, Reverend McElhenney tried to console Mother, but she was not having any part of it. Just then, the irritating, family dog began barking outside. I never understood why John kept that beagle dog. John never was much of a hunter. Sure, he would go off in the woods for hours, but he never came back with anything he had shot.

That dog's barking was quite annoying and Mother said, "Will

someone shut that mongrel up? My head is aching." Dr. Simpkins
offered to get her a medicinal remedy but she said, and this is very
important, she said, "No, I took something before dinner. It is
making me tired. I am going back to bed."

She stood up and began to leave the room. Naturally, Dr.
Simpkins offered to accompany her. But she turned him down,
insisting, "No, no; I will go myself. You all carry on and enjoy
yourselves. It will be good practice for when I am dead."

I see you find that remark a little shocking. Well, it most
certainly did not surprise any of us. Why, we had heard Mother
repeat that line at least a hundred times before! She tried to alarm
us with such outrageous contentions, but we had become inured
to all her silly claims. Believe you me, we had heard and seen it
all before. She had been acting that way since she turned forty—
always on the verge of death. On the other hand, newcomers could
be easily convinced that she had one foot already in the grave,
even doctors; and she reveled in all the attention she received from
them.

Well anyway, that tiresome dog began to bark more vigorously.
Consequently, Mother said, "Samuel, shoot that dog," and headed
out the doorway and up the stairs. The barking continued and
Samuel stood up. Margaret, being the kind-hearted person that she
is, shrieked.

"I am not going to shoot our dog," Samuel said. "I just wanted
to see what he is barking at."

"Probably just a rabbit," the Reverend counseled. "Come, sit
back down, Son."

Sure enough, the barking stopped and Samuel returned to his
seat. The situation with Mother and all the barking had unsettled
my nerves, so I asked the Reverend to pass me the brandy and
I had just a touch more. Dr. Simpkins joked that I had better be
careful or I might need his services more than Mother, but I re-

assured him that all I ever did was sip. Everyone laughed at the delightful banter and we all resumed eating and conversing.

Suddenly, we heard the horrifying shouts of "Hurrah! Hurrah! Hurrah!"[51] and the stomping of running boots. The door from the kitchen into the dining room was nearly blown from its hinges. It crashed into the wall and a group of six or so Yankee soldiers burst into the room. Before we knew what was what, they surrounded us, guns pointed in our faces. We were paralyzed in our seats and rendered mute by fear. With the exception of one man, a young officer who was quite exceptionally handsome, they seemed a horrible, nasty, dirty bunch of men, intent on no good.

Their leader, a sergeant named Richter, was an imposing figure. I would say he was in his late thirties, possibly early forties, tall and muscular with a full, dark beard. The handsome young officer was a surgeon and a captain; he was called Tobin. He was definitely in his late twenties or possibly early thirties, with a strong, angular face and mesmerizing eyes. Why, they were so blue they practically clashed with the red walls of the dining room! He was the only one among these Yankees who did not have a full, scraggly beard, just a well-trimmed goatee. It made him look distinguished and genteel, like he came from money. Come to think of it, his boots and other trimmings clearly marked that he came from money, considerable money I would say. The others, however, had no mind for grooming which is just like a vulgar Yankee. I tell you, I had certainly never seen Confederate soldiers looking so disheveled. They knew the importance of making a good appearance.

Well anyway, that Sergeant Richter walked around the table and looked us up and down and sideways as we sat waiting. We were quivering with fear. Now, when I say, "quivering," I mean quivering! I tell you, I was so scared for my life that I did not notice that I was still holding my wine glass and how, because my hand was shaking, I had sloshed brandy all over Mother's beautiful white tablecloth. Naturally, as soon as I regained a little composure and discovered this situation, I set down the glass.

As I said, that Sergeant Richter walked around the table and sized us up. His look was one of avarice combined with disgust. Finally, he stopped at the foot of the table and gripped the top of my brother's chair. With my niece, Sally, and my nephew, Samuel, on either side of him, he looked as though he could be their father instead of our enemy. Woe that he were!

While this was happening, there were other soldiers running about the house tearing things apart. However, we knew not of the destruction, for it was deadly quiet in the dining room—just like time was standing still in that room. As I well recall, you could not even hear the ticking of the long case clock in the hall which is usually so horribly loud that, even after all those years of hearing it tick and chime, I still found it an annoyance.

Anyway, that Sergeant Richter glared at us and, after what seemed like an eternity, he said with self-righteous contempt, "Would you look at this: there is a war going on and these people are having a dinner party! You ought to be ashamed of yourselves, celebrating like kings while young men are dying like dogs. Well, your little party is over." Then, he paused again and stared at us some more. "Now, before anyone gets hurt," he continued, "tell me where you have hidden the medical supplies." Medical supplies? Goodness me, what medical supplies? We did not have any medical supplies, but we were all too stunned and frightened to answer him as such.

So, he shouted at us, "Where are the medical supplies? Where are they?"

We had absolutely no idea what he was carrying on about. We were not hiding any medical supplies. We were simply innocent civilian bystanders. Naturally, though, we were all too frightened to speak up.

With an angry roar, Sergeant Richter picked up John's chair and smashed it against the fireplace. Pieces flew everywhere. "Tell me where they are," he roared.

Again, his command was met with silence as we shivered with fear. He picked up a disembodied chair leg in one of his powerful fists, placed the end of it in the fire, and made a torch. Brandishing his weapon of destruction, Sergeant Richter clenched his teeth and ordered, "Tell me now where those supplies are!" He waited a few moments more and then gloated, "No matter, we'll find them ourselves. And after we do, we will burn this house down."

Burn the house down! Oh my, what a horrid idea. As if this whole predicament were not alarming enough, to our extreme shock, Caroline jumped to her feet and exclaimed, "Wait! Please, you cannot burn the house down. My mother-in-law is ill. She is in her bed upstairs. If we try to move her, she will die for sure!" This outburst caused Margaret and myself to gasp in surprise and stare at each other. Firstly, Caroline never spoke up like that. She knew her place. Secondly, it was a bold-faced lie. There was not a thing in the world wrong with Mother.

My heart began the palpitations. Just what would that nasty sergeant do to us when he discovered the truth?

Chapter Eleven:
Full of Explanations and Surprises
As Told by Sergeant Ephraim Richter

If you wrote to me with the hope of receiving incriminating evidence of some kind, you have wasted your time. It was wartime. I was a soldier. I did what needed to be done. My cause was righteous. My actions were proper and justified.

I am responding to your query only because you too were a soldier and I respect your service to our country. No matter what you have likely heard to the contrary from those Confederate sympathizers you have already interviewed, I acted only as the law and my conscience dictated.

To understand what happened those days, you must know that 1) I firmly believe that every Christian had a duty to end the abominable institution of slavery, 2) I completely reject the notion of "innocent bystanders" during wartime, and 3) because I hold these two fundamental beliefs, I am a great admirer of General David Hunter.[52]

My first affirmation needs no explanation. If you do not understand the affront to all Christian morals that the system of slavery perpetrated, then you are lost, plain and simple. I know that most of my comrades were not fighting on behalf of the enslaved, but I was. My second declaration I will defend by asserting that every man, woman, and child of rational age on the home front was abetting one side or the other on the warfront. Some were actively assisting by raising funds or providing food, clothing, shelter, and other necessities for the war effort. The others were offering passive assistance through their silence. Our country is a democracy. Our elected officials respond to what we say. If people hold their tongues and do not speak out against atrocities, then they are complicit, plain and simple.

As for the third avowal of my high esteem for General Hunter, I will state simply that he is a man of integrity and principles—a true leader and not a politician like most of the men in our state and national capitals. Surprisingly, many people are not familiar with General Hunter's distinguished career. In case you are ignorant of his noble deeds, I will tell you a little about him. General Hunter took command of the Department of the South in March of 1862. In May of that year, he issued General Order Number Eleven. During the War, I carried it around in my breast pocket, along with a photograph of my wife and daughter. On bleak days when all hope seemed lost, they reminded me of what I was fighting for and what I would come back home to when it was all over.

The order said that because the states of Georgia, Florida and South Carolina had, "Deliberately declared themselves no longer under the protection of the United States of America, and had taken up arms against the said United States," it was a military necessity to declare them under martial law. Since, "Slavery and martial law in a free country are altogether incompatible," the persons in these three states held as slaves, are therefore declared forever free. President Lincoln rescinded the order because he did not want to upset the Border States. He always favored compromise over principle. I do not know why the South thought his election would threaten slavery. They certainly did not need to secede on account of him.

General Hunter, though, would not be deterred by politics. He sent a notice to Congress. He told those politicians that there was no such thing as a fugitive slave, only fugitive rebels, "Men who everywhere fly before the appearance of the National Flag." General Hunter stood in defiance and said that he would employ all loyal persons offering service in defense of the Union and for suppression of the rebellion no matter what color they be. I have set many of his inspiring speeches to memory. Not three months later, President Lincoln finally changed his mind and issued the Emancipation Proclamation. I have not committed that speech to memory. Poor martyred soul. He was a terrible speechwriter, not like General Hunter.

General Hunter is sometimes called "Black Dave" because he burned many buildings like Virginia Governor John Letcher's house, Mrs. Henrietta E. Lee's[53] home, and the buildings of the Virginia Military Institute. However, he did not burn the buildings out of malice. It was a calculated military maneuver. The War would never have been won without discomforting and demoralizing Southern civilians. We had to bring the proud and vainglorious South to its knees. We had to make their lives as wretched as they had made the lives of the slaves by taking away their nice homes, fancy clothes, and fine food, and replacing all their comforts with misery and fear. Otherwise, they might never have surrendered.

With that understood, I submit to you my account of what occurred on May 22 and May 23, 1863. As you requested, I will begin with a short history of myself and how I happened to be in western Virginia on those dates:

Before the War, I was a shipbuilder by trade. I built side-wheelers in New Albany, Indiana. There were six shipbuilding companies in town. At our peak, each company was laying down three boats at a time to keep up with demand and was turning out twenty-two packets a year. First ship I worked on was the *Eliza Battle*. She was as fine a ship as they come. Some called her "palatial." Her interior was as grand as any home I had ever known: rosewood paneling, Wilton carpeting, brocatelle, satin at twenty dollars a yard, Limoges china, and silver from Reed & Barton. We launched her in 1852. For six years there was not a more beautiful paddle steamer in the water. Then, one night in March of 1858, two men robbed her stateroom and set her on fire to cover their escape. With nearly 1200 bales of cotton aboard, she was quickly engulfed in flames and sank to the bottom of the Tombigbee River. People say she is a ghost ship now. Many claim to have seen her floating in those waters, fire a-blazing.

As you know, when the fighting began, President Lincoln called for 75,000 men to volunteer for three month's service. Ninety days, that was all. They were certain the war would be over by Christmas. We Hoosiers were only asked to contribute 7,500 men but 22,000 volunteered in those first few months. I am certain that ten times that number joined in all. In August of 1861, I mustered in to the Third Indiana Cavalry, Forty-fifth Regiment Company C.

Originally, I went to Camp Noble to enlist.[54] It had been set up on the state fairgrounds in New Albany and served as a muster point for all of the area regiments. Many of the fine men at Camp Noble died from disease during the training. Throughout the War, there were outbreaks of measles, pneumonia, and smallpox, dysentery, diarrhea, typhoid and cholera. By the grace of God, I managed to avoid them all. I have recently learned that the odds of dying in battle were one in eighteen. The odds of dying of disease were one in eight.

To inter the poor souls who died from disease, President Lincoln established the first national cemetery in 1862 right in New Albany. The government bought a fine piece of land from Dr. Charles

Bowman and laid out the grounds. Some people believe that Arlington was the first national cemetery, but it was not. Now that I have returned home to New Albany, every Sunday, after church, no matter the weather, I walk through the rows of graves. I visit the boys to let them know their sacrifice will always be remembered.

From Camp Noble, I was sent to Madison, Indiana. My company was then ordered to the Army of the Potomac. We were moved to the District of Columbia along with five other companies. There was great excitement. Before we left, many had their pictures made to send home to their wives and mothers.

We were loaded on steamboats and headed up the Ohio River. This trip was only the second time I had ever taken a ride on one of the boats that I had helped to build over the preceding twenty years. The men and I were in fine spirits. We were treated to a calliope concert and afterward joined in a hearty singing of "John Brown's Body" and "Hail Columbia." Some men took to the bottle, others sought comfort in the Bible, but most of us passed the time in innocent horseplay. Almost immediately, we gave each other nicknames. The practice began as a lark but proved helpful in coping with battlefield deaths. "Jackal" and "Buffalo" reminded you of storybook characters and it was easier to lose them than Robert Harrington and William Lane.

We did not have much in those early days, only our uniforms, spurs, and a blanket each. Of course, our officers, who had home resources to rely on, were brilliantly arrayed in their custom-made uniforms. Thanks to the generous loan to the state from James Lanier of Madison, we Hoosiers were actually better situated than the volunteers of other states. We were even issued drawers as part of our uniform. Most of the men had never worn them before. They didn't understand what they were. Some of the older men told these fellows that it was a special dress uniform to be worn on parade and they half believed it.

Unfortunately, like some other states, two of our Indiana regiments began the War wearing grey jackets. This situation often made it difficult to tell friend from foe.

Our journey on water was short. The river was low. We had to abandon our boats in Wheeling, Virginia and then march to Pittsburgh. The three-day journey was nearly sixty miles across mountainous terrain. Without any equipment or supplies, the men had to raid farms for wheat sacks or anything else that could be stuffed with hay to improvise a saddle. Clotheslines became makeshift stirrups. As we made our way, we were fortunate that the loyal citizens of Virginia and Pennsylvania who we encountered made us welcome and did their best to feed us.

When we arrived in Pittsburgh, we boarded railroad cars and soon arrived in our nation's capital. We camped in the northeastern outskirts of Washington City for almost three months, drilling on horseback. The government furnished us now with saddles, bridles, haversacks, canteens, sabers, and two horse pistols that fastened onto holsters on the front part of the saddles. As soon as we were ready, we were sent to Budd's Ferry, Maryland under the command of General Joseph Hooker. We became known as "Hooker's Horse Marines," and we saw plenty of action.

I was fairly adept in the saddle and not a bad shot, but my true talent lay in observation. I was a city boy. The country we traveled through was novel to me. So, I noticed everything about my new surroundings: the sights, sounds, and smells. From signs like ruts in the ground, trampled vegetation, the pitch of the bird calls, or the lingering stench of human existence, I could tell if troops were nearby or had passed through, if it was a large force or small, if they had artillery, and where they were most likely heading. Also, I was good with maps and a compass. A quick study and I knew where to go and how to get there.

Our officers discovered that I possessed these skills and often asked me to be a scout. I would leave camp, go behind enemy lines for a week or two, and return with valuable information about troop positions, strength, and movement. I traveled alone. Later, when I was promoted to Sergeant, I was put in charge of a group of scouts and we sometimes journeyed together. They were brave and talented young men.

At the start, we dressed as civilians. As the war went on, any healthy man who was not in uniform became suspect in the South. Therefore, sometimes we dressed in Confederate uniforms and tried to blend in, other times we were in our own uniforms and pretended to be deserters. I was never any good at counterfeit, so I usually kept my distance from people and sent my men on the missions that required talking. Otherwise, people might ask me questions and, if I could not sham the answers convincingly, I would have found my neck in a noose. Those two days in 1863 that you asked about were one of the few occasions during the course of the entire War that I had any direct contact with Southern civilians.

That May, my regiment, the Third Indiana Cavalry, was camped in Virginia, north of the Rappahannock River. We had just fought at Chancellorsville and were soon to fight the great cavalry battle now called the Battle of Brandy Station. (This battle decimated so many in our ranks that the surviving soldiers were detailed as a Headquarters Guard Unit until the regiment could be reconstituted). Medical supplies had become greatly depleted with no indication that they would be replenished. Word was that a hospital in White Sulphur Springs, Virginia had a considerable supply of ether, morphine, and chloroform. I was placed in charge of a small party of a dozen men with orders to confiscate these stocks. Assistant Surgeon James Tobin was assigned to accompany us to help identify the medicines we needed from those he thought did more harm than good. At first, with him being a captain and me only a sergeant, I did not like the idea of his joining my mission. But, he had no airs about him—was as easy-going as a man could be. He was happy to let me be in charge, so we got along fine.

My men, Captain Tobin, and I traveled southwest for approximately six days and arrived in White Sulphur Springs. Disguised as orderlies, two of my scouts infiltrated the facility while the rest of us waited, hidden in the woods nearby. Before the War, the facility had been a hotel,[55] a playground, really, where rich white Southerners could come to escape the heat of the coastal cities. I had never seen anything like it in regard to extravagance and waste. This was what they did with their slave labor: the main building was the size of an entire city block! While at one time the hotel must have catered to every frivolous desire of its guests, as a hospital, it could not meet the desperate needs of its occupants. Bandages and brandy, both made by the women of Greenbrier County, were all it had to offer its wounded patients.

However, my scouts were told of a home, located only a few miles to the west, where medical supplies were being stockpiled. They were told that the house harbored enough medicine to supply a battalion. I decided that we should investigate the situation.

We arrived midday at our destination. Certain that no Confederate troops were in the vicinity, we concealed our horses a short distance to the east of the house with only one man to guard them. We did not intend to be away for long. Also, even though the house was located at the intersection of two major roads, the surrounding terrain served to isolate it from neighboring farms. There was a sharp hill blocking access to the North, a river on the West, and woods to the South and East. While we were as safely sheltered as we could hope to be, the seclusion of the estate did not bode well for its inhabitants. It seemed as though we could basically do as we needed with impunity.

As we approached the house, a dog began to bark. Captain Tobin cleverly silenced the mutt with a strip of jerky. It appeared that no one had been alerted. I sent Private Foster ahead to assess the situation. He reported that the residents were all inside the house, eating dinner. Therefore, our search of the premises began with the outbuildings. We could not find anything of use aside from a pair of boots that I allowed Private Kelly to commandeer since the soles had separated on his.

As the men searched and came up empty-handed, it became clear to me that the medical supplies were being stored in the house. I debated whether to try to acquire them through a ruse, the scouts who had pretended to be orderlies in White Sulphur could request supplies for the hospital, or to simply take them by force. Because Private Foster had indicated that there were only women, children, and old men about, I figured that it would be more expedient to scare them into surrendering the supplies—we had already wasted enough time. There were five entries to the house on the ground level. (The owners clearly were not concerned about intruders). I divided my men, sending four to enter from the front and another three to enter from the side. I kept four men and Captain Tobin with me to subdue the occupants in the dining room. We entered through the kitchen door.

Once inside, I discovered that the occupants were not simply eating dinner, they were enjoying a bountiful feast. How could they be so selfish? Didn't they care about their men—cold, tired, hungry, afraid, suffering the worst of agonies? Their behavior made me irate. I am certain that you can understand my anger. To go from the battlefield to the hospital to this display of total disregard for anyone else was infuriating.

However, as angry as I was, I knew that my duty was to obtain the medical supplies, so I kept my head. I demanded that those selfish people tell me where they were hiding the supplies. They refused to divulge the location. So, I tried to scare them. I smashed a chair, made a torch, and like my hero General Hunter would have done, threatened to burn the house down. A woman stood up and claimed that her mother-in-law was bedridden and could not be moved. "A likely story," I said in disbelief.

A little girl seated to my left looked up at me and boldly said, "Oh no, Sir, it is true. Grandmother is very sick."

"You are an impertinent girl," I scolded.

"Oh, yes, Sir," she replied. "Grandmother says I am more outspoken than Senator Thaddeus Stevens.[56]"

"She does, does she?"

"Oh yes, Sir. And she also says I am more difficult than the seven labors of Hercules." I could not help myself; that remark made me chuckle. So, I said, "What is your name, child?"

"Sarah Anderson, Sir, but everyone calls me "Sally" because I am too sassy to be a Sarah."

"And how old are you, Sally?"

"I am nine years old, Sir. Nine long years"

"And tell me, little Sally, what does your mother do when she catches you being naughty, for instance, if she catches you telling a lie?" I said this as a warning, looking not at the girl but staring at the woman who had challenged me. I assumed she was the girl's mother.

"Actually, Sir, Grandmother is the one who does the punishing in this house, and she is very clever at devising punishments. Why only last week she caught me lowering our dog Skippy down the hole in the outhouse and she made me help Mrs. Weikle care for the awful twins."

"Sally, please," a gaunt, elderly man at the table interrupted, unsuccessfully trying to silence the girl. She continued.

"But, I promise you, Sir, my grandmother is very, very sick. She looks just like the plague victims. I have seen pictures of them in this book *The Horrors of the Black Death.*[57] There are pictures of plague masks and boils and sores and..."

"Sally, please!" The man insisted.

But the little imp had softened me a touch. So I said, "Well, little Sally, I have a daughter just your age. For her sake and yours, I shall have my surgeon examine your grandmother. If she is indeed too ill to be moved, I shall not burn down your house. But, if you have been lying to me, I shall deal with you all severely."

I called for Captain Tobin and asked him to find the sick woman and examine her. The outspoken woman offered to show him to the room. I did not trust her and I was certain Captain Tobin could find the room without assistance, so I ordered her to sit. As she returned to her seat she stated simply that the bedroom would be locked. I assumed that we had finally found where the supplies were hidden. I told her that we would break down the door and the woman offered to retrieve a key from the pantry. Then, little Sally chimed in and said that she had a key with her. To everyone's amazement, she picked up a rag doll[58] from her lap, placed it on the table, opened a seam in the doll's back, and removed a key. Captain Tobin took the key and left the room.

While I waited for a report from Captain Tobin on the woman's condition, and from the rest of my men, as to what supplies, if any, they had found, I decided to see if I could learn anything useful from these people.

Chapter Twelve:
With Further Revelations about the Heroine But Much Remaining Hidden Until Later
As Told by Caroline Anderson

I am not for sure how old I was when my eyesight started
to fail, but I have had trouble seeing things at a distance for as
long as I can remember. I can see perfectly fine to about the end
of my arm's reach, but beyond that point, the details get blurry.
One of the kindnesses that Mrs. Anderson had done for me was
to buy me a pair of spectacles. But, as I had mentioned before,
Frank had knocked them off my face earlier that day, and I had
not had a chance to find them that afternoon. So, when those
soldiers charged into the room at us, all I could make out was the
brightness of their enraged eyes, their mouths open in wide bellow,
and their hands gripped tightly on their guns. It was the most
terrifying sight I have ever witnessed. I remember pulling Sally
close to me, wrapping my arms around her, and ducking down a
bit to brace for a physical attack. But none came.

Instead, their leader hit us with words. They made no sense
to me at first for I was too scared to take any meaning, but then I
understood that he was threatening to burn down Elmhurst.

I was raised up in the hollers. I was the fifth of thirteen
children and the only girl among them until I was ten. Our house
was a wood shack with dirt floors and greased paper in the

windows. The best you could say about the place was that it kept the rain out... mostly. There surely was no privacy in that place. When my mama was pregnant with baby number nine, a neighbor friend who was visiting pointed at my mama's belly and joked to her and my father, "I guess you two don't know what causes that." My six year-old brother Willard answered back, "Like Hell they don't."

When that Sergeant Richter threatened to burn down my beautiful brick house with fine carpets across its polished oak floors, and beautiful glass-paned windows, I became bold. Even though the guns were pointed right at us and the soldiers looked like they would have no trouble using them, I was not going to lose my beloved house without a fight.

I had spent the past seven years caring for that place, scrubbing it clean, sewing curtains, and quilting coverlets. I knew every inch of that house like the back of my hand. So, I did something I had never ever done before: I spoke out. Not only that, but also I did something that I swore I would never be so mean as to do: I lied. I stood up and told that hateful sergeant that Mrs. Anderson was in her bed dying when I did not even believe there was the first thing wrong with her. Sally, who loved to tell stories and did not understand the danger, joined in the lie.

But that Union man was clever and he took me to task. He sent a surgeon to examine Mrs. Anderson. Although I imagined that she would put on quite a show for the surgeon, I worried that her performance would not be enough to convince a medical man that her passing was imminent. I shuddered to think of what that commander might do if he caught me in that lie.

My mother used to warn me that men would cut out the tongues of women who gossiped and lied. She used to tell tales of a woman named Philomela[59] who had her tongue cut out for being a gossip. Even after she had been so cruelly butchered, Philomela still did not learn her lesson. Instead, she became a weaver and told lies about people through her weaving. So they cut off her fingers as well. Mother's stories, as I am certain she intended, scared the living daylights out of me. They were part of the reason I always kept quiet. After the sergeant smashed up a chair the way he did, I was not at all for sure what violence he was capable of. I prayed it was not cutting out tongues and chopping off fingers.

He seemed to relish his position of power and our fear of him. But, for the time being, he held off on destroying anything more. Instead, he began to ask all sorts of questions of us as we waited for the surgeon's report. He walked up close to me and I tried to look him in the eye. But, his overpowering smell of sweat, bad teeth, and smoke forced me to turn my head. Hovering over me, he said, "This is your home, I presume."

Orpha, who had been unusually, but thankfully, quiet till that point was indignant. She shouted, "No!" but the sergeant glared at her and waited for me to reply.

"It is my mother-in-law's house," I corrected.

"Where is your husband?"

"I wish I knew."

"You are Confederates, no doubt."

"Most people in these parts sympathize with the Southern cause," Reverend McElhenney put in.

"And you do not?"

For some reason, I was twitching to talk. I would have liked to have said that I did not sympathize with any side, that the killing was horrible, and that my sympathy was only for people trying to get by and make do. But, my concern was for my house and the lives of the people in that dining room. Speaking my mind would only have angered that sergeant and put us all in worse danger, so, like always, I held my tongue. Whether it was from fear or good sense, everyone else remained quiet as well.

Before the sergeant could follow up on his question, two more soldiers entered with Hartwell at gunpoint. One of these soldiers approached and said, "Sergeant Richter, we searched the premises. We found no munitions or medical supplies, Sir, only him."

Hartwell usually went home each day after eating his dinner. However, he had decided to do me a favor and stay late to help clean up after the big meal. At the time the soldiers arrived, he had finished his dinner and had been upstairs, resting in one of the extra bedrooms over the kitchen. I looked up at him and tried to show how sorry I was that he was caught up in our trouble.

Sergeant Richter looked at me and asked, "Is this your slave?"

"We do not own slaves, Sir," I said sharply. "This is Mr. Finney, our handyman. He is a free man."

The sergeant asked Hartwell if my statement was true and Hartwell proudly agreed it was. Then the sergeant wanted to know if there was anyone else "hiding?" I tensed up as I remembered Frank, wondering if he was still about somewhere and what it might mean to our safety if they thought we were hiding enemy soldiers. But the Union soldiers had searched the grounds. I was for sure that they would have found Frank if he had not left. So, I figured that he was long gone and told Sergeant Richter that he had found us all. Sally piped up and said, "Well, Sir, there is the ghost of my dearly deceased brother." Reverend McElhenney tried to shush her but she continued, "Sorry, Sir, Reverend McElhenney says that I must not speak of him. But, if you stay long, I am certain you will meet him."

"I will be on the lookout," the sergeant replied with a shake of his head and what appeared to be an amused smile. Then, he threw the torched chair leg into the fire.

While we waited in stone-cold silence downstairs, we could hear the sounds of destruction coming from upstairs.

Chapter Thirteen:
In Which a Diagnosis is Given
As Told by Captain James Tobin

I have never set foot on Indiana soil. At the time I enlisted, I called no place "home." Assistant surgeons could sometimes be assigned to regiments on an as-needed basis. Evidently, the men of Indiana needed me.

I was born and raised in Philadelphia, City of Brotherly Love, and the most religiously tolerant. Although my family was quite comfortable monetarily, I was expected to have an occupation. I chose medicine. I left Philadelphia at the age of twenty to pursue my career and returned only twice: once for my mother's funeral and less than a year later for my father's. She died of a cancer; he died from a broken heart.

My only sibling was an older brother, Franklin. My senior by six years, he had grown accustomed to his life as an only child and resented the disruption to the household equilibrium that my birth initiated. Franklin was superbly clever and industrious, always earning the second highest grade in his class. At first, I idolized him and toddled in his footsteps; but he imparted to me in no uncertain terms that he thought me little more than a parasite. Initially, I was deeply wounded by his rebukes. As I grew, however, I learned to be less impressed with his accomplishments and more pleased with my own, for without expending any energy, I was first in my class. My ability to succeed effortlessly infuriated my hard-working brother. He was never unkind to me in any overt manner, and in regard for my parents, he maintained a civil albeit cold manner toward me.

When my father's will was executed, the estate was split between the two of us, and we each inherited a fortune. I was a student at the time, unsure of where, or even if, I might settle down. My chief concerns were hedonistic. Accordingly, having no definitive notion of what to do with my windfall, I decided to leave the money in trust for such time when either inspiration should strike or I should decide I was ready to be a "serious" fellow.

Immediately prior to the outbreak of the War, I was working in the District of Columbia for the United States Medical Department. With no incentive to earn money, I had applied for the position because it required far less of me than either private practice or hospital work. Both my peers and my superior officers in the Medical Department appreciated my lack of vocational aspirations because it rendered me far more affable and far less threatening to their future career advancements.

Life was indeed pleasant. I had no thought as to how the impending crisis would change my agreeable situation. My light duties afforded me copious time to socialize. Our nation's capital was, and remains, not much more than a country town, but it uniquely offered an ample supply of female clerks, who if you have not yet discovered for yourself, are a progressive breed. Word spread quickly among these liberal women that I had expertise in all manners of caring for the female anatomy. I applied my skills and services often.

When the hostilities began, I was sent to Camp Thomas[60] near Columbus, Ohio to perform physical assessments of recruits. Since the army accepted all regardless of their age, ailments, and handicaps, I was to weed out those who were unsuited to fight: asthmatic, consumptive, one-eyed, club-footed, I saw it all. I am certain that for every soldier on active duty who was discharged for wounds or sickness, three were sent home because they were disabled before enlistment.

At that time, the entire United States Medical Department was in a state of disarray under the ossified and useless Surgeon General Clement Finley.[61] Fortunately, the Sanitary Commission assumed the responsibility of providing medical services for the army. Under the direction of Frederick Law Olmsted[62], they sent inspection teams to the volunteer camps, examined the data that had been collected during the Crimean War[63], and improved the soldiers' health greatly by lobbying Congress to hire experienced cooks and providing more nourishing meals. Then, in April 1862, William Alexander Hammond became Surgeon General. The result: hospitals were better supplied; surgeons better trained, and record keeping improved. Hammond also hired Dr. Jonathan Letterman[64] who established a system for the safe and prompt removal of battlefield wounded to field hospitals using a permanent ambulance corps.

Unfortunately, Hammond found himself on the wrong side of politics with too many important people. Secretary of War Stanton trumped up charges against him, something absurd on the order of irregular purchases of medical furniture. First, Hammond was re-assigned. Eventually he was court-martialed. But, I hear that he is faring well in New York City, studying nervous and mental diseases—a field that is in great need of research.

Shortly after Hammond took office in 1862, I was re-assigned as well. This decision was not made for the betterment of either the troops or war effort, and certainly not for my improvement; rather, it was made to benefit one Major William Johnson. His wife had taken a strong fancy to me after I had treated her for a sprained ankle. The therapy was strictly clinical, but as I have learned, the mere touch of a woman's ankle by a man is often enough to incite in her an intense passion (the wrist as well). Although I had in no manner encouraged her infatuation, and maintained sufficient distance from her to prove to all my honest intentions, her jealous husband decided to widen the gulf—and to put me as closely in harm's way as possible. Major Johnson had a friend with the Third Indiana Cavalry who was pleased to retain my services for his troops. My days of ease were thus ended.

I had no noble dreams of service to my country or countrymen; yet, with this new position, close to one thousand men looked to me to help them in their time of need. I quickly lost my cavalier attitude and endeavored to serve them well. I was with them at Antietam and many other bloody battles. I prefer not to talk about what I saw and what I had to do. You were there. You know the conditions. Suffice it to say, I was able to put a small number of men back into action and send others home.

My days with the Third Indiana Cavalry vacillated between the intense mental and corporeal exertions of battlefield work, to the unrelenting vigor of the marches, to the equally inexorable tedium of camp life. I was initially thankful for the relative safety that my position afforded me as compared with my comrades: division hospitals were far to the rear of the fighting. However, the longer my service lasted, the less I cared about my own safety. Why should I live when so many others died? I realized that, in the grand scheme, my life was insignificant—it mattered only because I had the ability to help others. Therefore, I was determined to save as many men as I could, even if I had to die.

I began working in the regimental dressing station. I thought, perhaps, I would be better able than my predecessors to stabilize the wounded and prepare them to be transported. We had only earthworks or other natural defenses to protect us, and the battlefield casualties were far more gruesome than the wounded that were alive enough to arrive at my operating table, but I far preferred dispensing whiskey and applying dressings to amputating limbs.

That May in 1863, the men had just survived Chancellorsville and our medical supplies were depleted. Hearing that scouts were being sent to liberate some supplies from a Rebel hospital, I inquired into the possibility of joining the expedition. Sergeant Ephraim Richter commanded the small band of intrepid men selected for the mission. I believed Richter to be a good man: passionate but not zealous, at least, not that I had witnessed... to that date. I admired his conviction, something I clearly lacked.

The journey to the hospital was both arduous and exhilarating. To avoid discovery, we traveled in the early dawn hours and at night until two or three o'clock, adopting the Spanish custom of long midday siestas. (Oddly, the extreme state of anxiety and stress that the body experiences in situations such as these, permits one to sleep wherever and whenever the opportunity arises). Half of the time, our advance was hindered by heavy spring rain. The terrain was steep and grueling for our horses, but it offered the most breathtaking vistas. On the clear nights, the sky was so illuminated with stars that one could see for miles across the valleys.

Perhaps the most trying element, though, was the deference shown to me by the men. Sergeant Richter insisted on protocol and distinction of rank at all times. As a captain, I was only permitted to speak sociably with him; yet, his conversation was terse and limited to matters directly before us. Not only was I forbidden to converse with the others, but they were also obliged to silence all jovial exchanges when I was nearby. For the first time in my life, I was lonely.

When we arrived at our destination, we camped for a few

days while two scouts gathered information. Unfortunately, the hospital was sadly lacking anything of use; therefore, Sergeant Richter decided to investigate the possibility that their medical supplies were housed off-sight. We relocated ourselves to a house nearby, an attractive Neo-Georgian. There, we discovered that the residents were enjoying a lavish dinner. The scene outraged Richter. With what I originally assumed was merely an intent to scare the residents; he threatened to burn the house. Like a modern-day Queen Esther, a young woman pleaded with Richter to spare the home since her mother-in-law was too ill to leave the premises. Richter sent me to verify the claim.

On Richter's orders, I ascended the stairs and went to examine the old woman in her bedroom. The other scouts in our party had been busy searching the upstairs rooms and attic, but had not yet entered the dying woman's bedroom. The door was locked and would have required considerable effort to break open. It was, I discovered, oak, two inches thick. Private Brody approached me and whispered that the scouts assumed the supplies were in the bedroom. They were afraid that someone armed was inside the room standing guard over the cache; accordingly, they were planning to attack *en masse* once the other rooms had been searched. I presented the key to Private Brody and he signaled for his comrades to join him. I stood aside as they carefully unlocked the door, quietly turned the knob, and then burst inside with a yell meant to frighten the fight out of their foe. No shots were fired at them or by them. The only enemy that greeted these brave men was the old woman, slumbering in her bed.

Private Brody called out "All's clear" and I entered the room. The force of the soldiers' entry into her room did not appear to have disturbed the old woman's slumber. As the scouts began to look through her drawers and search for hidden compartments in the walls and floors, I approached her bed. She was well dressed and well groomed, looking as if the undertaker had already done his work. On her nightstand I noticed nearly two dozen medicinal bottles. All appeared to be empty or near to it. They had contained every conceivable treatment from laudanum to sarsaparilla. Many bore the label of Edward Robinson Squibb. Squibb had served as a surgeon in the Navy during the Mexican War. Appalled by the quality of medicines available on the ships, he established his own pharmaceutical laboratory in Brooklyn, New York, dedicated to creating uniformly pure drugs. Squibb also designed the lightweight pannier box that was adopted by the army for battlefield use that I, and most of my fellow surgeons, relied upon.

The nightstand additionally supported a row of attractive blue porcelain jars labeled, "W.P. Blasgrove, Druggist, Brooklyn, New York." One jar, containing a bright white powder, was the only vessel that lay unmolested. Because it was so commonly prescribed, I assumed the jar contained calomel, a mercury based compound used as a purgative. Hammond had just banned the substance because he determined that it was neither safe nor effective. It was generally administered to patients until they began to salivate uncontrollably or their mouths turned brown. Often these patients lost their teeth and hair, if they survived at all. I was pleased that the old woman had refrained from ingesting it that day.

The old woman certainly spared no expense in regard to treating her ailments. As the search of the estate yielded no hoard, the stories of hidden medical provisions that had brought us to this residence must have been exaggerated tales based on these supplies acquired only for personal usage.

As I examined the empty bottles, I noticed that the woman had awakened and was watching me. Her glazed eyes revealed highly constricted pupils, and she seemed to be having difficulty focusing. "You are awake," I said cheerfully.

"How could I sleep through all this commotion? Are you the

angel of death?" she asked with a weak voice.

"No, quite the opposite, I am a surgeon."

"A handsome one; I have two widowed daughters."

"I am sorry to hear that."

"No, I mean they need husbands."

"I will take that under advisement."

"Do."

"I came to see you, however."

Her face lit up in response to these words and her voice grew a little stronger. "Yes," she replied proudly, "the handsome men always come to visit with me. My friends have always been green with envy. Do you know the game 'Kneel to the wittiest, bow to the prettiest, and kiss the hand of the one you love most?' When I was a girl and played the game with my friends, I was always 'the prettiest.' But, I have had so few male visitors since the War began and fewer still since I took ill."

"You are unwell?"

"Can you not see that I am dying?"

"Perhaps if you sat up or walked about."

"I have not been out of this bed for months."

"How unfortunate! May I examine you?"

"Yes, yes, please do. I need a proper examination. None of the local doctors can determine what is causing my ailments."

I felt her forehead and cheeks. Her skin was cold and clammy. Then I took her pulse. It was weak. She pulled back the sleeve of her nightdress, revealing an arm covered in rash.

"Not very pretty," she complained. "I used to have such beautiful skin. Everyone said so. Fortunately, the rash is only on my arms and my back and not on my face. I have taken such good care of the skin on my face. See how few wrinkles I have? One reason I have so few wrinkles is because I keep my face taut. I never smile. People who smile often have horrible wrinkles about the mouth and eyes."

I examined the rash: pale red bumps that appeared to be urticaria, a temporary allergic reaction and not a life-threatening condition. Trying to better determine the nature and severity of her illness, I asked, "How long ago did this rash appear?"

Her eyelids growing heavy, she ignored this question. "You have a very gentle and soothing touch," she replied instead. With that statement, she closed her eyes and drifted back into what I presumed was a drug-induced sleep.

The scouts had finished their search and it yielded no rewards. Clearly, the only medicine in the room was in the old woman's body. We walked downstairs together to report to Sergeant Richter. I was not certain what to tell him. I observed no clear indication that the old woman was suffering from a serious disorder; yet, something strangely instinctive caused me to believe that she would not be alive come the morrow. Perhaps it was the slight rasp that I had heard in her breathing. It was faint; yet, I wondered if the allergic reaction that had brought about her rash might not now be manifesting itself in her lungs.

"Well, Tobin?" Richter asked.

"The scouts found nothing. From what I observed, the only medications present in this house were being used to treat the old woman, and she had consumed them all."

"And her health?"

Thinking on the distance between this house and its neighbors, I replied confidently, "She is indeed too infirm to be moved. She would likely die before she reached the nearest home."

Richter surveyed the room to see how the residents responded to my news. None seemed moved by this revelation. If anything, they seemed relieved to hear my diagnosis. "Any chance of recovery?" he asked of me, still watching the reaction of the family.

"Slim, Sir. I would say she will be gone by morning."

With that statement, the men among the party guests looked appropriately distraught and the women whimpered, but none looked surprised.

CHAPTER FOURTEEN:
Wherein Arrangements Are Made For the Captives
As told by Sergeant Ephraim Richter

The members of that household had no information of
any value. The selfish twits were almost oblivious to what was
happening around them. My men found no medical supplies.
Our mission had been nothing but a goose chase. To ensure that
something beneficial came from it, I decided to make good on my
threat to burn down the house and to teach those people a lesson
they would never forget. While I knew that discomforting those
people would help our cause, I could not legally or morally bring
about the death of an old woman. Captain Tobin said that she
was too ill to move, but unlikely to survive the night. I decided to
wait until the morning. Then, I would give those people their just
reward.

I knew that we would be safe inside the house. So, why not
enjoy a good meal and a comfortable night's rest? We were due.
The family and their friends had been having a party. All I did was
add a few more people to the guest list. Nothing in the Articles
of War or the Lieber Code prohibits that. But I could not risk
allowing any of them to leave the premises. So, I told them, "No
one is to leave this house. As long as you cooperate, no one will be
harmed."

An older gentleman asked, "What do you mean by 'cooperate?'"

"I mean be quiet, go to your rooms, go to sleep, whatever; just don't give me any trouble."

"Sir, if you will permit," the other old gentleman interjected, "I would like to stay with the sick woman until her time comes. That is, nevertheless, why I am here. I am Reverend John McElhenney and this is Dr. Simpkins. He has been tending to her physical needs."

At the mention of a doctor, I became excited. Perhaps he had some supplies or knew where some might be acquired. But, before I could say anything, he said, "I have no medicines myself. I have had no supply since the War began. My sister has had her own supplies for years. She had them sent from New York back in '61, before Sumter.[65] She claimed that drugs made in Brooklyn were superior and never let me treat her with my own. I do believe they have lost their potency over the years, otherwise they would have been donated for military use."

"Very well," I conceded none too happily. Then, I ordered two privates to take the preacher and the doctor to the sick woman's room, adding, "Stay in the room and keep watch over them. I trust no one." They left to do as commanded while I considered the arrangements for the remaining people.

My spunky friend Sally asked, "Can we go to the attic, Sir? I am never allowed up there. It is haunted."

"No," I replied. "You must have a bedroom, though?" She nodded her head with disappointment.

"Stevens," I ordered, "take my friend Sally and the other girl to her bedroom." Sally sighed in resignation and the three headed upstairs. Having discerned that two bedrooms remained, I sent the men to one and the women to the other, each with two soldiers to guard them. I ordered one private to keep watch and patrol outside the house, another to take some food to the private guarding the horses, apprise him of our plans, and keep him company until the morning, and allowed the remaining two to eat and find a comfortable place downstairs to sleep until I changed the watch.

"And me?" Captain Tobin asked.

"As you will, I suppose."

When the others had departed, I seated myself at the table. The food looked delicious, like one of those mirages you hear about from men who have been in the desert too long. I began to eat what was on the plate in front of me. The food was indeed like manna from Heaven. "The Lord be praised," I said to Captain Tobin. "It's been a long time since I've sat at a table and had a meal. Sure beats hardtack[80], boiled beef, and desecrated, I mean desiccated vegetables."

CHAPTER FIFTEEN:
In Which the Heroine Is Sent to Await Her Fate
As Told by Caroline Anderson

I walked up the stairs with my sisters-in-law and our two captors. Orpha and Margaret walked painfully slow, whining and whimpering every step of the way. The stair risers, which had always seemed sturdy, groaned in reply to each foot that was laid heavily down upon them. With one of the soldiers close by my side, I arrived at the top of the stairs considerably sooner than the other three. We stood and waited in the upstairs hallway next to Mrs. Anderson's bedroom. The door had been left open. I was able to see that the room had been ransacked. Mrs. Anderson's belongings were thrown willy-nilly about the room. Her clothes and her precious magazines were strewn all over the room. Had she been in her right spirit, she would have been angrier than a wet hen. While I was horrified to see the mess, I was relieved as well for nothing much appeared to have been permanently damaged that could not be put right with time and hard work.

Mrs. Anderson appeared to be sleeping. I could hear clearly that her breathing was labored. If I had not heard her at the dining table just a bit earlier, I too would have believed her near death from all the rasping and gasping noises. I understood now why the captain pronounced her to be so gravely ill. Dr. Simpkins and Reverend McElhenney were standing by Mrs. Anderson's bed.

The soldiers guarding them had turned their attention to me. They walked closer to my guard, made lewd gestures and jokes about me toward their comrade, and watched for Orpha and Margaret to arrive. With the soldiers' backs turned to them, Reverend McElhenney took advantage of the distraction and quietly asked Dr. Simpkins, "What happened?"

"Damned if I know. Oh, sorry, Reverend, nerves."

"Perhaps the old girl willed this upon herself."

"Perhaps. Do you think it was wise for us to remove ourselves from the others? What if the women need our protection? And the little girls?"

"The women are strong," Reverend McElhenney said. "And that Sally is the wiliest critter I have ever met. They can fend for themselves for now. I trust that the sergeant will keep them safe so long as Grace remains alive. It is our job to keep her strong: my prayers, your medicine."

Finally, Orpha and Margaret made their noisy progression past their mother's room. They were far too absorbed in their own misery to look into her room and notice the change in her health. We continued on together to the master bedroom. Like Mrs. Anderson's room, it looked like a mighty wind had blown on through. Margaret immediately threw herself across the bed and began weeping. Her hoop skirt protruded comically into the air. Orpha tried to comfort her while I did what was natural to me: I began putting the place back in order.

"That Yankee!" Orpha started in. "He just does not understand. If only he had let Reverend McElhenney explain."

"What difference would it make?" Margaret sobbed. "They are all monsters."

Orpha gasped and looked over at the soldiers who were standing on the other side of the room to be for sure they had not heard Margaret. They seemed to have taken no notice. "Hush,

Margaret," she scolded. Margaret sat up and looked at the soldiers with disgust.

"Did you not see how he acted? He was so smug and self-righteous. Just because men choose to fight does not mean that women have to suffer endlessly for their stupidity. So what if we were having a nice dinner? We deserve a reprieve every now and again."

"Amen to that."

"Does he imagine that his wife is home keeping a cloistered vigil? Hah! Even Penelope had suitors around her as she waited for mighty Odysseus to return."

"His behavior was most insulting."

As usual, I stayed apart from this conversation. At this time, however, Margaret took notice of me. "Caroline, why are you picking things up?" she squawked. "That Yankee is going to burn the house down. It does not matter whether it is tidy."

CHAPTER SIXTEEN:
A Very Short Chapter to Express Confusion
As Told by Sally Anderson

For the 1,239,543rd time in my life, I was sent to my room. My bedroom was a mess and for the first time in my life, the mess was not my fault. Fortunately, the soldiers that had searched my room were not particularly intelligent. They did not find any of the treasures I had hidden in my room. Actually, none of the soldiers were any good at searching for things. There was treasure buried all over our yard! Why, only last week we hid the silver under the hen house.

"Pirate" was the only game my grandmother ever played with me. She invented the game when my father left to go to war. Grandmother would give me precious things to bury like jewelry and gold coins. She said they were family heirlooms. We would pick a hiding place and I would dig the hole and bury them. Then we would make a treasure map to remember where to find it. The maps themselves were all hidden in a secret compartment in Grandmother's bedside table. I knew that Grandmother would be very pleased that the soldiers had not found any of our treasure, and I thought of what a good chuckle the two of us would have about how we had tricked them.

Becky and I walked into the room and stood, waiting for instructions. Our guard looked down at us. We stared up at him. Finally, I asked, "What do we do now, Sir?"

CHAPTER SEVENTEEN:
Full of Contemplations on the Nature of Freedom
As Told by Hartwell Finney

We was taken to Mista Samuel's room, just him and me and two mean lookin' soldiers. The place had been torn asunder. Mista Samuel shook his head at the sight of it, but just let it be. He sat down on his bed, picked up a ball, and began to fidget. There weren't no chairs in Mista Samuel's room so I made myself as comfortable as I could on the floor, leanin' aginst the foot of his bed. Now, I am not one who has ever had the chance to set still for long times, so I started to do what I believe most people do when they have too much time on their hands: I started to fret. Right now, everthin' was quiet and calm, but that could change in a heartbeat.

I could tell that Mista Samuel was thinkin' real hard. I wondered what he was thinkin' about. Was he frettin' about his fam'ly or just worried 'bout hisself? Fine'ly, he lay on his belly and peered down at me.

"That Union captain asked if you were a slave," he said to me. "Don't you feel like one? I sure do."

"Oh, no," I says.

"But you do not really have any freedom," he kept on. "You always have to do what my family commands."

"No," I says, "I choose to do what they aks of me. At my age and with this war on, I don't have many places to go, but it's still

111

my choice to stay here. I can walk away any time I want and no one can stop me."

"I would like to walk away from this place or run if I have to."

"You cain't."

"Why not?"

"Because you're too young to be out on your own."

Sayin' that made Mista Samuel angry. He sat bolt up. "I am not. That's why I hate it here. No one treats me like a man— except when it comes to doing work. I get a man's workload, but not a man's respect."

I understood how Mista Samuel was feelin' cause I had felt the same way when I was his age. Don't most boys? But, I also understood the other side so I tried to explain it to him. "Mista Samuel," I says, "your daddy may be gone, but your family still has money, and it is Miz Caroline not you who is worrying 'bout providin' for the family. Until you have that worry, you are not a man."

"Men have to be brave and strong not worried. Worrying is for women and yellow-bellies."

"You don't understand," I said.

Mista Samuel turned onto his back and stared at the ceiling. "Not your logic, I don't."

I was gonna keep on, but just then, another soldier came on into the room. He said real rough, "You, boy, up with you." Mista Samuel got on up off that bed lickety-split. But the soldier shook his head with disgust and said, "Not you, darkie over here. Sergeant wants to see you downstairs." Mista Samuel he set hisself back down on the bed and I went after the soldier.

CHAPTER EIGHTEEN:
Wherein We Learn More About the Captors
As Told by Captain James Tobin

I joined Richter at the dining table, as did the other scouts who had not yet been assigned duties. I was accustomed to fine dining. My family had employed a French chef and I often enjoyed gourmet meals at my friends' homes in both Philadelphia and Cambridge. Before I joined the Third Indiana, I would have gone hungry rather than eat off of someone else's plate, using their utensils. Now, however, I thought it a luxury to be able to eat at a table on china dishes with fine silver, and I cared not a whit that the place had originally been set for another. I suppose I could have used my own knife and fork that I kept in my haversack,[66] or found clean utensils in the sideboard, but I saw no reason to bother.

While deprivation had indeed lowered my standards in all regards, I truly believe that the food I ate that evening would have rivaled many a meal that I had been served before the war. The cook's use of seasoning was bold. The turkey was served with a plum sauce made with honey and sage. It was complemented by fresh asparagus in something that resembled a Hollandaise sauce, black-eyed peas in a light onion sauce, mashed turnips, sliced bread and butter, and a delightful rhubarb and potato gratin. We all had begun to eat with the gusto of starvation but soon slowed our pace to savor each bite.

At one point, Richter stopped eating and became thoughtful. He sent Private Dodd to bring the colored man to him, explaining that he had a few more questions to ask. After Dodd left, Richter dismissed the other scouts in order that they have an opportunity to sleep for a few hours. Once the two of us were alone in the room, he poured us each a glass of brandy.

"I never imagined we would be taking women, children and old men prisoner," I said.

"A taste of their own medicine: imprisoning those who imprison others," Richter retorted.

"An interesting codicil to the moral code," I mused.

"It's only for one night. It's no hardship for them and a tremendous relief for us."

"Do not misunderstand me. I am happy to stay: I have not enjoyed female company in eleven months and here there are three somewhat attractive women who have not seen a healthy man between the ages of twenty and fifty in at least an equivalent time period. No need to leave on my behalf."

Richter was about to express his disapproval with my last remark when Dodd returned with the colored man.

CHAPTER NINETEEN:
More Musings on the Nature of Freedom
As Told by Hartwell Finney

I was taken down the stairs to appear b'fore the officer. His name was Richter. He aksed me my name again and I told him. Then he said that he wanted to know the truth and was I a slave.

"Oh, No, Sir," I said.

That officer Richter he looked in disbelief, so I says, "Missus Anderson she don't hold none for slavery like she used to cause she don't want no coloreds livin' on her land or in her house no more, and Miz. Caroline, she don't believe in it. She's too kind-hearted."

"She is, eh?"

"Oh, yessir. She's the most kind-hearted, white woman I know."

He took a moment to consider this info'mation. Then he aks me, "Are there many free Negroes in the area?"

"Depends on what you think 'many' is," I said.

"Yes, I suppose so," he said, and then he said "let me rephrase my question: how many free Negroes are there?"

"Well, Sir, there are about two hundred of us in Greenbrier County."[67]

Now all this time, that officer Richter was sippin' on some of our brandy and right about now he finished his glass and poured hisself another. "What do they do?" he aksed me.

"Most used to work for the White Sulphur Springs Company, waitin' on them fancy ho-tel guests who prob'ly thought they was slaves. But the ho-tel is a hospital now so don't none of them have jobs now."

"What are they doing then?"

"They's gettin' by. Some folks say that they'd been better off if'n they was slaves 'cause then they'd always be guaranteed a house and a meal, but I know that ain't so cause I know freedom is the most important thing of all. I know 'cause I used to be in bondage but now I's free. Ain't nothin' more important than freedom.

But if you don't believe me, you can aks the Good Reverend McElhenney upstairs. You see I aksed the Good Reverend once how come they be so many bad things happenin' like killin' and stealin', and he said it's because God wants us to have the free will and if God stopped people from doin' bad things then God would be takin' away their free will. So you see, even God thinks freedom is more important than anything else, more important than kindness and decency. He wants us to choose to be good, but it's our choice and we can choose the other way. We ain't meant to have good in our lives all the time, but we are always meant to have freedom."

CHAPTER TWENTY:
Wherein One of the Prisoners Considers the Danger of Her Situation
As Told by Orpha McClung

We were upstairs in the master bedroom. Margaret had finally quit her wailing and we were sitting on the bed, wondering what was to become of us. The two young ruffians who were guarding us were sitting on the floor leaning against the door as if to leave no doubt that we were their prisoners and at their mercy. They were eyeing us and talking to each other in low tones about what one could only assume were vulgar thoughts. For some foolish reason, Caroline was still tidying the room.

The house was very quiet. I heard the clock downstairs chiming the hour like the town crier—six o'clock and all was not well. Finally, Margaret broke the silence and announced, "Well, this is a bore."

"Hush, Margaret," I warned. "They will hear you."

"Who cares if they do?" she said flippantly. "What are they going to do?"

"For shame! How can you say such a thing? You never know what a man is capable of during war times."[68]

Although Margaret was never a reader, when I was young, I had actually read quite a bit about war and the behavior of soldiers. My father's library had many history books, and history,

117

naturally, is full of wars. My mother and my father did not know
that I would sneak into the library to read these books, and I am
for certain they could never have conceived that the topic of war
would have interested me, otherwise they most likely would have
barred me from looking at them. For some reason, I liked to read
about the Vikings and pirates and the Romans and especially the
knights. How I enjoyed reading about King Arthur! One day,
when I was about fourteen or fifteen and I was becoming aware
of some of the more unsavory aspects of life, I finally discovered
what was meant in my reading when they said that villages were
looted, pillaged, and sacked. They were speaking, naturally, of all
the burning and destroying of things and, well... the despoilment
of women.

Oh, the horror of it! Is there anything more deviant and cruel?

Looking back, however, I must say, while many properties
were destroyed and goods were certainly pillaged throughout the
South, the general conduct of the soldiers on both sides during
that monstrous war that the North brought down upon us was
actually a great deal more civil than in those previous wars that
I had read about in the history books. Why, with all the soldiers
running about Greenbrier County, I never did hear of one instance
of sexual violation involving a white woman. If there had been
one, I would have known, believe you me. Even if a woman did
not make an official report to the authorities or tell a single friend
about what had transpired, she could never truly hide the brutal
violation of her body and soul. Her devastation would show in
her face, posture, and general countenance. She would be a broken
woman. I know because I have seen it on far too many accounts.
In my charitable work, I have assisted several women who have
been the victims of this heinous crime, and at the hands of a
family member—two when they were only little girls!

I also knew of a young woman in Richmond who was

assaulted by the boy who had been courting her. Fortunately for her, the miscreant had bragged about his deeds to an acquaintance, and this man testified in her behalf at the trial, otherwise she might not have had justice. You see, under the law, a woman must prove that she did not consent to the sexual violation and, in many instances, the law allows an assailant to "persuade" a woman into giving her consent by beating her or holding a knife to her throat. Alas! The administration of the law is entirely unjust in regard to women in cases of sexual violation. Girls as young as ten years of age have been accused of enticing men. Why, I even heard of one instance where a judge dismissed the case before him because he declared that if the victim were a true lady, and not a woman of ill repute, she would be too ashamed to come forward with the accusation!

Although it pains me, I will say one thing favorable about Mr. Lincoln. He issued General Orders Number 100, which I have heard many refer to as the Lieber Code, which established a code of conduct for how the Yankee soldiers should treat civilians. It made the violation of a woman a crime punishable by death. This decree must have had some level of effectiveness for, during the War, I never read in the papers of any molestations. If the Yankees had been defiling our women, I am convinced something would have printed in the papers to remind us of the necessity of creating our own government, one that would not tolerate such abominable behavior. But, as I said, I never heard of or read about the ravishment of white women... at least not any more than occurred before or after the War.

As to the treatment of colored women, I could not say. No one ever talked about it. But, I suppose again that the situation was no worse than what they suffered before the War.

Still, it was only 1863 at the time of that horrific incident that we are discussing. The War, as you know, still had two more years to go. The situation could only deteriorate as to incivility, and I was not about to be a victim of any physical violence or allow my daughter, my sister, and Mother either. I am not certain how I could have defended us against those armed brutes, but I would have done my best.

Chapter Twenty-one:
In Which We Learn of a Soldier's Kindness To the Children

As Told by Sally Anderson

The soldier guarding us stated that he assumed we could play. We did. Oh, I have not properly told you who "we" was. "We" was my cousin Becky and me. Becky was three years older but she still very much enjoyed playing games with me. This was because she was basically the only child in her home and had no one else to play with, ever. Her sister Hazeltine was nineteen and was married and living in Richmond. She also had two older brothers but they had both moved to Ohio. At first, Aunt Orpha would read us letters from them telling of their many successes in business and social standing and the like. But, when the war started, both of them joined the Union army and their names were never mentioned by anyone in the family ever again.

Becky was everything that I was not: quiet, hardworking, obedient, kind. She was ever so nice and I enjoyed playing with her. Her only problems were 1) that she did not have too much of an imagination, and 2) she did not like our games to include anything bloody or with too much sickness or death. Becky owned a magnificent doll with a china head and china hands named Charlotte. Unlike other times, she had not brought Charlotte with her that day. In fact, she had not brought any toys with her. Aunt

Orpha was forcing her to act like a grownup. At first, Becky tried to act like she did not want to play dolls, but she saw me having ever so much fun and couldn't resist.

Unfortunately, I did not have a china doll. I had one once. I named her Lucinda. But Lucinda's head was sort of accidentally smashed. So all I had now was Emmeline, a ragdoll that Caroline had made for me shortly after Lucinda's demise when I was terribly sad and everyone said that "it" was a lesson to me. Emmeline was very beautiful for a ragdoll. In particular, she had the loveliest dresses. Caroline would make a new dress for her every time her old dress would become ripped or destroyed in some manner, which was usually once a month, but sometimes longer.

I also had a stuffed dog that Father had bought for me in Richmond when I was very young. I had loved most of the stuffing out of the dog so that he could no longer sit unassisted but had to spend his days lying down. When I was three, I had named him "Bumdog." The Bumdog was a magical creature and he always rescued people when they were in trouble.

"We" were playing a game where Emmeline was trapped under an avalanche mudslide and the Bumdog was digging them out. To our delight, our soldier guard asked if he could join us. His name was Private Stevens but he said that everyone called him "Scant."

Scant did not want to be Emmeline, so he got to be the Bumdog; only Scant said that he did not like the name "Bumdog," which I thought was very funny given his silly nickname: "Scant." For purposes of being friendly, though, I allowed him to change the Bumdog's name to "Rab" after some story that he had read. We made him... I mean we asked him to tell us the story of Rab,[69] which he did. Scant also did a most excellent voice as Rab the Dog and we very much enjoyed playing dolls with him.

CHAPTER TWENTY-TWO:
Further Thoughts on Freedom
As Told by Hartwell Finney

When the sergeant was done aksin' me questions, he had the
soldier bring me back to Mista Samuel's room. Mista Samuel
was settin' on his bed readin' a newspaper as he liked to do. I sat
myself back down on the floor. There weren't nothin' for me to
look at so I looked on up at that paper; but, truth be told, it were
mostly a bunch of squiggles to me except for the letters "a," "b,"
and "c." I saw a few of them sprinkled here 'n there on that paper.

I knew those letters 'cause for awhile there'd been a pit school[70]
down at the other end a' the Second Creek and I'd snuck off a few
times to join in. I wanted to learn to read the Bible. But, the white
folks done found out about the schoolin' and a course they were
afraid of what might happen if coloreds were educated—thought
we would read about freedom and come to realize that slavery was
wrong. Hah! Don't take no book to teach a person that lesson, no,
Sir. But, they run the teacher out a' the county for fear of bein'
lynched and I never learned to read.

Mista Samuel saw me lookin' at him and he stopped his readin'
and aksed me what the sergeant had wanted. I told him that the
sergeant had just wanted to be for sure that I was no slave.

"He did not let you go home once he found out you were free?"

"No. That sergeant is a smart man, Mista Samuel. Cain't take no chances on no one. Too dangerous. He couldn't know where I'd run off to and what I might do." Mista Samuel didn't take no mind to what I had said and he let out a groan to prove it. So I reminded Mista Samuel of how smart that the officer Richter was when had called Mista Samuel a man b'fore.

"When?"

"When he sent us to these rooms. He said men go in the one and the women go in the other. He called you a man." Mista Samuel considered this. So I said, "Sho' is nice to be called a man, ain't it?"

Chapter Twenty-three:
In Which an Antagonist Sets His Sights On the Heroine
As Told by Captain James Tobin

When I finished my one glass of brandy, I asked Richter if he would like me to check on the sick woman. He replied that there was no hurry and that he had seen a library and would retire among the books to enjoy a few minutes alone. That being the case, I told him that I would spend my time with one of our fine hostesses.

"They'll be no disrespecting a woman on my watch," he warned.

I smiled and re-assured him that I had never disrespected a woman; in fact, I had nothing but respect for the comforts a woman gives a man. "Besides," I informed him, "the old lady told me that they were all widows."

"Widows, eh? I suppose it's all right then, as long as they are willing."

"The women I have known have always been extremely ready, willing, and able."

At first, he smiled at my remark, but then he looked disgusted. "You don't traffic with prostitutes, do you?"

"No! I most certainly do not. I am a medical man. The diseases spread amongst that population are appalling. More importantly, the trade is debasing and shameful. I value women. I have no desire to take advantage of one. I could never take pleasure in a relationship unless it was a meeting of equals with like-minded goals."

"At least we agree there," he grumbled, and seemed satisfied. I began to take my leave when a quizzical look appeared upon his face. "Are you just going to march in there and proposition the lot of them?"

"My poor Puritanical friend, you have no idea how such matters are conducted, do you?"

"None, I'm proud to say. I married my second cousin. Never courted anyone. For curiosity's sake, enlighten me."

"Well, I will concoct some reason to speak with one of them separately. If she seems receptive, I will carry on the conversation until an intimacy is established. If not, I will try with another."

"And if none of them are receptive?"

"If it comes to that, I will sleep alone. Say, the woman who spoke up, she was the most handsome of the three."

"You noticed?" he asked with disdain.

"You did not?" I replied with astonishment. Richter bowed his head and looked sheepish. "Of course you did," I continued. "You are only human after all. You did not happen to catch her name, did you?"

"I probably shouldn't tell you, but... Anderson. Her name is, Anderson."

"Thank you."

I took out a bottle of 4711 Eau de Cologne[71] that I always carry in my pouch, splashed a few drops on my neck, bid Sergeant Richter a pleasant evening, and ascended the stairs once again. At the end of the hall was a bench before a window that overlooked the street. I decided that it would serve as an excellent place to begin an intimacy, especially since the doors to the bedrooms were now all shut. The space was public yet still afforded privacy. With a plan forming in my mind, I passed the old woman's bedroom, knocked on the first door I came to, and discovered that it was the room to which Richter had sent the men. I apologized for the interruption and continued with my quest.

I knocked on the next door, and it was opened for me. As I stood in the doorway, I looked more closely at the three women inside. Two of them were sitting on the bed. They were clearly sisters and the daughters of the sick woman. The family resemblance in their dark, round eyes and uncommonly thin lips was strong. Also, like their mother, they had attempted to mask their advancing age through excessive grooming. Their gowns were far too ornate and low cut for the decorum expected of a war widow and the numerous ribbons that festooned their hair made them appear childish not youthful. Both had dark hair and both were exceptionally tall, characteristics that should have made them comely; but one was overweight, while the other was too lean. The former snarled and turned her back on me with indignation while the latter batted her eyes and smiled flirtatiously, revealing repugnantly stained teeth (stains this severe were most likely the result of frequent tobacco usage[72]. If you did not encounter any Southern women during your service, tobacco chewing and snuff rubbing are common. Most homes contain spittoons and the women are as equally accomplished in expectorating as any man).

I turned my attention to the third. She sat apart from the other two with a book in her lap, waiting for the news I had come to deliver. I quickly determined that she could not be related to the others by birth for she was slender, her features delicate, and her eyes were almond-shaped and light. I also decided that she was probably a score younger than the other two: most likely in her late teens or early twenties. Her light brown hair was neither braided nor curled or embellished in any way and wisps had fallen loose from the knot she had tied at the nape of her neck. Her deep purple dress was plain but of fine cloth and excellent fit. Although the bodice was high-necked and buttoned to the top, it flattered her figure and I was much more inclined to try to discover what was hidden under those buttons than to trifle with the goods flaunted in plain site by the other two.

"Mrs. Anderson?" I queried. "May I have a word with you in private?" Her trepidation was apparent, but she rose and silently followed me as the other two women hissed like geese. I led Mrs. Anderson to the aforementioned bench. "Please, have a seat," I requested. She obeyed and I continued, "My name is James Tobin. I want to apologize for this… disruption to your evening and your home."

"We were not having a dinner party."

"No?"

"Not in the sense of a celebration. My mother-in-law decided that with all the men dying in the war, an elaborate funeral for her would be inappropriate. Instead of a funeral she wanted one, last, pleasant meal with her family before she died. I was only trying to fulfill her dying request."

"How thoughtful. Did you prepare the meal?"

"Yes, but we have not eaten this well in over a year—since my husband left."

"You do not have to justify the situation to me. I only meant to say that you are an excellent cook. The food was divine. Your family is very fortunate."

"Pardon?"

"That was a compliment."

I waited for her to respond, but she remained quiet and looked puzzled. To break the tension and ingratiate myself to her, I explained that my mother was a wonderful woman, but a terrible cook. Her lima beans were so hard you could break a tooth trying to chew them. When I was a child, my siblings and I would swallow them whole with glasses of water. We would have truly relished a meal like the one she prepared. I neglected to tell her that as soon as my father had earned enough money, he had remedied the situation by hiring a chef to the relief of us all, especially my mother.

Mrs. Anderson was perplexed by my affability and remained stoic. I smiled and continued my attempt to earn her trust. "We were told by an informant that you were hiding munitions and medical supplies. Clearly, the information was false," I remarked.

"Now that you searched the house and you know we are innocent, are you still going to burn it down?"

"Innocent?" I joked. "Your mother-in-law had enough medicine in her room to supply a battalion."

"For her personal use, we are not aiding the Rebels. Please take whatever she had that is of use and let us be."

"Unfortunately, there was nothing left of any use."

"Then, can't you simply go?" she pleaded.

All I could do was shrug. "Orders are orders."

"How many homes have you burned?" She asked woefully.

"Me, personally? None."

She looked at me with disbelief.

"I am a surgeon. I do not generally participate in scouting or other such missions. As I said, we were told that you were hiding medical supplies. I was asked to help identify and collect them."

With that statement, her demeanor changed and she became more cordial. She called me "Sir," and asked for permission to see the children, to be certain they were not frightened. I could see no harm in her proposal; accordingly, I consented.

We first visited the boy. He was sitting on the bed and made no attempt to rise when we entered. I thought his behavior quite rude for a lad. However, the colored man, Finney, jumped to his feet. The boy seemed to take affront to Mrs. Anderson's visit and asked her what had prompted it. When she responded that she was concerned for his welfare, he turned his back to her and said with exasperation, "I am fine. Of course I am. I am not a little child." I was appalled that a youth would speak in such a tone to an adult; but, since my concern was in wooing the woman and not in disciplining the child, I held my tongue. Besides, I did not know the family dynamics. At first glance, I had assumed she was mother to the two children. Now, I could see that she was not much older than the boy. Perhaps they were siblings. That relationship could explain his behavior, although not excuse it.

She inquired about the colored man's well-being. He eyed me suspiciously and stated that he was fine and that she should look to her own care and to remember Barbree Allen and Pretty Polly. I was uncertain as to his reference, but Mrs. Anderson appeared to comprehend. She acknowledged his remarks in a friendly manner and glanced anxiously back at the boy. We then went to the next bedroom to look in on the little girls. When we opened the bedroom door, the two girls were sitting on the floor with the scout who had been assigned to guard them. He appeared to be playing dolls with them. He quickly stood at attention, his face burning with embarrassment. I chuckled.

"Hello, Mother," little Sally said with a wink.

"Hello, Dear. I was worried about you," Mrs. Anderson replied.

"Oh, Mother, no need to worry; we are having ever so much fun."

"I am glad."

"As you were," I said with a smile to the soldier and with that, we left the room and closed the door. I could tell Mrs. Anderson was feeling some relief in knowing that the children were safe. Perhaps she could relax now and turn her attentions to her own needs.

Unfortunately, but appropriately, her home was still paramount among her concerns. She asked if she could go to Sergeant Richter to plead her case to obtain a pardon from his terrible sentence. I told her that I believed it was too soon and that she should allow him a little more time to reflect upon the circumstances. She nodded with understanding. Moving forward with my agenda, I noted that the air was awfully stuffy upstairs and suggested that we should sit outside and wait together for Sergeant Richter to calm down. She agreed.

We went outside to a lovely patio that overlooked the river to the West. It would afford an especially beautiful view of the forthcoming sunset. The patio was furnished with two wrought iron chairs on either side of a matching two-person iron settee that faced the river. I escorted her to the settee. As decorum required, I remained standing at first. I was certain that upon winning her trust, she would allow me to sit next to her. We would then be quite close.

To divert her attention from the unpleasantness of the situation at hand, I decided to engage her with conversation that would be both common and comfortable: the weather. "It is much more pleasant out here," I began. "I am glad that winter is over. I do love the scents and sights of spring. I had never seen redbud before coming south. The display this past spring was magnificent." To her credit, she was not easily distracted.

"Do you truly believe that my mother-in-law will be dead by morning?" she asked with concern.

"She seemed quite ill to me, but I suppose time will tell. Your mother-in-law may be the greatest thespian I have ever seen."

She laughed at my remark and then asked, "How long have you been practicing medicine?"

"Twelve years, if you include my schooling."

"You must enjoy it."

"Most of my career has been quite banal," I confessed. "People die. But, every once in a while I would cure someone, and when I did, I would get the most overwhelming sense of triumph, knowing that I had cheated death. When I was assigned to the cavalry, I had hoped to feel that sense of victory every day. But, it is not as I imagined. Death claims far too many for me to rejoice in any of my own achievements. "

"Where did you train?"

"I studied at the Medical School of Harvard. I selected Harvard because Massachusetts is one of the few states that allow the use of cadavers for medical study. Imagine trying to learn how to heal the human body without properly looking at it and touching it."

"Do people often donate their bodies?"

"No. In fact, after John Brown's raid on Harper's Ferry, students from Winchester Medical College went to the battle site to look for unclaimed bodies. As I heard tell, they only found one. Poor soul turned out to be none other than John Brown's son. When federal troops captured the town of Winchester last year, they recovered the boy's remains. Then, they burned the college buildings to the ground."

Looking back, I see that although I did most of the talking that night, she clearly controlled the conversation; yet, I was delighted to share my thoughts with her. No man in the Third Cavalry had asked about my background or my ideas about medical education and practices. My conversations with my comrades were more visceral. We spoke of escapades, excursions to extraordinary locales, fights with interesting foe, and encounters with beautiful or loose women; yes, much of the talk centered on our exploits with women.

She asked mostly about my family. I had wonderful memories to tell of my childhood: days when I would rise early in the morning to begin my adventures, and would go to bed at night filled with anticipation for the next day's quests. My parents adored each other and their children.

I did omit the bigotry we sometimes endured due to my family's religious practices. My father warned me that these prejudices would increase when I left Philadelphia and that I should expect to be taunted and excluded. In our community, I was always the golden child, most popular with the boys, girls, and adults. I could not fathom being spurned simply on account of a heritage that I had not chosen. Accordingly, when I moved to Cambridge to begin my medical studies, I joined the Unitarian Church. Hailing from the City of Brotherly Love, my classmates assumed that my initial lack of knowledge of the hymns and other church rituals stemmed from a Quaker upbringing. I did nothing to abuse them of that notion. It was far more acceptable to them for me to be a Quaker or any type of Christian than what I was or rather what I am and I suppose always shall be even if I do not practice.

CHAPTER TWENTY-FOUR:
More Trouble Begins to Brew
As Told by Orpha McClung

Some time had passed. We were sitting on the bed trying
as best as possible to remain calm before the impending doom.
Margaret was thinking about that handsome surgeon. She was
prattling on quite a bit about him and didn't he have striking eyes
and wasn't he finely dressed. For, as much as he was an enemy
invader, that Captain Tobin truly was the finest looking man
either of us had ever laid eyes upon—physically that is. I cannot
speak for his character but to say that all of those Yankees were
barbarians—taking us hostage, for shame! Naturally, Margaret
wondered what Captain Tobin wanted with Caroline.

I politely tried to change the subject. Being a devoted daughter,
but not wanting to alert our captors, I quietly asked Margaret if
she supposed Mother had truly taken a turn for the worse. She
replied, rather too loudly, that she did not see how. Mother was in
perfect health at dinner. I agreed.

Margaret then turned the conversation right back to the
handsome surgeon. She was upset that he had called on Caroline
when he should have come for one of us because we were
Mother's daughters after all and Caroline was not. I told that silly
sister of mine that the doctor had no way of knowing who was
kin to whom. Since Caroline had been so brazen as to speak up to

that sergeant, it was only natural that he should think she mattered more than she did. This logic was so clear that it even made sense to Margaret.

But she could not get her mind off that fine looking man and said that she wished he had chosen her to speak with in private. Then, she reminded me of earlier that day in the library when we were wishing that we could converse with a decent-looking man. We both looked over at that same moment to the two soldiers who were guarding us. They clearly did not fit that description. The only advantage they had was their youth. But, they were paying us no heed in that regard either. Trying to look on the bright side, I told Margaret not to worry; that I was for sure the doctor would tire of Caroline's company soon enough, and she said, "Who wouldn't?"

Chapter Twenty-Five:
In Which the Villain Reveals His True and Noble Motives

As told by Sergeant Ephraim Richter

After finishing a most delicious and rejuvenating meal, I
retired to the library for some much needed rest. I had only been in
a room like this once before, in the home of a wealthy family back
in New Albany. My father had worked at the Phoenix Foundry[73]
in New Albany. He earned an impressive sum of around $1,000 a
year in wages. Still, my parents wanted a different life for me, more
genteel, less dangerous. They were hoping I would enter the legal
profession.

We did not have any public schools in New Albany at the
time, but a teacher, Mr. Chapman, had set up a small school in his
house. My mother took on work to afford the fees. She became
a housemaid to the Gibsons, one of the most prominent families
in town. As soon as I was of sufficient age, I contributed to our
family's income. I worked as a messenger at Charles Wible's
shipyard. After my lessons were over, I would scurry back and
forth between the different yards, delivering progress updates,
questions, and answers. When the quitting–time whistle blew,
I would pick my mother up at her work, and we would walk
home together. If Mother needed more time to finish her tasks, I
would wait in the Gibsons' library for her. Old Mrs. Gibson was

extremely liberal and gave me permission to borrow books, one at a time.

When I was thirteen, my father died in an accident at the foundry and my formal education ended. I began work in earnest at the shipyards, gaining skills and increased pay with every year. Mother continued to work for the Gibsons. I was still entitled to borrow books and I saw no shame in doing so.

I have no regrets that I did not become a lawyer. I take great pride in my work. My home may not be palatial like the Gibsons, but it's respectable. My daughter attends the public school. New Albany was the first consolidated school district in the state and had the first public high school. I am proud that my wife has never had to take on work, even during all those years when I was away at war.

The library in the Rebel home was not as ornate as the Gibson's library, but it had an excellent array of books. I walked over to the bookshelves and began to look at the titles. Many were law books and other such treatises. They held no interest to me. As I moved around the room, I discovered a section devoted to history books and the tome little Sally had mentioned, *The Horrors of the Black Death*. The surrounding titles sounded equally morbid. I wondered what else that little imp had gotten into.

Finally, to the left of the fireplace, I discovered the novels. My eyes were immediately drawn to gold letters on a black field spelling out the name *Ivanhoe*.[74] The novel was a favorite of mine—one of only four books that I own. I pulled the volume out from the shelf. This copy was much finer than the one I own. The pages had gilded edges. The leather binding was as soft as a pair of dress gloves and was embossed with gold. The spine appeared to have never been cracked. Either the owner of the book took impeccable care of his volumes, or he had not read it as often as I, if at all. With so many other books to choose from, I doubted that he would have read it five times.

As you know, reading[75] was one of the few pleasures we soldiers had. Most of the men could read. Those who couldn't often learned how. The greatest supply of reading materials was newspapers sent from home. In camp, we always had a fine supply of the *New Albany Daily Ledger*. Also, there were dime novels aplenty like Beadle's *East and West* and *Gold Fiend* that I bought from a sutler and read over and over again. But, there were never enough books of quality. This room was a feast for my eyes. I ran my fingers along the book spines to be certain again that I was not having one of those mirage experiences. Then, I gripped the cold mantle of the fireplace and hung my head.

Before the War, my family would all sit by the fire on a Friday night such as it was. I would have my daughter Rosie on my lap and I would read to her. My wife, Ruth, would knit. A more devoted family man you've never seen. I had always wanted a son, but God had not blessed us with one at that time. I wondered if perhaps when I returned, if I returned, there would still be time for Ruth and me. These thoughts made me lonesome. There was no place I would have rather been at that moment than home with my wife and daughter. I stared into the unlit fireplace.

My reverie was interrupted by Private Walton. He was standing in the doorway with the preacher and requested permission to enter. "Granted," I said gruffly and sat myself down behind a large walnut desk. It matched the bookcases and was most likely made by the same craftsman. "What is it?" I asked. "Has the woman died?"

"No," the preacher replied. "She is still with us, thank the Lord. However, I would like to know if there is anything I can do to improve this situation; to protect the family."

"There is nothing you can do. We must let time run its course and see where it all leads. But since you are here, have a seat." I gestured to a wingback chair that was cattycorner to the desk. He sat. "Answer me this," I said, "you don't preach against slavery, do you?"

"The institution of slavery? No."

"Why not?"

"The Bible does not speak against it. God took the Jews out of bondage in Egypt, but he never ended slavery. In fact, he cursed Ham and made him and all of his descendants slaves."

"But we are merely men, not God. What gives us the right to decide who is to be free and who a slave? If God gave man free will, then it must be the work of the Devil to take that away."

"I have no desire to argue the merits of slavery. You are obviously quite passionate about the subject."

"Extremely. I used to be as callous as you in regard to the sufferings of others, but all that changed when I witnessed the brutality first-hand."

I told the preacher my story: how even though I had always believed that slavery was a sin, I had been willing to overlook it as I did the sins of the drunkards and fornicators and other moral deviants. I had believed in following the gospel word of Saint Matthew to remove the plank of wood from my own eye before worrying about the speck of sawdust in my neighbor's. I had no true understanding of the total evil of that institution: that slavery was not only the act of putting a human being in bondage, it was also the various means of physical and emotional torture that perpetuated the system. I could not begin to imagine the cruelty that one man could inflict upon another. Slavery was an outrage, a blight upon our Christian nation, a grand wooden fortress of evil, and not a plank or a speck of sawdust.

My awakening occurred in 1859. I was on a business trip. Oh, what a business I saw! It was my first trip on a paddle steamer, the boats I had built and loved for so many years. I was excited and proud to be representing my company on the trip. We were headed for New Orleans, but I only got as far as Greenville, Mississippi. What I saw in Greenville made me so repulsed, I had to turn back.

Our boat docked in Greenville and we had a day to explore the town. You cannot imagine the horrors that I encountered in that God forsaken place. Do not forget, I survived the slaughter of Antietam. I shall forever have those grisly images from Sharpsburg seared into my brain; but truly, those memories pale in comparison to my remembrances of Greenville. As awful as it was, the soldiers at Antietam died with dignity. No matter what their reasons were for joining up, they were serving noble and selfless causes. Preserving the Union, serving your country, ending slavery, and proving your manhood, are all worthy motives.

The suffering I witnessed in Greenville was inflicted upon the innocent for no other reason except the benefit and pleasure of others. I saw one Negro man who bore deep scars across his back from the whippings he had received. Another man I saw that day had a log and chain[76] placed upon his legs and he was forced to drag them around. His crime? He had tried to run away from slavery. I was told that he was fortunate not to have his foot cut off.

The most horrific experience that I witnessed was a slave auction. Selling humans like cattle? It was disgusting. I will never forget the sound of the auctioneer's voice. It still haunts me, for it was the very sound of Evil. It had an eerie, lilting, calmness that made the hair stand up on the back of my neck. Listening to him talk was like drinking cyanide in sweet milk.

At the moment I came upon the auction, a young woman and her infant daughter were set before the crowd. "Two for the price of one," the auctioneer boasted. The crowd roared with laughter. I couldn't help but stare incredulously as the frightened woman tried to maintain her dignity.

My associate with whom I had been exploring the city was anxious and wanted to leave. But, I could not abandon that woman to such a fate. When the bidding started, I joined in. I bought her. I bought a human being. I had no idea where I would get the money I pledged: sixteen hundred dollars was more money than I made in two years. In the end, I was able to procure a loan. Barings Bank was willing to finance almost any slave purchase.

Then, I brought her back to New Albany and set her free. It was the best I could do. I joined with others and we started an emancipation society. The Town Clock Church[77] became a stop on the Underground Railroad. But, it wasn't enough. So, when the war started and I had the chance to free millions, how could I stay home by the fireside with my Ruth and Rosie?

When I finished my story, the preacher looked uncomfortable. I glared at him with disdain, and then rose and walked over turned to stare again at the cold fireplace with its unlit logs.

Chapter Twenty-six:
A Changing of the Guard
As Told by Sally Anderson

We were having a most wonderful evening playing games of all sorts with Scant when another soldier entered the room. Scant jumped to his feet and tried to make it appear as though he had not actually been playing with us. The new soldier informed our friend that the time had come for him to eat his supper. While this news greatly excited Scant, Becky and I were very disappointed. We made him... I mean we asked him to promise to return to us later when he was able. The new soldier seemed surprised by our behavior. Scant explained to him that he grew up with four sisters. This declaration answered many of my questions about him as well.

CHAPTER TWENTY-SEVEN:
More Changes to the Order of Things
As Told by Hartwell Finney

We was settin' around Mista Samuel's room for a long time.
My old bottom was getting mighty sore from settin' on the floor all
that time, but I knew better than to complain. I tried to busy my
mind by thinkin' bout happy times and singin' songs in my head.
Mista Samuel was still lookin' through his passel a newspapers.

Then, outta nowhere, a soldier done burst into the room with
the Good Reverend McElhenney. Mista Samuel and I both stood
in respect for him. Mista Samuel aksed the Good Reverend why he
was in the room with us. The Reverend said for Mista Samuel and
me not to be alarmed. Was a mix up is all. Then, he aksed Mista
Samuel how he was a doin'. Mista Samuel puffed hisself up and
said he was fine. Then, the Good Reverend aksed me and I said I's
fine and been through worse.

There bein' no other place for him to rest his old bones, the
Good Reverend set hisself on the bed with Mista Samuel. He
noticed what Mista Samuel had been about and said that it was
quite a collection of clippins he had. Mista Samuel said that he
liked to read 'bout the war and the Good Reverend aksed if he
was lookin' for news of his daddy. Mista Samuel said he was, but
mostly he liked readin' about the men his age who were fightin'
and all the different places they gets to see. The Good Reverend

picked up summa the clippins and they talked 'bout who each boy
was and what he'd done and where he'd been. They called one
boy a "powder monkey"[78] and said he was in the navy and Mista
Samuel wanted to know if'n the Reverend had ever been on a ship
b'fore. The Good Reverend said he'd been on a riverboat but not
on the ocean. Mista Samuel said he'd like to sail the ocean and go
far away.

The new soldier stayed in the room with us and another
one left the room. It were startin' to get cold, so I aksed the two
soldiers if I could make a fire and the new soldier said Mista
Samuel should do it, seein' as how I weren't no slave. Then he told
us about President Lincoln and the E-man-cipation[79] and how the
President was makin' a new state for these parts and there weren't
gonna be no slavery nor freeman's papers no more. The Good
Reverend didn't say nothin' contrarywise to all this, so I figured it
had to be true, and I let out a deep breath and whispered, "Praise
the Lord."

Mista Samuel didn't say nothin' either. I s'pose he'd read 'bout
the E-man-cipation in his newspapers, 'cause he got up off the bed
and made that fire.

Chapter Twenty-eight:
Respite
As Told by Caroline Anderson

In spite of the awful circumstances, I was actually enjoying myself. Don't get me wrong: I was sick with worry about my home; but, after looking in on the children, I was no longer afraid that the soldiers were going to harm them in any way. Also, I hoped and prayed that Mrs. Anderson was not truly dying, and that if she was still too sick to move in the morning when the soldiers were ready to leave, the sergeant would spare the house. With those ideas somewhat settled in my mind, I decided to make the best of the situation.

Even though Captain Tobin was my captor, he spoke respectfully to me and did not look down upon me as everyone else always did. I know it sounds horribly selfish, but I was flattered that a well-mannered, well-educated, and wealthy man like Captain Tobin had taken notice of me. I should add that he was also an especially fine-looking man and was much closer in age to me than my husband. Funny thing is that Mr. Anderson was supposed to be my protector, but I was always afraid to look at him closely, while Captain Tobin was my attacker and I could not take my eyes off of his face. I remember his looks so well that I could probably paint you a picture. He had curly, chestnut brown hair, angular cheekbones, a perfectly-trimmed goatee on his square jaw, straight teeth that looked white as Mrs. Anderson's pearls when he smiled, and expressive aquamarine eyes. I had never before understood why someone named a blue-green color after water since all the streams and rivers I had seen were clear or had turned brown with all the mud in the spring, but I realized that it was an appropriate name because Captain Tobin's eyes looked like pools of water. I could not stop staring into them and felt as though I was drowning, but in a good way if that makes any sense.

Captain Tobin had taken a seat next to me on the settee but was still maintaining a respectable distance. As we sat on the patio together, he talked with such good humor that it truly was a delight to listen to him. His conversation was different from anything that I had ever heard before from a man. He talked unguardedly about his personal experiences and opinions. He took me into his confidence in such a way as it seemed as if he was confessing his soul. I wondered if he was always that open or if he had simply discovered that sincerity was a quality women found attractive. Talking, as he did, in this unconcealed manner certainly established an intimacy and it probably made most women more receptive to familiars greater than just sitting close and conversing about the weather or some other inane subject. I admit that I was drawn to him from the start, but as Hartwell had warned me, I had no intention of being so charmed that I would compromise myself.

Although Captain Tobin's accent was decidedly northern, his voice had a beautiful, rich tone and he pronounced every word with perfect elocution like I am trying to learn in my class. He was very animated when he talked and used his hands a great deal— gesticulating, I believe is the correct term. The total effect was quite theatrical and exciting.

I heard the clock chime eight and knew that we had been talking well on over an hour—almost two. He was telling me what it was like to grow up in Philadelphia, when of a sudden he stopped. "What is the matter?" I asked getting fearful again. Looking concerned hisself, he held up his hand to shush me.

"I heard something," he whispered. We both listened carefully and heard a rustling sound coming from around back. My stomach knotted up. I quickly worried that Confederate soldiers had heard tell that the Yankees were here and had come to run them off. Would there be fighting? Captain Tobin stood up and gently patted my shoulder to indicate that I should remain seated. I reached out and grabbed him by the sleeve, trying to hold him back and keep him safe from the danger. He smiled at my concern and gently removed my hand, pressing it between his for assurance. Then, he walked quietly to the edge of the house and carefully peered around back.

Captain Tobin let out a sigh of relief and I relaxed as well. He turned, smiled at me, and motioned for me to come see what had caused the unusual sound. The noise turned out only to be our beagle dog Skippy, licking Frank's empty plate. As the evening had wore on, I had forgotten all about Frank. I was for sure that Frank had dropped the plate outside the kitchen door as he always did when he left. I was relieved to know that Frank was indeed long gone.

Captain Tobin smiled kindly at Skippy, opened his pouch, took out a piece of hardtack, and threw it to the dog. Skippy sniffed it suspiciously and looked up at Captain Tobin who apologized. "Sorry, no more jerky. That biscuit is all I have." Skippy took up the hardtack and began to bury it under a nearby bush. Captain Tobin chuckled and said, "You are right to bury it. Perhaps a few days underground will soften it enough to be edible." Then, he returned his attention to me.

"What are you staring at?" he asked.

"There is something very different about you, different from the others."

"I like dogs."

"That is not it," I said, and then I realized what it was. "You do not have that same haunted look the others have."

"Haunted?"

"Yes, they have a darkness about the eyes that makes their eye sockets seem twice as deep as they ought to be. The look of death, I suppose."

"Yes, I know the visage well. It is the look that overtakes one's countenance after one has killed a man."

"Why don't you look that way then?"

"I have never killed anyone."

"You haven't?"

"No! I am a surgeon. My sole aim is to save lives. I do not even possess a weapon." He raised his arms as if in surrender to illustrate his point. "No rifle, no sabre. I am a city boy. Not only have I never owned a gun, but also I have never fired one."

"Well don't that just frost your berries," I said with surprise. I certainly had never before met a white man who had not fired a gun. A boy from western Virginia would have been ashamed if he had not shot his first buck by age ten.

Captain Tobin laughed at my backwoods expression, offered me an arm, and escorted me back around to the patio.

CHAPTER TWENTY-NINE:
Wherein a Party Truly Begins
As Told by Orpha McClung

I do not know what was happening in the rest of the house, but Margaret and I had clearly been forgotten. I tell you, we were not accustomed to be set aside like that with no means of amusing ourselves. It was torture. As is my kindly nature, I put asunder my own worries and tried my best to comfort my sister. "When this is over, think of the story we will have to tell," I said as gaily as I could.

But with her stubborn temperament, Margaret was impossible to console. "Oh yes," she said facetiously, "we will call our story 'The Night We Almost Died of Boredom.'"

"The first part of the story was certainly exciting enough," I reasoned.

"Well, not anymore."

"The night is still young."

"Yes, yes it is," Margaret declared defiantly. Then she jumped on up and started to search furiously through the dresser drawers. Her fury put the soldiers on alarm. They drew their weapons and demanded to know just what she was up to. Margaret said in her pretty voice that she was looking for some playing cards and that we could use some entertainment ever so badly. One soldier said that he had a deck and Margaret became giddy. "Well, let's play," she declared. Then, she pulled the quilt off of the bed and set it on the floor. "There now," she said, "it will be like we are having a picnic."

All four of us sat down on the quilt and we introduced ourselves. The two soldiers were Mr. Jedediah Walker and Mr. Thomas Irving. They had silly nicknames[81] for each other: Spike and Bird, but in spite of the degrading situation, Margaret and I maintained as much gentility as possible and we continued to address them formally.

Unlike the other soldiers, these two were wearing street clothes instead of uniforms. Naturally, we were curious to know why. They said it was because they were scouts and wearing street clothes helped them fit in better. Margaret laughed and said "Oh, honey, around here there is not a healthy man your age for miles. You would stick out like a sore thumb no matter what you wore, even if it was a Confederate uniform." They said that some of the scouts did actually dress in Confederate uniforms, but that, of course, made them spies which was an entirely different story from being a scout. Spies were hung on the spot while scouts were taken prisoner. Later on, when I heard tale of the prison camps, I thought they might have been more fortunate to be caught as spies and die quickly then to languish and starve in a prison.[82]

Margaret asked them how they came to be scouts. Mr. Walker told us that their captain said one day that he needed some men for an extra dangerous duty. "I looked at Spike here and we were both curious. We wanted to know what this extra dangerous duty was. Only way to find out was to volunteer." Margaret and I both commented that they were very brave and they looked most pleased with themselves.

CHAPTER THIRTY:
In Which Daylight and Inhibitions Recede
As Told by Caroline Anderson

The sun was setting. Captain Tobin had once again taken a seat next to me, only he sat closer now. I was surprised by how nice he smelled: like citrus and herbs. I wondered how far they all had traveled since he looked so fresh. I thought to ask him where they had come from and where they were headed, but even though it was only polite conversation and curiosity, I did not dare speak such thoughts to him for fear that he might think me a spy, trying to gain information about troop movement. It certainly was remarkable that no significant traces of dirt or perspiration appeared anywhere on his face or hands, and his clothes were particularly clean. His white shirt looked as if they had been recently pressed and the collar and cuffs had no dark rings. I knew that sutlers[83] and some of the soldiers' wives followed the troops to provide laundry and other services. Captain Tobin was clearly paying someone to launder his shirts. His regiment, he said, was under the control of General Joseph Hooker who, even in his short time in command, was well known for the band of prostitutes that had attached themselves to his division. They became known as "Hooker's Brigade." Perhaps Captain Tobin paid for their services as well.

We sat together on the settee and watched the sun go down

over the river. It was a lovely sight. At that time, he was singing the praises of the Sanitary Commission and Frederick Law Olmsted. I liked that name. I told myself that if I were ever to have a son, I would name him after Frederick Law Olmsted. I suppose Captain Tobin could see that I had gotten a bit dreamy. He thought it was because he was boring me with all of the medical and military talk.

"Not at all," I said. "It is fascinating."

"I am pleased you consider it so. I have not been in the company of a lady in a long time. I was afraid the war had turned me into a brute."

"Actually," I confessed, "not only do I find your stories and information to be interesting; but also, to be entirely honest, I find it remarkable that you are taking so much time with me and seem to care about my opinions. I have never actually had a lengthy conversation with a man before. I do not suppose any man has ever considered me worthy."

I meant the comment as a warning of sorts to Captain Tobin, a way to let him know that I was from low circumstances and not of his breeding. However, he understood it to be an invitation and moved closer to me. "How strange," he said. "I feel so comfortable with you, so natural. I feel I could pour my heart out to you." I looked at him carefully, trying to decide if he was being sincere. His words sounded hollow but he looked earnest. I was not for sure how to respond, so I thought it best to be coy.

"My, my, such words. Your sweet talking and your handsome looks must get you far."

"I will take that remark as a compliment," he replied cheerfully.

Just then, I began to suppose. Captain Tobin had told me much about his parents and siblings. Did he have a wife that he failed to mention? Perhaps there was a kindly, patient, honest woman waiting back at home for him.

"I wonder, are you married, Captain Tobin?" I asked.

"No, most definitely not. The married men I know are all hen-pecked. I have always wanted my freedom."

"And are you free?"

"Yes," he replied looking especially thoughtful. "But I have come to realize that there is a price for my freedom. No one is missing me, wondering if I am safe. I have not received a single letter since I left Washington. If I die, there will be no one to mourn me."

CHAPTER THIRTY-ONE:
A Short Tale to Illustrate the Cunning of Women
As Told by Sally Anderson

Our new guard was named Ritter. He was not a pleasant person. Although he allowed Becky and me to resume our play, he stood by the door and did not join in even after we asked him very nicely to do so. However, just standing around is quite boring, even for a soldier. Ritter began to walk about the room, looking for something of interest. He noticed my picture of Nancy Hart[84] on the nightstand. She was a most magnificent woman and it is no wonder that the picture caught his eye. After looking it over some, he asked us who she was. I told him.

Nancy Hart was a spy. Union forces captured her and put her in the Summersville jail; but her striking beauty tormented her captors. They allowed her to roam the jail at will, and to walk in the courtyard with a soldier escort on warm evenings. One night, a guard succumbed to her charms. She asked him if she could examine his pistol. He agreed. She shot him in the head and escaped to freedom.

"Nancy Hart is my hero," I declared. Ritter smiled uncomfortably and held his gun a little tighter.

Chapter Thirty-two:
Full of Conjecture and Confessions
As Told by Captain James Tobin

The sunset had been resplendent. Caroline and I were now sitting close together in the beautiful blue twilight. Although she had also permitted me the intimacy of calling her by her given name, she continued to address me formally, maintaining a respectable distance between us. Consequently, I was not certain how far this relationship could progress. However, after that brief but memorable encounter with the other two women, I was determined to succeed with her or sleep alone.

My greatest concern was whether tender feelings for her husband would prevent any further developments between us. How devoted had Mr. Anderson been to his young wife before he left home? Had there been a heart-wrenching, sorrowful parting? Did she miss him? My inclination was to believe that he had been inattentive.

I had often been with neglected wives. They were most appreciative of my services and the least likely to harbor expectations of a long-term attachment, wanting no more than to be valued for an evening or two. Professors' wives were especially vulnerable to my ministrations. Their husbands often had their minds set on lofty reflection rather than the napes of their wives' necks or the softness of their inner thighs. My attention to these

156

women's needs was generally tempting enough to overwhelm any concerns for the duties owed to a negligent husband: the longer the neglect, the quicker the consent. I brazenly considered my interactions with these women to be within the boundaries of medical care since we were all much improved in body and spirit afterward. I even had a husband or two thank me for curing their wives' melancholia.

Caroline had presently remarked that she had never truly conversed with a man. This comment denoted poorly for her husband and boded well for me. I delved further and she told me that her husband was a quiet man; that his mother and sisters had always done the talking in the family. He claimed that he married Caroline because she was the meekest girl in Greenbrier County, and he wanted an obedient wife. I took issue with the description of her as "meek."

"I usually am," she rejoined.

"That is a shame. I like strong women."

"Especially ones bold enough to have relations with you even though her family and preacher will know of her behavior?"

"Yes, especially those," I chuckled. Despite my attempt at subtlety, she had understood my implications all too well. She began to say something in response, but stopped. "What is it?" I asked.

"Nothing."

"Tell me."

"No, it is too forward."

"No matter; after tonight, you will never see me again."

Her recognition as to the veracity of this statement emboldened her. "Very well," she began, "I was simply wondering, why any woman would ever want to do that."

"Do what?"

"Have carnal relations. Unless, of course, she wanted to have a baby, what would the temptation be?"

"Intimacy, pleasure."

"Come now, how could any woman find it pleasurable?"

"I can show you."

"Now I believe the serpent said the same to Eve and look where it got her: with child and cast out of Eden. The same will happen to me if I listen to you."

"Is this Eden?"

"It is a good deal more like it than the place where I was raised up."

"And what was that like?"

"Thirteen children in a filthy three-room house with dirt floors. And my brothers were meaner than a sack full of copperheads. Now do you understand why I am attached to this place? It is comfortable and clean and, until tonight, it was safe."

"But, you and your husband, you shared no intimacy, no physical pleasure, no love?"

"There was decency. My husband was a well-respected man and a good provider for his family."

"And that is enough?"

"It should be."

"Should it? Is that truly all you desire?"

"Is anyone ever satisfied?"

"No, not even Eve," I reminded her. "She had it all and still she took a bite out of that apple."

CHAPTER THIRTY-THREE:
Merriment
As Told by Orpha McClung

We had been playing euchre.[85] It was the most popular game at that time. Nobody who knew better played anything else. The boys had lit a fire and it was a rather cozy scene. Mr. Irving had been carrying some fortification, so he passed his flask around for us all to share. The time just seemed to fly on by. I remember hearing the clock chime nine and then ten o'clock.

Naturally, with such a friendly setting, the boys wanted to learn more about our marital situation. We told them we were widows and was it not a great shame. I explained that Margaret's husband died before the war with the typhus[86] outbreak of '55. Margaret got weepy and recalled that her husband was a very delicate man. I took part in the recollection and explained that her husband was so delicate that they never had children. While I surely meant no harm in my remark, Margaret took exception to it and snapped, "Just what are you implying?"

"Not a thing," I replied innocently.

"Well, her husband died of a social disease last year," Margaret announced.

"For shame!" I declared.

"Sorry, Dear, but it is undeniably true and you know it is."

"How about some music?" Mr. Irving suggested.

He took out a harmonica and played a short, mournful tune.

"My, my, but you two are just full of surprises," I said admiringly.

Then Margaret told them of the gay parties we used to have at Elmhurst: musical parties and fish fries the likes of which you have never seen. Why the fish just seemed to jump out of the river into our brother's hands. Often at these soirées, our brother John would take out his fiddle and play and we would dance until late into the night. Other times we would have the most spectacular bonfires.

Mr. Irving said that he could play and asked if John's fiddle was handy. I knew it was. I had seen Caroline pick it up earlier when she was tidying. I went over to the wardrobe, opened the doors, and there it was. I waved it proudly and they all cheered.

After he tuned the fiddle, Mr. Irving played a sweet song and we applauded. He told us it was called "Aura Lee."[87] As you know, that song came to be admired by all fashionable people throughout the country and we were most definitely the first to hear it in Greenbrier County.

Margaret said she was tired of sad songs and asked him to liven it up a bit and play something we could dance to. Mr. Irving played a peppy tune. Mr. Walker took Margaret's hand and they began to dance as I clapped along. "My turn next," I sang out.

Chapter Thirty-four:
Still Another Change in the Order of Things
As Told by Sally Anderson

Although Private Ritter had settled down on my bed, he looked quite uncomfortable. I thought that perhaps some amusing talk might set him at ease.

"We have not had this much excitement in our house since the baby pig incident," I said. Becky giggled.

"What happened?" he inquired.

I was pleased that Private Ritter wanted us to tell him our story. For a man who did not like to play games, he certainly did enjoy storytelling. I told him that when I was six years old, my parents went to visit my Aunt Beulah in Richmond for a week and Becky came over to play. I had a baby pig in my doll carriage but I told Becky that it was my baby brother. Well, Becky went home and told her mother who told Mrs. Bell. By the end of the week, our house was filled with people coming to see the baby that was half pig, half boy.

We giggled quite a bit remembering how funny it had been. Then Becky began to cry. Ritter asked me what the matter was but I did not know so I just shrugged my shoulders.

"Make her stop that," he ordered.

"What is wrong, Becky?" I inquired.

"I want my momma. I want my momma."

Ritter was extremely put out by her behavior. "Who's her mother?" he demanded to know. I explained that her mother was my Aunt Orpha and that she was most likely in my parent's bedroom at that time. As Becky's wailing had increased in volume, Ritter decided that it would be best if we took Becky to her mother. I led them across the hall.

My aunts had been having as much if not more fun than we had. However, they stopped their dancing and music playing when we entered. Aunt Orpha scooped Becky up in her big arms and then sat on the bed with Becky in her lap. Ritter complained "'Damn'—his words not mine." I promise you that he said it and that I would never say such a thing except in a direct quote. He said, "Damn, I can't believe you two are in here dancing and playing cards while I'm stuck with these crazy babies." But one of the soldiers in that room countered that they had not had any food yet.

While all this was occurring, I was thinking about the commanding officer, Sergeant Richter. I liked him and he certainly seemed more entertaining than this motley crew. I also was not certain that he would approve of our gathering. After all, he had specifically separated us from each other. So I said to Private Ritter, "Excuse me, Sir, but do you think we should tell the sergeant about these modifications to the arrangements he made?" One of the soldiers agreed with me and another suggested that he would speak with the sergeant and find something to eat for his comrade and himself. The others all agreed with the plan and everyone seemed quite pleased. I asked if I could accompany the soldier. At first he said "No!" but Ritter persuaded him to take me. Now, I was quite pleased too.

We went to the library to call on Sergeant Richter. He was at my father's desk, writing letters it appeared. The soldier, whose name I learned was Private Irving, explained to Sergeant Richter about Becky's distress and allowing her to be with Aunt Orpha. Sergeant Richter understood. He was no longer angry and had decided that our family posed no danger to him or his troops. He told Private Irving that he was changing his order and from then on would only keep one man as a sentry to allow the others to sleep. He said Pauley would have the first watch and that the others should stay where they were and get some sleep until he called for them, and that Private Irving should relay the sergeant's new orders to everyone. Private Irving asked Sergeant Richter if it would be all right if they played their music for a little while longer. Sergeant Richter said, "Why not? It's a good cover if any of the neighbors should happen by and get suspicious. The family was having a party, after all. But, we need sleep." He pulled out a pocket watch and checked the time and told Private Irving that the music had to end by midnight. Then he dismissed Private Irving.

As Private Irving was leaving, Sergeant Richter became aware of my presence. He said, "Little Sally, I did not see you before. What brings you here when you haven't been sent for and I explicitly sent you to your room?"

"Excuse my impertinence, Sir, but I thought perhaps I could be of some service to you."

"And how could a child, and a girl no less, be of any assistance to me?"

"Well, Sir, I thought I could provide you with some valuable information. I know many important things."

"I'm certain you do. Was there anything in particular you wanted to tell me?"

"Ah, well… no, Sir, nothing in particular. Is there anything you would like to know about? In my memoirs, I have written down everything interesting that has ever happened to me or anyone I know both in person or that I feel like I know because I have read so much about them." Sergeant Richter looked interested in my memoirs.

Since my father had left home, I had been using his desk as my own. I went over to it, opened the top left-side drawer, produced one copy of my memoirs, and handed it to Sergeant Richter. He scanned it for approximately twelve and one half seconds and pronounced that it looked "fascinating." I assured him that it was and said that he was welcome to keep that copy since I had four others.

"When do you find the time? Don't you have chores to do?"

"Not many, Sir. Caro... I mean, Mother likes to keep me out of trouble."

"A wise woman. I think she would be much happier if you were in bed right now, don't you?"

"But, I am not sleepy."

"You need to go to bed."

"Perhaps if you told me a bedtime story..."

Chapter Thirty-Five:
In Which the Heroine and the Antagonist Metaphorically Play with Fire and He Gets Burned
As Told by Captain James Tobin

Music began to play in a room upstairs. We could clearly hear the vibrant melodies through an open window. Since ample starlight illuminated the patio, I invited Caroline to dance. She stated that she did not know how, that she had never danced before. "No matter" I replied as the violinist hit a wrong note. "Simply follow my lead."

"I have always wanted to learn," she confided with a blush and eagerly awaited my next move. I offered her my hand and she shyly accepted it. Then, I raised her to her feet. Her hand was slender, with long, tapered fingers, graceful but clearly well worked. Her knuckles were bright red as if she had recently punched someone. I took her other hand into mine and scrutinized it as well. The condition was the same as the other with only the addition of a small gold band that sat loosely on her finger and looked as though it might fall off at any moment. The ring had clearly never been sized for her willowy finger.

I lightly rubbed one of her scarlet knuckles and teased, "I see you are a prizefighter."

She blushed and turned her gaze downward.

I clasped her right hand properly for the dance and positioned her left on my shoulder. Then, placing my left hand on her shoulder blade, I gently pulled her close. She stared up into my eyes. As I paused to relish the moment, the song ended.

"Oh, no" she said with great disappointment. We both waited a moment and listened with hope. A new tune soon began. It was the Fireman's Polka[88]. If you are not familiar with it, the piece commences slowly to represent the firemen lollygagging about a firehouse with little to do. "Da dum, da dum, da dum, da dum; da dum, da dum dum dum." In response to the tempo, I lead Caroline in an easy waltz. We took a few awkward turns, but she quickly relaxed and we were able to move in tandem. With a few more turns she had learned the simple steps. Interestingly, she never asked any questions or looked down at her feet as most beginners do; rather, she kept her eyes focused on mine. Instead of relying on verbal or visual instructions, she trusted in her sense of touch, or proximity if you will, anticipating and reacting to my movements. I moved my left hand to the small of her back and placed my steps between her legs to decrease the space that separated us.

With a joyous shout of "Fire! Fire! Fire!" from the company upstairs, the music abruptly changed its pace and became an exceptionally fast polka, representing the firemen rushing to extinguish a blaze. "Ba ba ba da da ba da, ba ba ba da da da." Holding tight to Caroline's back, I reeled her around the patio with broad steps. At times she was lifted off the ground. Her smile was radiant and she never tore her gaze from mine.

When the music ended, we stopped dancing but neither of us loosened our hold on each other. We were breathing heavily. Another song began yet we did not dance. Looking closely at her face I realized that what I had originally described as "pleasing" was truly exquisite, especially now with her jubilant smile. Her skin, I discovered, was flawless, and although it was colored from the sun, a quality considered by most to be highly undesirable, it was a soft hue that complimented the tones of her light brown eyes and hair. It was far more attractive than the stark white skin that society women prized. I was also quite taken with the slight dimple in her chin that I had previously overlooked.

Caroline reminded me of an opal. A quick look at the stone and one only sees a smooth pearly surface. But a closer examination reveals many brilliant colors. One simply needs to take the time to view it from different angles and turn it to catch the light.

I actually know of many people who believe the opal to be an evil stone that can bring poor health and even death to its owner. This notion is, of course, utter nonsense. Interestingly, the myth has its origins some thirty years ago with Sir Walter Scott's novel *Anne of Geierstein*, the maid of the mist. In the story, an enchantress named Lady Hermione wears an opal in her hair that reflects her moods. It shines brilliantly when she is happy and flashes red when she is irate. Lady Hermione dies when a drop of holy water falls on her opal and destroys its color. She turns to ash.

People assumed that Scott had written the tale as a warning on the dangers of the stone. I have heard that within months of the novel's publication in 1829, the opal market crashed and prices plummeted fifty percent. To counteract this phenomenon and protect British interests in Australian opals, Queen Victoria tried to persuade others to wear the gems and was known to give them as gifts. The superstition continued, however. My mother never owned any opals. She favored sapphires.

As I held Caroline close, I began to appreciate the beauty of the gem in my arms. Her cheeks were flush; her breathing was fast and deep. Was it from the exercise or the intimacy of the dance? Caroline quickly became uncomfortable with my scrutiny and bit her lower lip. "Now, what are you staring at?" she asked, breaking the silence.

"Your lips," I replied. "They are chapped."

"Chapped lips, chapped hands, I am a farm girl."

My instincts as a doctor took over. "Here, I have a salve," I said as I retrieved a tin from my pouch. Yet, rather than allow her to apply the salve, I opened the tin, dipped my finger in the unguent, placed my other hand under her chin, and gently wiped the balm across her plump, inviting lips, top and bottom. What began as a medical procedure became a most bold and sensual experience. "That is better," I said in a whispered tone, still playing the kindly doctor. She was transfixed. The opportunity I had been waiting for all evening finally presented itself. Slowly, I moved my lips closer to hers and was about to kiss her... when a clock loudly chimed eleven and broke the spell. Caroline moved away abruptly.

"My goodness, it is late," she said nervously. "You must be exhausted."

"I had thought I would be abed sooner," I replied snidely.

"The clock that just chimed was my father-in-law's pride and joy," she chattered nervously. "He had it sent here from England. Just think, to get here, that clock had to cross the ocean and travel over the mountains—what a journey! You might want to have a look at it."

I certainly did not care to view the clock. Quite the contrary, I resented it. Our intimacy had progressed so far only to be undone by its chiming! As I sulked, she prattled on. "I am for sure that you would be most impressed with its craftsmanship. My favorite feature is the Moonphase arch because the man in the moon had the sweetest, pouty face, rosy cheeks, and dimpled chin. There is also a painting on the moonphase of the sea and another painting of the quaintest country cottage and I like to imagine that someday I might live in a house like that with my husband and my children. Also, written on the dial is the motto, 'Let not the sun go down on your wrath.' I believe that is an excellent credo, don't you?"

Her query was met with my indignant silence. Undeterred, she continued with plaintive reflection, "Come tomorrow, it will be burned to dust."

"With as many people as I have seen killed, it is difficult for me to feel sorry for the demise of a piece of furniture," I retorted. "Do you care more for objects than people?"

"No! But without furniture and houses and respectable clothes, people are nothing more than animals. I know because I lived with a pack of animals before I came here. All they cared about was eating and copulating and beating things up—laughing at other people's misfortunes. You all are no different. Just look at the way you soldiers behave: ransacking and burning houses! You live in the wild like beasts, so you behave like beasts."

This accusation raised my dander. I moved closer to her and she retreated until I had her backed up against the house. I hovered over her, menacingly and said, "I am a beast, eh?"

"Touch me and I will scream and scratch at you."

"Oh really? And I am the animal?"

I looked closely at her face. Her eyes implored me to understand. My anger gave way to disappointment. I stepped away and, ignoring propriety, sat down on the settee as she remained standing, her back against the wall. "No need to worry, I will not touch you," I said as I turned my back to her. "I have not sunk that low yet."

She tried to explain her position. "I have been taking care of this house since I was little more than a child. I have worked my fingers to the bone to make it beautiful. I cannot let it burn without a fight." Her tone changed from a plea to defiance and she announced, "I believe we have waited long enough. With your permission, I am going to speak with the sergeant now."

"Certainly, do as you see fit. But, you are wrong. A house is just a house. It is the people in it that make it a home. And even without furniture and fancy clothes, the things that make us human remain," I turned to face her again and continued "kindness and compassion and..."

Suddenly, a gunshot rang out and I felt a searing pain in my left triceps. I quickly got to my feet, grabbed hold of Caroline who was standing paralyzed with surprise and fear, and pulled her into the house for safety. I inspected my upper arm. I was bleeding heavily.

CHAPTER THIRTY-SIX:
Full of Confrontation and Calamity
As Told by Sally Anderson

Sergeant Richter had sent me to my room with yet another soldier. He did not bother to tell me his name. He had a most hostile demeanor, so I thought it best not to ask. As soon as we arrived in my room, he ordered me to go to sleep on the floor. He lay down on the bed and was quickly snoring away. I was not the least bit sleepy and had no intention of missing anything exciting that might happen.

I sat down upon my window seat and looked out. Down below on the patio, Caroline and the dashing, surgeon captain were conversing. From what I could see of the expressions on their faces, and also from how close they were sitting to each other, I could tell that they were discussing something very fascinating. I was tempted to open my window to hear what they were saying, but I knew that the noise from raising the sash would alert them to my presence, and history had proven that whenever adults knew that I was around, the fascinating conversations ended. So, I pressed my ear against the window. I could hear their voices, (well, mostly the captain's), but still could not understand what they were saying.

My neck began to ache from the crooked position that I was holding my head. As I straightened up, I looked across the way and saw something moving in the hayloft. I knew that it could only be one thing: Frank. He was Caroline's brother. Everyone, even the most proper-speaking people, referred to him as "no count." I called him a "master of trouble." He frightened me.

Frank would often come around when he needed a meal and a place to sleep. I could tell that Caroline did not like him either. She was always very nervous when he was around. I had seen Frank earlier that day, toting around a jug of whiskey; but I had been distracted by our company and had forgotten all about him. I had seen him go up to the hayloft too. It was his favorite place to hide. There were so many places to lie down in the soft hay where no one could find you, especially in the dark. It was no wonder the soldiers had not found him when they searched the grounds.

Frank was quite good at hiding—almost as good as I am. Grandmother never knew when Frank would come by. She thought she knew everything that happened in our house, but she did not know the half of it. I knew that Frank had joined up and I wondered what sort mischief he was about, away from the other troops and on his own. So, I focused my attention on the barn and saw him clearly. He had gotten down on his belly, like the snake that he was, and was laying at the edge of the opening of the loft. Then, a shot rang out. Before anyone could stop me, I ran straight downstairs to see what had transpired.

Several of us rushed into the downstairs' hall: Sergeant Richter, my friend Scant, some other soldiers, the surgeon captain, and Caroline. Sergeant Richter demanded to know what was happening. The surgeon captain said that there was a bushwhacker outside. He was cringing with pain and holding his arm and the blood was oozing through his fingers. It was the bloodiest thing I had ever seen in real life! The sight of real blood actually made me feel a bit sick to my stomach. It was not like looking at pictures!

Sergeant Richter sent Caroline to fetch Dr. Simpkins to attend to the bleeding and she ran right up the stairs. Then, looking like he had fire in his head with smoke coming out of his ears, Sergeant Richter said to the scouts through his very, clenched teeth, "Get him!"

The soldiers rushed out the door and I ran after them. I threw myself at Scant and grabbed hold of him by the leg shouting, "No! Wait!"

He tried to shake me off but I held tight.

"Get off me girl," he yelled.

"No," I sobbed. "He will kill you. I do not want you to die."

Scant bent down and shook me by the shoulders.

"What are you talking about?"

"It's Frank. He is in the hayloft. He is vermin and he will kill you."

"Is there anyone else?"

"No. Just him. He has been hiding there all day."

And then Scant cursed. He said, "Damn," and some other words that I had never heard before and cannot exactly remember what they were and "how did we miss him?"

Just then, one of the soldiers saw something move in the field and he fired his gun. The sound made me shriek and I began to cry harder. Scant called to the other soldiers, "He's up in the hayloft." Then he spoke gently to me and said, "Let me do my job now. You get inside where it's safe." But, I just could not let go. So he used his strength and removed my hands from his leg. Tears were still streaming down my face, but I sat quietly now and watched what happened.

Even though it was night, I saw everything as clearly as if it was day. Frank was still in the hayloft opening. He was loading his gun. His eyes were wide open with a look of terror. He must have been under the influence of the whiskey when he fired at the surgeon captain or perhaps he did not realize that there were other soldiers about. Otherwise, he would have remained hidden until the soldiers left or tried to sneak out when they were not looking. Frank was cunning and, as far as I could ever tell, the most important concern to him was his own self. He never would have attempted something so definitely suicidal.

Scant and the others crept up to the barn. They dragged the ladder around so they could enter the hayloft from outside. Two of the soldiers climbed the ladder as the others stood with their guns ready. Frank loaded his gun again![89] I suppose in his fear, he forgot that it was already loaded. Then, everything happened at once. Frank jumped up so he could point his gun down at the soldiers on the ladder and fired. The recoil from his overloaded gun sent him flying backward. His shot hit one of the soldiers who fell to the ground. The other soldiers fired back at Frank. Then, with wild shouts of "Hurrah," three soldiers charged up the ladder and raced into the loft to try to get to Frank before he had time to reload. Suddenly, all was quiet, eerie quiet. A big cloud of grey gun smoke hung in the air. Then, one lone gunshot rang out.

CHAPTER THIRTY-SEVEN:
The Great Conflagration
As Told by Caroline Anderson

I came rushing down the stairs with Dr. Simpkins. We took Captain Tobin into my sewing room and then Dr. Simpkins sent me out of the room. No one was paying me any mind so I sat on the bottom stair and waited nervously. I was extremely jumpy but I made myself sit still. Sergeant Richter was pacing by the back door.

After a short volley of fire, a single gunshot rang out. Then, the place became real quiet. After what seemed like an age, two soldiers came on up to the door and Sergeant Richter let them into the hall.

"Got him, Sir," one said. "He was Secesh."

Then the other added, "We looked around, Sir. Don't look like there are any more."

"You looked around before, too," Sergeant Richter shouted at them.

"With all due respect, Sir, he might not have been here when we first arrived—might have snuck in."

Sergeant Richter nodded in agreement but did not look convinced by the argument. His fists were clenched as if he might punch someone and he was breathing hard. The soldier continued, "He'd been positioned in the hayloft, Sir. We put him out of our misery."

"Any of our boys hurt?"

"Davis was killed, Sir."

Sergeant Richter threw back his head and let out a roar as if he were trying to shout down the mountains. He took a few deep breaths as he lowered his head and regained his composure. "We'll have to bury him here," he said with sadness in his voice. "Find a nice spot." Then he looked me in the eyes with a piercing look of hatred and spite and said; "Check the barn and all those other buildings again for any hidden medical supplies. Knock down the walls and dig up the ground if you need to. And when you are finished, burn them all. We'll see if that flushes out any more vermin."

"What about any animals, Sir?" the private asked.

Sergeant Richter turned his attention back to the soldier and replied, "Let 'em go free. There's nothing we can do with them right now."

"Yes, Sir."

"And send Private Roush to check on Daniels and Murphy and the horses. Have him report back at once."

"Yes, Sir."

The men left to carry out the orders they had been given. At first I was frozen in my seat. Then I ran up to Sergeant Richter in a panic. "No, don't. Please don't," I pleaded. But that sergeant, he just turned his back on me and went on into the sewing room with Captain Tobin and Dr. Simpkins and closed the door. I ran outside toward the barn. I tried to hold my skirts out of the way, but with that awful hoop that I was wearing, my shoe caught on a hem and I fell to the ground in a big puddle of mud. Without my spectacles, the scene was a big blur. Still, I was able to make out the soldiers as they set fire to the hen house and the wood shed. The chickens were running about, squawking, and Skippy was barking at the soldiers. It must have been an awful noise, but all I could hear was my heart, pounding in my ears.

I saw one of the soldiers swat at Skippy with the butt of his gun and I feared for the dog's safety. I called out his name and, although I could not hear the sound of my voice, Skippy heard it and came running to me. I held him close and comforted him. He remained vigilant and confused but he stopped his barking. Some soldiers were leading Big Red out of the barn in preparation for it to be burned. I remembered Frank in the hayloft. As horrible as Frank had been to me and everyone else, it would have been meaner still to leave him up in the loft to burn. It just was not right.

Finding my strength, I got up and put Skippy inside the kitchen where he would be safe and, while inside; I quickly removed that ridiculous hoop. Then, I ran outside toward the barn and climbed the ladder. As I scrambled into the loft, I practically fell on Frank's dead body. At first, all I could focus on was a brass buckle around his middle. It was nothing my family could have afforded so I figured he either took it off another man through gambling or off of a corpse. Then, I saw his face. I had never seen a man shot dead before. They had shot him through the forehead. The sight of it made me wretch. I turned away and tried to take deep breaths, but my dinner would not stay down.

When my heaving stomach finally quieted, I turned and saw a soldier who had climbed in after me. Laughing at my misery, he said, "Lady, you gotta get out of here."

"Please, can we move him?" I asked.

"How do you expect me to get him down from here? Toss him outta the loft? He got what he deserved, the no good bushwhacker." The soldier took firm hold of my arm and dragged me toward the ladder. "Now, get down that ladder before I throw you down."

I climbed down, but my legs were shaking so frightfully that my foot missed a rung and I fell half the distance, landing on my stomach. Watching me fall, that soldier laughed again. When he was down on the ground, he grabbed my arm again, pulled me up a bit, and then dragged me a short distance away where he joined up with two other soldiers. The three men then took torches and set fire to the barn. With all the straw inside as fuel, the flames quickly consumed the building. I looked on with horror. The heat was stifling and I began to choke on the smoke.

"Stand back you stupid woman," one of the three soldiers yelled at me. But I could not move. He slapped my face, but I still did not move. Then the first soldier from the group grabbed my arm once more and dragged me into the house.

Chapter Thirty-eight:
Wherein a Servant Proves Himself a Loyal Friend
As Told by Hartwell Finney

Nothin' much happened for the next several hours. They was playing music in the bedroom next door—sounded like they was dancin' and havin' a good time. The Good Reverend said it was probably for the best, and that the more we could keep the soldiers occupied with happy things like that, the less likely it would be for them to do harm to anybody or anything. A course, the Good Reverend was right about it all. The soldiers in our room seemed to be enjoyin' the music. They set themselves down on the floor and talked quietly to each other. I saw one soldier's foot tappin' to the beat and the other was noddin' his head around in time with the music… well, as best he could.

It had become nice and warm in the room and everybody was happy like all we had to do was wait until mornin' and it would all be over. I saw the Good Reverend drift on off to sleep, so I closed my eyes and did the same.

But, oh! oh! oh! I was awakened by the sound of a gunshot. A course that could only mean no good. Both of the soldiers done jump to their feet and the one says, "Stay here, I'll go see what's happened," and he run off. The other picked up his gun and pointed it at us. He listened real hard to see if he could figure out what was happening. We heard rushin' around and Sally a'wailin' and the sergeant was hollerin' out orders.

Fine'ly that soldier who was watchin' us got tired a waitin' around. He told Mista Samuel and the Good Reverend to come with him and they went down the stairs to see what was happenin', leavin' me behind. I walked out into the hall and saw that the doors had all been flung open and that everyone had left the rooms. I was all alone upstairs except for Missus Anderson who was still sleepin' in her bed. What was I to do?

I thought about leavin', a course. No one was payin' me no 'tention and I coulda been long gone. But, where would I go? I could run down to where I knew the Confederates were and tell them what was a happenin'. That didn't make no sense. I didn't like that these Northern soldiers had taken us prisoner and were gonna burn down the house and now there was gunfire, but they was the ones fightin' aginst slavery. I didn't want to do them no harm.

I knew I could just go home and be safe and rid of the whole situation, but I was afeared of what the soldiers might do to the Anderson fam'ly if I disappeared. I didn't want them to get hurt none on my account, 'specially not Miz Caroline or little Sally. So I decided to stay put. After a while, though, I had to slip on out to take care of some a nature's business. I knew there'd be hell to pay if I had used a chamber pot inside the house instead a doin' my business outside.

When I got on outside the house, it were like the Armageddon. Everything was burnin' and the soldiers and animals was runnin' about. So, I got a little scared. I started to walk away. But, as I walked on by that kitchen garden, it reminded me of all the kindnesses that Miz Caroline had done for me and I turned back around and went into the house to be sure that she was safe.

CHAPTER THIRTY-NINE:
That Includes Another Important Revelation about our Heroine's Fate
As Told by Orpha McClung

We had all heard the gunshot and ensuing commotion. Our soldier guards ran out of the room, leaving Margaret, Becky, and myself all alone. We were very frightened. At first we simply stayed in the room, but then it became perfectly clear to us that the sergeant had started burning things and we were afraid that we would be burned alive in the house. So we ran down the stairs and found that practically everyone was gathered in the downstairs hallway by the back door. Naturally, everyone was talking at once, trying to discover what on earth was happening.

A sharpshooter loyal to the Confederate cause had been in the hayloft. No one knew the fellow's identity. One of our captors was questioning Sally rather brusquely, as if she might actually know who the shooter was, but for the first time in her life, that little imp was mute. The sergeant had ordered that the sheds and barn be burned. Everything out back was aflame. Even if the soldiers had not been guarding the door, no one in his right mind would have gone outside near the conflagration.

But Caroline was certainly not in her right mind that night. She had been out there doing Lord knows what. A soldier had captured her and brought her back inside. She was pale and covered with straw and soot. Perhaps she and some of the soldiers had been rutting in the barn when the fire started. Margaret was thinking like-mindedly and asked that little hussy what on earth she had been up to with her hair a mess and all that straw on her skirts. Caroline did not catch Margaret's meaning and mumbled something about the chickens and the horse and the dog. Then, I thought perhaps Caroline was still foolishly trying to save the house. With nothing else than that girl's best interest at heart, I tried to stop her from continuing her lies and other dangerous actions. I said, "I do not know why you are so worried about this house, Caroline. You know Mother changed her will after John left. She gave Elmhurst to me and Margaret," and Margaret added, "as soon as Mother is gone, you are gone too."

Then, that nasty Sergeant Richter entered the hallway with Dr. Simpkins. That was when we discovered that the handsome surgeon had been shot. With a smile as big as the man in the moon, Margaret quickly volunteered to nurse the surgeon. I do believe she thought that she was going to wind up married to that man just like Virginia Alderson had done with her patient. I reminded Margaret that she had no experience whatsoever with nursing and that if anyone should be looking after the surgeon, it should be me. "After all," I said, "who has been taking care of Mother all this time?"

Margaret insisted that she had been helping just as much as I had with Mother and I thought it best not to start an argument with her. Someone needed to be an adult about the situation and I also had Becky to look after whereas, childless as she was, she had no one but herself. Margaret promised Dr. Simpkins that she would stay awake all night with the handsome surgeon to watch for fever and tend to his needs. Dr. Simpkins said that although her offer was especially kind, the patient would probably not need such attention. Margaret was not to be deterred and Dr. Simpkins relented. She winked at me and twinkled her fingers and went on inside Caroline's sewing room. She even closed the door behind her. For shame!

The sergeant ordered the rest of us all to return to our rooms and to get some sleep. He said that he wanted absolute silence. We did as he commanded.

Chapter Forty:
Full of Confrontations and Confessions
As Told by Caroline Anderson

Although Sergeant Richter had told us in no uncertain terms to return to our rooms, I followed him into the library. He was sitting at my husband's desk and I was taken aback. With his dark, full beard and stature, he bore a striking resemblance to my husband. Sergeant Richter glared at me and barked, "What are you doing?"

"Forgive me," I explained. "There is some whiskey hidden in here. I thought I might take it to Captain Tobin before I retired to my bedroom."

"Fine," he grumbled.

I walked to the bookshelf and pulled out a dummy book that hid a whiskey bottle inside. I had discovered it one day when I was dusting, but never let on to my husband or anyone else that I knew about it. It was hidden for a reason. I suppose my husband had been keeping it a secret from his mother and perhaps his father had done so before. Grace Anderson allowed a little brandy to be served, but she strongly disapproved of whiskey. Madame Lola Montez wrote repeatedly that temperance, exercise, and cleanliness were the keys to beauty and a good life. I am not for sure who my husband obtained his supply of whiskey from, but from the look of the bottle, I figured that it was mountain moonshine. I had seen enough of it in my childhood home to know. My daddy and brothers kept a still out by the woodshed. Perhaps Mr. Anderson had some poor client who had to pay for his legal services in whiskey.

I opened the book, took out the bottle and a small glass that also hid in there, and put the book back on the shelf as Sergeant Richter watched.

"How clever," he remarked.

That was all.

I crossed the room and was about to leave when I could not stop myself from speaking up again. I had to try one more time to save the house. So, I mustered up a sweet voice and said to him, "I do not know whether this would matter to you, but this house is called Elmhurst. It was built about fifty years ago and was a well-respected establishment."

"Why would that matter to me?" he said sharply.

I continued to try to endear him to the place. "President Martin Van Buren visited here and Senator Henry Clay. They decorated the house with patriotic bunting in his honor and he was extremely complimentary of the accommodations and the cooking."

"So?"

"This house is more than just a building. It has a history. There are memories and stories that will be lost if you burn it down; people and happenings that should be remembered."

"I'm too tired for this. Leave me," he ordered.

I lowered my head in defeat. "Yes, Sir," I said quietly and obediently. Then I lifted my head back up and took a good, strong look at Sergeant Richter. The scene was strangely familiar. The way that Sergeant Richter looked behind that desk, leaning back in the chair, reminded me of a night some two years before: the night my husband had called me into his library for the first time.

Back then, I was sixteen, and I was a servant to the Andersons. I had come to their household when I was but eleven years. Mr.

Anderson's first wife Dreama, needed help caring for her brood. It consisted of five children at that time. She had three more afterward, but none to survive past their first year. Sally was only two years old at that time and she was already a heap of trouble for her mama. According to Mrs. Anderson, Sally started walking at nine and a half months and got into everything. By the time she was twenty months old, she was talking in full sentences and my goodness the things she said! Dreama just could not keep up with her.

The Andersons had always had slaves to raise up their children, but Grace Anderson's suspicions had grown and she insisted that they get a white girl to do the work. I do not know what the arrangements were with my parents or how they were made. One Sunday after church, a stern-looking, fat man from Mr. Anderson's law firm (who I never saw again after that day), approached my mamma and me. He gave my mamma a sack with what appeared to be some coins in it and told me to get in his carriage. With fear and astonishment, I looked up at my mamma. She silently nodded her head and began to walk off. She did not look particularly sad, just beat, like a tired, old work horse.

I was not sad either. I was a bit scared of what was to come, but I figured that it had to be better than what was now behind me. It was better, much. As I said before, I had a warm, clean, dry place to live, my own bed and bed sheets, nicer clothes to wear, and the work was much easier. At first, I was only responsible for helping with the young 'uns. As time went on and I was trained up, I did more and more for the family. But, I enjoyed the work. Perhaps I am simple, but I get a great amount of pride out of how fine a room looks when everything is clean and tidy and set just right.

My mistress Dreama was Mr. Anderson's second cousin. Their marriage had been arranged by their parents and the best I can say is that neither one seemed to mind the arrangement. He was gone all day at work and secluded in his library at night... except on the occasions that they had guests. Dreama was a kind, chatty woman who was always in a dither. She was thankful for the order I brought to her life. She also appreciated my cooking: not so much in words but in actions; she consumed large quantities of it. As a result of time, pregnancies, and her enjoyment of blackberry pie, Dreama came to resemble an English bulldog.

In January 1861, the diphtheria came through. Dreama and three of her children were taken, leaving only Samuel and Sally. Two months later, Mr. Anderson called me in. Although I cleaned the room, I had never been in the library when he was at home. He forbade anyone to enter uninvited, and I had never known him to invite a female into his lair. I was frightened. No mistress and only two young 'uns, I thought he was going to dismiss me.

Mr. Anderson was sitting at his desk working on some papers when I entered. He leaned back in his chair and looked me over carefully. I waited patiently. I am for sure that I was trembling. Finally, he said, "You have been with our family a long time, Caroline: five or six years, if I am not mistaken."

"Yes, Sir," I agreed.

"You have been a good servant: an invisible servant. I like that."

"Thank you, Sir."

His next words surprised me. Instead of terminating my employment, he said, "I called you here tonight because I have an extra duty I shall need you to perform. I am a good, Christian man, Caroline. But, like all men, I have needs. Since your mistress died, these needs have not been met. Out of respect for her, I cannot marry for at least four more months, and, of course, a man of my position cannot frequent a bawdy house or risk having an illegitimate child. There is really only one solution. Do you understand what I am saying?"

I understood. He smiled and continued. "I plan to do right by you. After the mourning period, we shall be wed. It will be a big step up for you in the world and it will cause quite a stir I daresay; but, I like you. You are quiet and obedient." Then, he paused a moment to think. I felt his eyes all over me. Finally, he asked, "Can you read or write?"

"No, Sir."

"Very well, I shall teach you. It will be the perfect pretext for us to meet at night. We can have your first lesson right now," he announced with a smile of self-satisfaction. Then he stood up from behind the desk and walked over to me. He took my hand in his and looked it over. Unlike Dreama's hands that looked all white and smooth like a china doll, mine were red and chapped. He patted my hand and led me over to the couch.

"Now, Caroline, remove your boots and your drawers, lie down on your back, and lift up your skirts."

It was an order I could not refuse. If I had not done what he was asking of me, I was for sure that I would be dismissed and neither John nor Grace Anderson would find another situation for me. Where was I to go? I had been alone at Elmhurst. I had no friends to turn to. I doubted that my parents would take me back in their home. Even if they did, I dreaded returning to that filthy place where my body bruised from the whuppings I got. As far as I knew, there was only one job available for young, illiterate women, and that required me to lie down on my back and lift up my skirts for many different men.

So, I did what Mr. Anderson said. I did what every wife is expected to do for her husband. I sat down on that couch and began to remove my boots. My hands trembled a little as I unfastened the laces, and I took quite a bit of time to accomplish the extremely simple task. But, Mr. Anderson was patient. He was always patient. He did not offer to help, just stood by and watched as I fumbled.

When my boots were off, he calmly but firmly said, "Stockings and drawers now." Standing back up, I carefully removed my stockings and drawers in a way that would reveal as little of my flesh as possible—a skill perfected from my years of sharing living space with my brothers. He chuckled and said, "'Then the eyes of both were opened, and they knew that they were naked. And they sewed fig leaves together and made themselves loincloths.' Your modesty does you credit, Caroline. Now, lie down on your back and lift up your skirts." Reluctantly, I lay down and pulled up my skirts. "That is a good girl," he said, and he smiled again, because he liked what he saw.

I stopped the memory there. Dwelling on the bad served no purpose. Mr. Anderson had been true to his word. He had taught me to read and he had married me. I was not a quick learner but I was determined and dedicated. I worked hard to improve my vocabulary in order to be able to understand more difficult readings. Every night after I had finished my household duties, I would sit alone with a book. No one ever wanted for my company, so it made no never-mind what I did. Each family member of the Anderson household was always burrowed in their own den, amusing themselves in one way or another.

I especially enjoyed reading Charles Dickens because the people in his stories were in situations much worse than mine had been and then, through some miraculous discovery, their lives always ended up wonderful. The tales were mighty similar to the imaginings that I had when I was a little girl. I kept hoping that like Pip or Oliver Twist, my life at Elmhurst was only a trying time, just a stop in my journey, and that if I was strong, my life would improve as theirs did.

Mr. Anderson never saw fit to teach me to write. He did not see the need of it. He said it would be a waste of paper and ink.

We certainly did not have a fancy wedding. One day in September, shortly after my seventeenth birthday, he called me into his office, told me that his mourning was over and it was time for us to marry. Then, he told me to change into my best Sunday dress. He gathered up his mama and the three of us rode into town. We went to the church where Reverend McElhenney was waiting for us along with Mr. Anderson's law partner. After a few quick words, it was all over and we rode back to Elmhurst. As Mr. Anderson's wife, the only piece that really changed in my life is that I no longer slept by myself in one of the rooms over the kitchen. But, even in the master bedroom, in that beautiful rosewood bed, sleeping side-by-side and then some with my husband, I was still very much alone.

My sisters-in-law were outraged by the marriage, as were the many women who had been hoping to be in my place. Most people assumed that Mr. Anderson had married me because he had gotten me with child. Fortunately, that situation was not true and never came to be. Mr. Anderson did not want any more children. He never gave a moment of his time to Samuel or Sally and, as far as I could see, he was not the least bit concerned about a legacy or continuing the family name. Our matrimonial relations were not intended for either procreation or pleasure. They were a burden to us both.

Mr. Anderson said that we fornicated because he was a prisoner to his desires. He believed that lust was a sin and it made men weak. He especially hated the fact that poor white trash like me could have power over a man of breeding and refinement like him; but, try as he did to deny himself, he could not stop wanting me in a carnal way. Mr. Anderson always seemed like a pot about to boil over when he would have relations with me, like he could not wait another minute and wanted to get it all over as soon as possible, and he always insisted that we remain somewhat clothed during the act. He said that he would be the devil's slave forever if he saw me completely naked.

As for my part, I never wanted Mr. Anderson to desire me. And I certainly did not want to become like my mama, popping out a baby every year. Mr. Anderson was a good man, but he frightened me. I was not ever worried that he might strike me. He never struck anyone that I know of—never even raised his voice when he was angry. That was the frightening part. It was not natural. I expected that one day he would explode with rage, and then who knew what he might do? I often wondered if this had something to do with his disappearance.

Surprisingly, Mrs. Anderson was actually pleased with the marriage. One reason why was because if Mr. Anderson had married someone else, she would have had to adjust to a new person moving into her home. Another benefit to Mrs. Anderson of my marriage to her son was that she no longer had to pay my parents the meager sum she had been giving them for my labors. She now had a servant for free.

I did try hard to be a good wife and a good mother to Samuel and Sally. I had read stories in the Anderson's library about happy families. I wanted to be like them. I took care of everyone as best as I could and did nice things for them. I polished up the house for Mrs. Anderson, I cooked special meals, I bought albums for Samuel to put his newspaper clippings in, and I made pretty dresses for both Mrs. Anderson and Sally. As for my husband, after living with his mother and his sisters and their nasty, wagging tongues, I understood that the most important way that I could please him was to never, ever speak up. I never did. He certainly seemed to appreciate the quiet.

But, that Sergeant Richter was a different matter. He deserved a piece of my mind for what he had done to us and to Elmhurst. So, I looked him square in the face and I said, "I do hope your wife never finds Confederate troops destroying her home."

He scoffed at the thought. "They will never go that far north.

There is no reason to." Then he warned me, "Your side may be winning now, but in the end, we will prevail. Justice is on our side. God is on our side."

"I do not have a side."

"Yes you do. There is no neutrality in this war. Even if you do not own slaves, you are still complicit. How can you carry on your everyday activities and ignore the sufferings of your fellow man?"

"I do not ignore it, but what would you have had me do?"

"I don't know, but there is always something you can do."

"In my position? Why, I have had no more power to do anything for slaves than one of your soldiers can do about an order you give. They cannot disobey no matter how cruel and pointless. Not if they value their lives."

"My orders are never cruel and pointless."

"Is that so? Tell me then, what is the point in burning down this house?"

"To demoralize you and give my men a sense of victory— make them believe we are making progress in this wretched war."

"Suppose your men do not want to demoralize us? Suppose they like us or at least pity us. Do they have any say in the matter?"

"Of course they don't."

"Then how are conscripted soldiers any different than the Negro slaves? Aren't they all working against their will to make someone else's life better and certainly not their own?"

"You have twisted everything around. We are fighting for a better future for everyone. Yes, we soldiers must temporarily sacrifice some freedom and perhaps even our lives. And our women on the home front must make do without their men and without many of the niceties they are accustomed to, because life is nothing without freedom—absolutely nothing. Who would want to live in a world without liberty? No one with any self-respect and humanity puts their personal security above justice."

Was he right? I stopped arguing and thought about what he had just said. I realized that throughout my life, I had always chosen security over liberty. Where had it gotten me? All the cooking and sewing and cleaning would not mean a thing after the house was burned. That was why I had been fighting so hard to save Elmhurst. It was all I had. It was all I was. What a thought! Captain Tobin had remarked that if he were to die in the war, no one would mourn his death. I was no different. To my family, both back in the hollers and at Elmhurst, all I had ever signified was as a servant. I had no pleasant memories of time spent with others.

Then, I thought about my conversation with Captain Tobin. He had asked me if Elmhurst was Eden. I knew it was not. Eden was like the stories I had read about with happy, loving families. I thought about old Eve in the Garden of Eden. I had never understood why she had risked being banished from Paradise by taking a bite of that apple. I did not believe it was in a woman's nature to jeopardize her safety. The female always protected her nest. But, at that moment I realized that Eve's story had always been told to me by men. They thought that women were weak and given to temptation.

Thinking on it that way, I realized that the story was not actually about temptation. It was about free will. "My goodness," I said aloud without meaning to. "That is why she did it. That is why Eve ate that apple. She wanted freedom. She was tired of always being told what to do—even by God. For better or worse, she made her own choice." As I spoke these words, the clock began to chime midnight.

"What are you talking about, Woman?"

I looked at the sergeant and thought, "Let him burn the place down!"

"I am sorry to have taken your time," is all I said. Then, I walked out the door, leaving Sergeant Richter baffled.

I went on over to my sewing room to deliver the whiskey. Feeling bold and ornery, I did not even knock on the closed door before entering. I expected to find Margaret in the room, flirting away with Captain Tobin... or worse. But, surprisingly, she was gone already and he was asleep in the bed. Dr. Simpson had torn up a bed sheet to make bandages for him. His bloody clothes were lying on the floor. I set the whiskey bottle and glass down on the bedside table and picked up his torn shirt and jacket. Against the white of his shirt my hands looked terrible filthy. So, I went over to the dresser where a water jug and a basin rested along with a bar of my lavender soap. All my preparations for the evening seemed so silly now. I should have listened to Hartwell's warning and fled the house instead of hosting a party.

I rinsed out my mouth and washed my sooty hands and face. The smell of the lavender was soothing. After re-arranging my hair some to get it out of my eyes and off my neck, I set myself down in a chair, picked up a needle and thread, and began to repair Captain Tobin's clothes. I decided against washing the blood out of his shirt and jacket for fear that they would still be wet come the morning time when he would be in need of them; but, the sleeves would need patches. Fortunately, I had plenty of navy blue and white fabric to use. As I took up my scissors to cut away the frayed bits and form a smooth working edge, I noticed that the holes in the garments resembled hearts. I cut the sleeve of his jacket out in a complete circle so as to make the patch blend in as best as possible, but on the shirtsleeve, I kept the patch in the heart shape and sewed it up with red thread, giggling to myself about my orneriness. I was making Captain Tobin wear his heart out on his sleeve!

All the while I was working, I could hear the soldiers outside shouting to each other as they watched over the burning buildings.

They were trying to contain the damage to the outbuildings until the morning when the final judgment would be rendered on the house.

I sewed carefully, but the work was simple and I was quickly finished with the repairs. The familiar task of sewing actually helped to restore my calm. Once I had finished, there was no need for me to stay in that room any longer. I should have gotten up and gone somewhere else in the house—curled up to sleep in a corner undisturbed. But, I could not make myself leave Captain Tobin. As sinful as it was, I just wanted to sit there and watch him as he slept. His bandaged arm was above the coverlet but the rest of him was tucked snugly under. Fortunately, his wound did not seem to be too troubling and he looked in peace.

I found myself wishing that I had not backed away before when we were dancing, that we had indeed kissed. I thought about how pleasurable it felt when he put that salve on my lips—so gentle and unhurried. I also began to wish that he had been in truth, that he enjoyed my company for real, and that he had not just been playing me for a fool with his sugary words. Half of me was certain that he was a man on the make. But, the other half was thinking that he had changed as the evening had went on. Was I imagining it? And what did it matter? I was still a married woman and in a few hours we would never see each other again.

Breaking away from these thoughts, I realized that the room had grown quite cold. Although I could hardly bear the thought of building a fire—for all the blazes outside and yet to come, I did not want Captain Tobin, in his weakened, condition to catch a chill. So, I went over to the fireplace, started a small fire to warm the room up, and then sat back in my chair to resume my vigil.

In a bit, Captain Tobin woke and sat up. He was bare-chested. I was surprised by how muscular he was for a man whose work was not intended to include heavy physical toil. It clearly required more exertion than I realized. He was as fit as any laborer I had ever seen. Under the direction of Grace Anderson, my husband took good care of his body and, although he did not have the paunchy belly that marked most men of his age and status, he had acquired a softness that contrasted greatly with Captain Tobin's lean, youthful body.

Mind you, the only times I had seen Mr. Anderson without his clothes on was in glimpses, as he was dressing. Mr. Anderson was very insistent that civilized folks did not run about without their clothes on. Yet here was Captain Tobin, the most considerate and well-mannered man I had ever met, making no attempt to cover himself. Rather, he glared at me defiantly, saying, "Sorry I got my blood on your precious furniture."

I said nothing in reply but poured him a shot of whiskey instead. He sniffed the glass to determine its contents, then quickly threw it back and handed me the empty glass.

"Another?" I offered.

"No, thank you."

"Forgive me, Captain Tobin," I pleaded. "I was wrong. People are much more important than furniture. Some people at least. I just had not met anyone who was before tonight."

"And I have never met a woman who would admit she was wrong," he said lightening up a little.

"I suppose we have been socializing with the wrong sorts."

"Too true," he said with a smile.

"How is your arm?"

"It is only a flesh wound. I will be fine as long as infection does not set in."

"Fine enough to be leaving in the morning?" I asked with a mixture of relief and regret.

"Yes."

Then I realized that based on Margaret's threats, I too would be leaving in the morning. If Mrs. Anderson improved, Sergeant

Richter would burn the house. If she did not, Orpha and Margaret would throw me out. I said as much to Captain Tobin and he asked me where I thought I would go.

"Someplace up North, away from the fighting. Do you have any suggestions?"

"How about Philadelphia?"

"Do you plan to return there after the war?"

"If I survive."

"And you want me to be there waiting for you?" I inquired in disbelief.

"Yes, I have come to realize now that what I truly desire is a home and someone to come home to. Well, not just someone… you. You are a beautiful woman, Caroline. You are an excellent homemaker, you are a great listener, but you are feisty too. If I could direct that passion you feel for your home toward my personage, I would be a happy man." Then he got to his feet and said, "Let us go upstairs and ask your preacher friend to marry us." At first I thought he was in jest, but when I realized that he was in truth, I reminded him that I was still married. He said that since we were all for sure that Mr. Anderson was dead, he could not see how anyone could object, even Reverend McElhenney. I wondered just what the old Reverend would say. Would he think that Captain Tobin had taken leave of his senses? As far as I knew, he had never questioned why one of the most prominent men in Greenbrier County would want to marry me; perhaps he would understand that another man could feel the same way. Or maybe he would think that the whole marriage idea was a sham that Captain Tobin was using to bed me, and that he had no intention of ever meeting his marital obligations after that night. I am for sure the reverend would understand that motivation more than Captain Tobin wanting to spend the rest of his life with a chawbacon.

All I said to Captain Tobin, though, was that I thought he was rushing into things. He disagreed and explained, "I am a soldier. Time speeds up when death can come at any moment. I would have died tonight if I had not suddenly turned to face you. That bushwhacker would have hit me directly in the heart." He paused for a moment and then he said, "In point of fact, when you think about it, we have had a proper courting."

"How do you figure that?"

"We met at a dinner party, talked, danced, strolled. We have probably spent more time together tonight than most couples do when they are courting. I know I have told you more about myself than I have ever told anyone. And you said that we talked more tonight than you did in all your years with your husband."

"That is true."

"I will admit that my intentions were less than pure when the evening began... but you knew that all along, didn't you?"

I nodded.

"Then, why did you stay with me all night? Why are you here now?"

"Moth to a flame."

Chapter Forty-one:
Grace
As Told by Captain James Tobin

To be certain, I felt more like the moth than the flame. I got down from the bed and walked over to her. Taking her hand in mine, I kissed the top of it like a gentleman with his lady. Then, I turned her hand over and kissed the inside of her wrist like a lover. Still holding her hand, I ran her wrist along my face so I could feel its softness. Finally, I carefully laced my fingers among hers and leaned in for a gentle kiss on the lips.

Placing my cheek next to hers, I whispered in her ear, "I know it is sudden, but I do believe that I have fallen in love with you, Caroline." Lest you believe me to be a complete rake, I should inform you that my avowal was sincere. You might assume that I had often made such assertions in order to achieve my lusty goals; but I assure you that aside from affirmations to my mother of an entirely different sort of love, I had never before uttered those words to a woman. Even though I had several long relationships with dynamic women, they never aroused in me the ardor that I felt toward Caroline.

She gasped in response to my declaration. I held her closer. As we stood cheek-to-cheek, I felt a tear trickle from her eye. I pulled back and kissed her wet cheek. I was ready to ask her why she was crying, but the expression on her face supplied the answer.

It was a countenance worn by most of the neglected wives I had known: a mixture of adoration, surprise, disbelief, and remorse. However, the depth of the emotion displayed on Caroline's face was greater than I had hereto with observed. As I began to think about the comments that she had made throughout the evening, I understood that not only had her husband failed to express love or appreciation for her, but most likely he had never even regarded her with respect.

I thought about the manner in which the other two women had reacted when we left the master bedroom earlier that day. I had assumed their sneers were directed toward me. Now, I comprehended that they were expressing contempt for Caroline. I also remembered the boy Samuel's rebuff. Undoubtedly, no adult in Caroline's family had any consideration for her and the children were being taught to act in the same manner.

With all that I had witnessed on the battlefield: the fear and agony that accompanied the desperate struggle to survive, Caroline's sorrow should have seemed trivial to me. Yet, I realized that her battle was one of monumental importance for the body can endure more pain than the soul. What is more, I understood that the most compelling factor drawing me to Caroline was that she and I were actually both fighting for the same cause: a war on loneliness and isolation. My previously described behavior, reckless and suicidal as it was, had not been prompted by a lack of corporeal pleasures as I had previously believed; instead, it was induced by my need for a genuine and honest connection with another person.

Through her grace that evening, Caroline had begun to fill the emptiness of my shallow existence. With a desperate desire to fill the void in our lives, I held her tightly and kissed her lips fervently. Our passion seemed equal.

Then, the clock in the hall struck one. She abruptly broke away from me and walked toward the door. I assumed that she had come to her senses, that propriety was the victor over passion, and that she would be returning to her bedroom upstairs. I sat back down on the bed with a plaintive sigh. Mind you, at that point, I was not forlorn because our physical relationship had failed to progress. As I said, I no longer viewed Caroline as merely a means of providing temporary comfort; rather, I was simply wretched over the thought that we would never again spend any time together. I desired nothing more than to be in her company, for the remainder of that night... and forever.

Yet, instead of departing, she turned a key in the door and locked it. "I do not know why, but the key to this room is different than all the others," she explained. "Not even Sally has a copy. We are safe in here." Then, to my further surprise, and delight, she pulled the pins out of her hair and it cascaded down her back. This simple act changed her appearance from that of a graceful and wistful Raphael Madonna to an ethereal and sensual Pre-Raphaelite goddess. After combing through her newly freed locks, her hands went to her top button. "Like Adam and Eve," she whispered and began removing her filthy dress.

The next two hours seemed both to pass like a mere blink of the eyes and to last like a lifetime of experiences. When we heard the clock strike three, she became fearful for my safety lest I have no repose at all. We drifted off to sleep in each other's arms. I slept more soundly than I had since I was a child.

None but the worst of blackguards would say any more about what transpired between us that night; but, you should know that I discovered scars on her back that confirmed a history of physical abuse. Concurrently, she discovered the truth of my religion and my race, something that I cannot hide in intimate situations. Not surprising, the practice of circumcision was entirely unknown to her... and a bit of a shock. She had certainly never met anyone

Jewish before. When I explained to her that I was a Jew, she innocently asked, "Like Jesus?"

"Yes," I replied sheepishly.

She seemed extremely pleased with my connection to the one proclaimed as the king of the Jews. He was her only reference at first, but then she recalled another less agreeable association.

"And Judas?" she inquired further.

"Him as well," I concurred.

CHAPTER FORTY-TWO:
In Which a Boy Is Permitted to Become a Man
As Told by Sergeant Ephraim Richter

The house was quiet. I lay down on the sofa in the library and closed my eyes, chastising myself for letting my guard down and allowing that bushwacker to kill one man and wound another. Would Captain Tobin or any of my men report that I had been too lax? Had I been? Should I have insisted that every man except the sentry remain inside? Would Captain Tobin be able to continue his duties as a surgeon? That damn Captain Tobin and his damnable lust! If he had not gone outside to philander with that woman, none of this would have ever happened. I thanked the Lord that Daniels and the horses were fine.

As I re-played the evenings events to look for missed cues, I heard a knock on the door.

"Permission to enter, Sir," a young, male voice queried. I sat up, turned, and saw the Anderson boy in the doorway.

"Granted."

The boy straightened his posture and approached with an exaggerated swagger. He was clearly trying to look manly.

"What is it with you people?" I grumbled. "Who let you down here?"

"No one, Sir. Everyone is asleep, just as you ordered. I came on my own."

Now, there was some fine soldiering on the part of my scouts:

allowing him to slip by! I made a mental note to reprimand the soldiers watching this lad and continued to question him.

"Why are you here?"

"I want to join up, Sir. I am an excellent marksman. I could be a sharpshooter."

"Really? Have you ever fired at anything that was firing back at you?"

"No, Sir. But I have won three shooting matches already against men twice my age or older."

"How old are you?"

"Old enough, Sir. I read an article about a boy who wanted to enlist, so he wrote the number eighteen on a piece of paper and he placed it in his shoe so he could honestly say that he was 'over eighteen' when the recruiter asked." The boy laughed nervously. I was not amused. I stood and scowled at him. He continued, but did not back down.

"Sir, I am fifteen, Sir. But, there are many men my age who are distinguishing themselves in battle."

"Why do you want to fight?"

"I hate it here. I am always working for nothing and no thanks, and nothing exciting ever happens. I'm tired of being stuck at home with the yellow bellies and the women. I want to be with men and see more of the world than these hills."

"Does it matter to you which side you fight on?"

"No, Sir, not really. Union pay is thirteen dollars a month, Confederates only get eleven."

"And that is all that matters to you."

"To be honest, Sir, I do not really understand what the fighting is about. Seems to me like men just need to fight every so often. After a while, the politicians do not even try to compromise. If the War had not started, I was planning to go to Annapolis to try to be a naval officer."

"Have you considered that we might have to fight against your father?"

"No, Sir. Nobody believes that he is still alive. But it would not matter anyway if he were. He never cared about me. He left without even saying 'goodbye.'"

"What about your mother?"

"She is dead." He must have noticed my confusion for he explained, "The woman you met, Caroline, she is my father's second wife. She tries to act like my mother, but she is most certainly not. She is only four years older than me. She should be my girlfriend and not my mother. You see what it's like here? I have got nothing to hold me to this place and every reason to leave."

I started to say that if I had a son, I would never let him be a part of the carnage. But, as I looked at this boy's eager face, I realized that if he were my son, I would indeed let him go. I would have no other choice. He was keen to prove his manhood. With no understanding of the slaughter, how could he not desire to do his part? I could never describe the horrors to him in a way that he could grasp because he could not comprehend that he was mortal. He was young, invincible.

"You are set on joining up?"

"Yes, Sir."

"You're a big lad. You look strong. If I don't take you, Johnny Reb will, and I'd rather not have you shooting at me."

"Does that mean you are taking me?"

"Yes, I am taking you."

"Huzzah!"

"Now go and get some sleep. It may be the last night of peaceful sleep you ever have."

I shook the boy's hand and walked him to the door. He began to leave, then turned and saluted. I returned his salute and watched as he headed up the stairs, two at a time. I walked over to the back door and stepped outside. The air was still filled with smoke, but the fires had died down. Privates O'Reilly and Adams were keeping an eye on the embers, ensuring that nothing else ignited.

I returned to the library and walked over to the desk. Running my hand across its smooth leather top, I admired the beauty of the craftsmanship. The copy of *Ivanhoe* was waiting for me at the desktop's end. I picked it up, lay down on the sofa, and read until I fell asleep. I did not stir again, did not hear even the chiming of the clock outside my door, until it rang at six.

Chapter Forty-Three:
Settling Down for the Night
As Told by Orpha McClung

The day had been unbearably long and arduous and I was actually quite thankful that Sergeant Richter had ended our revelries. I trudged up the stairs one more time to the master bedroom. However, when the door to the room was closed, I realized that my daughter and I were alone in a bedroom with two Yankee soldiers. I am certain that my face must have turned white with fear. I looked around the room for something that I could use as a weapon to fend them off, but nothing availed itself. I would just have to rely on my voice to shriek and holler for help if they broke the boundaries of decorum. Naturally, I began to whimper a smidge as I knew that there would be no rest for the weary. I would have to keep a watch on those two men all night long.

As luck and good fortune would have it, Margaret came right on through the door in less than ten minutes. She said that all the Captain did while she was tending to him was sleep, that it was a terrible bore to just sit and watch him, and that nursing was a chore that should be reserved for women like Virginia Alderson who were more simple-minded. I was extremely relieved to have her company and felt certain that we three would be safe to sleep if we huddled together on the bed.

While Margaret and I were not going to undress, we asked Mr. Irving and Mr. Walker to turn around while we removed our hoops and corsets. Then, Margaret, Becky, and myself lay down upon the bed and fell asleep. We permitted Mr. Irving and Mr. Walker to use some of Caroline's garments to make a comfortable nest for themselves on the floor.

CHAPTER FORTY-FOUR:
Sweet Dreams
As Told by Sally Anderson

I was very pleased that Sergeant Richter had permitted Scant to return to my room. It was just the two of us this time and I do not believe I said even a peep the rest of the night. He sat upright against the headboard of my bed and let me snuggle up next to him. Then he sang me a lullaby[90] that I had never heard before about a bonnie bairn and a castle in the sky. He had a very fine singing voice and although the story in his song was quite fascinating, I fell fast asleep.

Chapter Forty-five:
Smoldering
As Told by Hartwell Finney

We was all sent back to our rooms to wait 'til the mornin'. That old wood floor in Mista Samuel's room was a rough place to sleep, but the soldiers lay down on the one side of the room and I found myself a corner in the other. The Good Reverend, he lay his weary head down on the bed next to Mista Samuel. But when Mista Samuel thinks everyone is asleep, he done snuck outta the room.

Mista Samuel was always sneakin' around and I didn't know what he might do. For months he'd been goin' on down the Salt Sulfa Pike to the cave where the Confedrates were minin' salt petre. He told his grandmammy that he was a goin' to Mista Houston's school down on Mista Humphrey's farm, but he was actchly helpin' to make the gunpowder. So I was afeared that night that Mista Samuel was gonna go try to find some of his Confederate friends and then Lord a'mighty what mighta happened!

Here it was that I had come back to that house when I coulda been long gone and now Mista Samuel was gonna get us all killed.

But, weren't no time 'till Mista Samuel came back. He couldn't have gone far. Maybe he'd just gone to take care a Nature's business. 'Cept, 'stead of crawlin' back on the bed straightways, Mista Samuel creeped around a bit and packed hisself a little bag with important things in it. Then he lay hisself down on the floor next to the soldiers. I was sho' I knew the meanin' a that.

My back was aching something awful, so I woke up a piece before the dawn. I stood up and stretched a bit. Then, I looked out Mista Samuel's window. Smoke was still billowin' from the burnt buildin's. Otherwise, it was all peaceful and looked like it was gonna be a pretty day.

Then, I heard the soldiers stirring a bit. So I laid myself back down again and pretended to be asleep.

Chapter Forty-six:
In Which the Heroine and Her Hero Part
As Told by Caroline Anderson

I hardly slept a wink that night. I did not want to lose a minute
of my time with Captain Tobin. When the clock would strike the
hour, I would silently curse it, wishing that the time would just
stand still. I tried my best to set everything about him to memory:
how he looked, smelled, and felt lying with his arms around me.
I was afraid that the new day would signify the return of an old
attitude: that in the morning light he would remember that he was
fighting a war, that he was a rich, educated Northerner while I was
just a poor, ignorant Southerner.

Captain Tobin was up with the sun and my fears came true.
He rose quickly from the bed and began to dress, whispering, "It is
imperative that we not be seen together." I nodded in agreement.
We dressed in silence.

However, when he was fully clothed and ready to take his leave
of me, he surprised me by asking, "May I write to you?"

My stomach knotted up. I started to tell him that I could
not write, but I was too ashamed to say those words to him. I
swallowed hard and said, "I do not know where I will be."

He pulled out a pencil and a piece of paper from his haversack
and wrote his brother's name and address on it. He said that his
brother was in Washington and had an important position in

the Department of State. Mail posted to him was guaranteed to be delivered safely and, even though he and his brother had not corresponded in over two years, his brother would always be able to find him.

"Do you suppose they will post a letter to a Yankee official around here?"

"This area is soon to be part of a new state, a Union state. There will always be Union troops nearby to post it."

I took the address in my hands and looked it over.

"If your letters do not reach me, I will come looking for you after the war," he said and added with a chuckle, "I mean it is a promise and not a threat."

I smiled back at him and wondered if he truly would come looking for me and how long it might actually be till the war ended. Also, I worried whether he would be able to find me, and what the hard years might turn us into.

Then, I realized that if Mr. Anderson were somehow still alive, he could come looking for me as well. I did not think he would, though. Even if he did, I vowed that I would never go back to him. He took no more note of me than his horse: he needed our services and that was all. He kept us both comfortably sheltered and well fed, and he never beat us, but he let us know that he was the master and we were the beasts of burden. I decided that if Mr. Anderson came looking for me, I would run away and never let anyone find me.

Still, I wanted to know for sure what I could expect. "Do you suppose this brother of yours could find out what happened to my husband?"

"I will ask."

He went back to his pouch and took out a small, glass bottle with a beautiful gold and blue label on it. "Something to remember me by," he said and placed it on the dresser. It was his bottle of Eau de Cologne. I picked up a thimble and presented it to him. It was a silly gift, perhaps, but he smiled and tucked it away in his jacket pocket. We kissed one last time. Then, he walked out the door to find Sergeant Richter and the other soldiers. Out of instinct, I started to make up the bed and tidy up the room and then I stopped, laughed a little to myself, and went upstairs to check on Sally and Samuel.

Chapter Forty-seven:
With Unhappy Revelations
As Told by Orpha McClung

Dr. Simpkins had spent the night watching over Mother. Alas! When he awoke in the morning, he discovered that she had passed in her sleep. Naturally, his first instinct was to inform Margaret and myself that Mother had gone to her reward. We were devastated. Margaret began to wail and so Dr. Simpkins took her into his arms and tried his best to comfort her, but he too was whimpering. I had to remain strong not only because I was the eldest surviving child, but also because I had to serve as an example for my Becky. However, she began to cry as well when she heard Margaret carrying on. Together, they created quite a noise.

The commotion brought everyone into the upstairs hallway where we had gathered. I informed them of the situation. Reverend McElhenney offered his condolences and said a prayer for Mother. His words were very soothing but Margaret was inconsolable.

"Oh, Reverend McElhenney, what are we going to do?" she cried.

"Come now, all will be well. She's gone to a better place," he counseled. Then, knowing that we needed to keep ourselves in good health and tend to our own essentials after such a difficult evening, he said, "Caroline, why don't you start preparing breakfast."

"Who could eat at a time like this?" Margaret whined.

"We must carry on. We will need our strength for the days to come." Caroline turned to leave and do as Reverend McElhenney bid, but Margaret stopped that little vixen in her tracks saying, "Wait! Where have you been all night, Caroline?"

Sally replied, "With me, of course," and walked on over and put her arm around Caroline's waist. Then, she added, "I will help you downstairs, Mother," which was an odd thing for her to call Caroline. At that moment, she looked sincerely sweet and loving. If I did not know better, I would have sworn she had some sort of behavior altering epiphany. More likely, she knew that her days at Elmhurst were numbered and needed to endear herself to Caroline because neither Margaret nor I wanted a strange, impudent child living with us, even if she was our brother's progeny. I could never have her in my home because she and all her mischief was a bad influence on my darling Becky. Margaret could not take that child because Margaret hoped to remarry—not that there was much chance of it, though, with the serious decline in the male population.

Before anyone could do a thing, Hartwell chimed in. "Excuse me for interrupting," he said, "but where are the soldiers?"

With all the ado surrounding Mother's passing, we had not noticed that the soldiers were not about. Then Caroline noticed someone else was missing from our group. Frantically, she cried, "Where is Samuel?" "Has anyone seen Samuel?" Then she charged down the stairs with the rest of us following as quickly as we could.

When we arrived at the bottom of the stairs, we espied that nasty Sergeant Richter and the dashing Captain Tobin at the door. They both looked especially well rested and in much better spirits than they had when they first arrived. We held our breaths as we waited for Sergeant Richter to pronounce his decision about the future of Elmhurst. He looked us over once more before rendering his judgment. Finally, he said, "We are leaving. I have decided to spare your home."

"Praise the Lord!" I declared in relief. We all began to congratulate one another on our better fortune with the exception of Caroline who continued to stare right at Sergeant Richter.

"Where is Samuel?" she demanded to know.

"He's coming with us," the sergeant replied coldly. The news came as no surprise to us. Anyone who knew Samuel knew that he had the wanderlust and it was only a matter of time and opportunity before he went off. It was his nature and could not be helped. Rather than accept the facts of the matter, silly Caroline began to cry and plead with the sergeant. "No, you can't. Not Samuel. He is just a boy."

"He thinks he's a man."

"No, please, not Samuel."

"He is determined to be a part of this war and he is safer with me than he is running off with any troop of insurgents he can find."

Then that handsome surgeon added, "I will help look after him, Mrs. Anderson. I shall be certain he writes to you, and I shall do everything in my power to bring him home safely."

"Please, Sir, may I say goodbye to him?" Caroline begged.

"Don't make a scene," Sergeant Richter replied.

"I won't. But, before he goes away, he needs to know that someone cares about him."

"Fine. The rest of you need to remain here."

CHAPTER FORTY-EIGHT:
In Which Tearful Goodbyes are Uttered and Hopeful Plans are Laid
As Told by Caroline Anderson

We walked on out to the front yard. The soldiers were waiting for their officers. They were lazing about and laughing. Samuel was in the thick of it and appeared elated until he saw me coming. He scowled at me. The soldiers stood at attention and Samuel followed their lead. I walked on up to him.

"What do you want?"

"To say goodbye and wish you well." I took his hands in mine and he allowed me to hold them a moment. Then he broke free. He looked down and started scuffing the dirt with the toe of his shoe.

"God be with you, Samuel," I said with tears streaming down my face.

He straightened up and looked at me. "God be with you too, Caroline," he said, appearing more at peace with himself than ever before.

"Right! Troops, let's march," Sergeant Richter barked. Samuel and the other soldiers turned and began to walk away. Captain Tobin lingered a moment. "Goodbye, Caroline. I shall watch out for the boy. Write to me." I could not speak for the tears. "I will see you when the War is over," he promised. Then, he took my hands and held them to his lips for a last embrace. Upon releasing my hands, he turned away and ran a bit to catch up with the others.

As I stood, once again watching the men in my life disappear down that old dirt road, I heard Hartwell approaching from behind. "If it is all right with you, Miz Caroline, I'll be headin' home now."

"Yes, of course," I replied.

"I'll be back tomorrow to make a coffin for Mrs. Anderson. Then we'll get you and Sally moved someplace safe."

"Thank you, Hartwell. You are such a dear. I'm sorry to have put you in danger's way." I choked on a sob and continued, "I will not be able to give you any work after tomorrow."

"That's a'right, Miz Caroline. Don't believe I'll be needin' your job any more. Them soldiers said we all is gonna have new laws real soon and I won't need to carry no freeman's papers." Hartwell smiled at the thought.

"That will be wonderful. Something good is finally coming from this horrible war."

Hartwell nodded. "See you tomorrow, Miz Caroline," he said and began to walk away, whistling a merry tune.

I was next approached by Sally who put her arm around my waist as she had done earlier that morning but never before. I returned her embrace.

"Will Samuel be alright?" she asked.

"I don't know, but I do believe that they will look out for him as best they can."

"Looks like it is just the two of us now."

"I suppose so."

"What are we going to do?"

"I am not for sure." I took her hand and we started to walk back into the house. She swung her arm and skipped as we went.

"Let's move to New York and start our own circus just like Mr. Barnum," she suggested excitedly.

"Now there is a thought."

"Or we could move to Boston and become tattoo artists like Martin Hildebrandt[91]. I have been reading all about him. He injects ink into men's skin with a needle and makes pictures that last forever. How does that sound?"

"Interesting."

"Or we could join a theater. I could be an actress and you could sew costumes. Or we could …"

Chapter Forty-nine:
Parting Words
As Told by Sergeant Ephraim Richter

We headed north toward Culpepper, Virginia to join again with the Third Indiana Cavalry. I reported the events of our scouting mission to my commanders: one man killed, one wounded, horses in good health, one new recruit, one new horse acquired, and one rebel killed. That was all that needed to be said. I made no incident report for the buildings burned. They were immaterial. What mattered was that we had returned empty-handed. We had not acquired the crucial medical supplies. I took some solace in knowing that the enemy was also critically low and prayed that assistance would arrive soon for our brave men and the fine surgeons who tended them.

In the end, I decided to spare the house. I simply couldn't bring myself to burn all those books. Instead, I confiscated *Ivanhoe* and five short novels to share with my comrades. I decided that this action would do more to boost morale among the troops than burning down the house.

There is no more to the story. The incident was nothing but a sorry waste of time and resources. More pressing missions awaited us. Shortly after we arrived back in camp, we engaged the enemy at Brandy Station. Soon after came Gettysburg. Then, we had the Battle of the Wilderness, Cold Harbor, Opequan, and Five Forks, not to mention countless skirmishes.

I looked out for young Samuel. Many assumed that he was my son. He proved to be a fine marksman and an excellent soldier. By the War's end, he was nearly eighteen and was sporting a beard. Samuel was determined to make soldiering his career. As the end of the Confederacy began to draw near, he talked of going west to fight Indians or of attending the Naval Academy in Annapolis.

A gunshot wound in the thigh (fortunately I was not hit with a bone-shattering Minie ball) ended my military service in February of 1865. Thanks to Captain Tobin's skills at dressing wounds and preventing infection, my leg was spared amputation. I only have a slight limp when I walk. After nearly four years of scouting and fighting, I returned home—back to work at the shipyards, back to my wife Ruth and my little Rosie. Rose was eleven years old by then. She had matured greatly since I had left her four years prior. But, she was as sweet and loving as ever, and fortunately not too old to sit in her father's lap by the fire on a Friday night. Only now, we take turns reading aloud.

The heroic men of the Third Indiana Cavalry were present at Appomattox Court House for Lee's surrender and for the Grand Review[92] in Washington. They mustered out last month.

CHAPTER FIFTY:
True Emancipation
As Told by Hartwell Finney

I came back the next day and made that coffin for Missus Anderson. They laid her to rest in the cemet'ry at the Presbyterian Church. Before that old woman was in the ground, Miz Orpha and Miz Margaret picked through the house like turkey buzzards, fightin' over who would get what. After I finished with the coffin, I was finished with the Andersons exceptin' the little dog Skippy who I took to live with me. I said a big goodbye to Miz Caroline. Couldn't help but start to cry for I knew I was gonna miss her somethin' awful. She cried too and then we hugged for a long time and that was that. Don't know where she is or what's become a' her.

On account a' the E-man-cipation, I was fine'ly through with workin'. A course I still work in my own garden and on my own house but I don't got to work for nobody else. Also, I fine'ly figured out what to do with the rest a' my money. I used it to help some a' the slaves who was now free get their start in life. Couldn't give them no forty acres and a mule[93]. But, I kept one acre for myself and divided up the rest a' my prop'aty into half acre lots. I paid to build some houses on 'em, and then I gave it all away. Now I got six fam'lies livin' beside me. We ain't doin' well, but we's all doin' fine. And we's real happy to be free. As I said, Ain't nothin' more important than freedom.

CHAPTER FIFTY-ONE:
Expected Outcomes
As Told by Orpha McClung

Even though the soldiers had left, Margaret was still carrying on: "looing" like a cow whose calf had been taken away. Dr. Simpkins' and Reverend McElhenney looked as if they had been beat. I suppose it must have hurt their manly pride to have been so utterly useless. Therefore, as usual, it was up to me to take control of the situation. I knew that we all needed to go back to our homes and set things right before we returned to care for Mother and Elmhurst. Consequently, I went outside to see what remained in regard to a conveyance back to town.

Fortunately, Margaret's barouche had remained unmolested. Margaret's horse, however, had gone missing. We assumed that the soldiers had absconded with him. Margaret's horse, Stormy he was called, was a Saddlebred. He had been raised near Blue Sulphur Springs by Mr. Andrew Davis Johnston and was kin to Traveller, General Lee's faithful steed. I am certain that the crass man who had absconded with Stormy had significantly less distinctive breeding.

The Anderson family horse had, however, remained on the premises. He was old and tired and of no use militarily. Hartwell hitched him to the barouche, Reverend McElhenney, Dr. Simpkins, Margaret, Becky and myself all settled ourselves inside, and we returned to the relative safety and comforts of our homes (I am certain Mrs. McElhenney must have been sick with worry when her husband had failed to return home that night).

The best way to cope with grief is to keep oneself busy with mundane chores. Naturally, that is what I did. First thing was to arrange Mother's funeral. Since Mother had left copious instructions as to what should be done, this task was easily accomplished with the exception of one detail. Surprisingly, Mother wanted to be embalmed. Embalming was not the custom at that time in western Virginia. Mother had most likely read about the practice in her magazines—at that time it was only being used as a way to preserve the bodies of Yankee officers, to allow them to be sent home to their wives and mothers. I simply did not know of anyone around who could perform that office for her, so we had to let nature take its course.

Other than that, we had everything arranged precisely as she wished. As Mother directed, we laid her out in the parlor in the mauve-colored gown that Caroline had sewn for her two years earlier when satin could be had at a reasonable price. Mother selected this dress to be buried in because she believed that purple color would counteract any greening of the skin that might occur. She was decidedly wrong in this regard. However, the long sleeves on the dress did work to hide an ugly rash that she had developed. Additionally, Mother had specified fragrant flowers in the room to mask any unpleasant odors, so we filled the parlor with lily of the valley. They proved quite effective.

Second, we needed to assess the damage at Elmhurst. Here again, Mother's diligence made the work lighter. She had taken a thorough inventory only a few years back. Margaret and I carefully went through the inventory to be certain that nothing had gone missing during the invasion. The soldiers had destroyed all of the outbuildings and made a mess of the kitchen and dining room, but surprisingly, they had not taken a thing—not even John's fiddle that Mr. Irving had played so well! Our friends who visited Elmhurst to pay their respects to Mother were quite appalled at the damage and ever-so impressed with our strength and resilience.

Third, I had to get with the lawyers about Mother's will and the transfer of Elmhurst and its contents. We discovered that Mother had stubbornly clung to the hope that John was still alive and had not actually changed her will as she had indicated to Margaret and myself. She had, however, written in her will that if John were to predecease, the property would all belong equally to Margaret and myself and not to Caroline. I have not mentioned this previously because I am a charitable woman and do not like to speak ugly, but Caroline was... how shall I say it delicately? Caroline was white trash. There was no doubt in Mother's mind or mine that if Caroline had taken possession of Elmhurst, it would have been destroyed in no time. Caroline was from "the hollers" as they say around here, and those people simply do not know how to take care of anything. Now, I know that is unkind to say, but it is true.

Nothing much could happen until we could determine unequivocally that John had died. So, Margaret and I simply mustered up our strength and carried on.

CHAPTER FIFTY-TWO:
Where Treasure is Uncovered
As Told by Sally Anderson

After the soldiers left, Orpha and Margaret got very busy with a lawyer and grandmother's will. Nothing could be legally decided until father was officially pronounced dead. Still, my aunts decided to send me to Richmond under the care of the Murdaughs, some relatives of my mother. Although she tried to keep me with her, Caroline could do nothing about the situation since she was not my legal guardian and Orpha was. Caroline moved up north somewhere, although no one will tell me where. When I get old enough to be on my own, I am going to find her.

Before we left Elmhurst, Caroline and I dug up the buried treasure. Like noble pirates in league together, we split the booty between us. Well, actually, Caroline only took a very little— some jewelry that had been my mother's that my father had said belonged to Caroline after she married him. The jewelry had been in my grandmother's possession. Caroline never had the temerity to ask Grandmother for them. If only I had known. I have temerity.

I wanted Caroline to take more of the treasure. I wanted her to have enough money to buy a pleasant cottage and never have to work again, but Caroline insisted that she had plenty, and that also she wanted me to have enough to have my own house when I grew up and to make certain that I did not have to get married unless I wanted to. That logic seemed quite reasonable to me. We hid my portion of the treasure in the trunk that I took with me to Richmond so neither Orpha nor Margaret would know about it and try to take it away from me. Not to worry, it is still hidden safely.

The Murdaughs did not appear to enjoy my company. They sent me here to Mrs. Pegram's school where I spend most of my time reading. I very much enjoy my lessons in literature and science, but I very much do not enjoy the lessons in grammar, etiquette, and mathematics. Also, I sometimes have a gay time with the other girls. Last winter we had five big snowstorms. I convinced some of the other girls to line up with me on Franklin Street and throw snowballs at the soldiers. One day a group of soldiers fired back at us and we had a most excellent snowball fight.

Miss Pegram says that I have a fascinating vocabulary but she wishes that I would learn to improve my restraint as to how often I exercise it. This may well be the greatest compliment I have ever received.

Chapter Fifty-Three:
In Which the Heroine Finally Begins a New Life
As Told by Caroline Anderson

In the end, it was decided that since I was of no kin to her, Sally was to live with relatives in Richmond. The Murdaughs came and collected her at Grace Anderson's funeral the following Friday. You say they sent her to a boarding school? I tried to contact her—dictated letters that Mrs. Mundy wrote down for me. But, I sent the letters care of the Murdaughs. I suppose they did not forward my letters to Sally, for I never heard a word in reply, and I am for sure she would have written.

Orpha and Margaret allowed that I could remain at Elmhurst until their mother's funeral, mostly so I would help them entertain callers and pack the place up for them. Over the next three days, they went through the house claiming this and that for themselves and arguing over who got what. One of their biggest fights was over who would take possession of Samuel's glass marbles. Orpha claimed that they were rightfully hers because they had belonged to her two sons prior to being Samuel's; Margaret insisted that she should have them because she had given them to Samuel as a gift. Imagine! After everything that was happening to folks and had happened to us, fighting over tiny pieces of glass! Surprisingly, neither of them wanted the beautiful long case clock that I had fretted over. They made plans to sell it and split the gains.

After those two had finished scavenging, they told me that I could take the remaining items that neither of them cared for and would not fetch a price; but, I did not want anything that would remind me of that house any more. All I kept for myself was my clothing and some soap. I made certain that it all fit in a bag that I could easily carry.

During that time, Orpha and Margaret arrived everyday at sunrise and remained until dusk. I knew that I did not need to obey them anymore, but old habits die hard. Besides, where was I to go and how was I to get there? There were no trains or stages that I could ride to get out of town. The trains were being sabotaged and attacked or used for military transport, and the roads were riddled with danger from marauding troops — both Union and Confederate. No one with any sense was taking to the roads. With the shame of being cast out, I had no desire to try to find a place in town to stay and I could never go back to the hollers.

Fortunately, the day after Orpha and Margaret finished their packing, exactly like Hartwell said, the Union troops that he had warned me of came on through. I say "fortunately" because they became my saviors. Company F of the First New York Cavalry[94], Lincoln's Cavalry as they were known, had been sent south to search out Confederate General John Imboden and his men who had been skulking their regiment's posts in the northern part of our state. They never found Imboden but they found me. I was alone at Elmhurst when they arrived and completely at their mercy. Thank goodness they were merciful toward me.

They did not take me by surprise. Unlike the scouts of the Third Indiana, these New York Cavalrymen arrived kicking up a dust cloud of noise. They were a lively bunch. I easily could have hidden from them but somehow I knew that they would do right by me.

They were headed north toward their post in Winchester and

invited me to travel with them. Because I had permission and they had authority, we raided what remained of Elmhurst, packing up all useful food supplies, herbs, cooking utensils and the like. I had hoped to have them help me to bury Frank, but the embers of the barn were still too hot even to get near enough to find Frank's body let alone move it. I am truly sad to learn that he remained unburied all that time. Thank you for notifying the authorities to fetch him.

I remained with the First New York Cavalry for the next five months, serving mostly as a cook and laundress but also as a nurse. There were many educated and artistic men among their ranks. They had a literary society that debated military and political questions as well as a theater troop that performed short plays. I learned the truth in what Captain Tobin had said to me: it did not matter that we were living in tents with dirt floors and sleeping on bunks; even without furniture and fancy clothes, the things that make us human remain. However, I was not entirely wrong, neither. The War could turn men into beasts in the blink of an eye. Less than a year after I left them, my friends from Lincoln's Cavalry were responsible for some horrible deeds in Lexington, Virginia.

During the time that I was in Winchester, sutlers Lynda and Lanny Howe had allowed me to share their tent. They were a kindly, elderly couple. When they decided to return to their home in Annapolis, I decided to join them. Samuel was always talking about the place. I thought perhaps he might settle here after the War. But, I have not seen nor heard a word about Samuel since that day he left. Not that I imagine he would ever want to see me again for he certainly seemed to resent my presence in his life, but I still care about him and hope the best for him. I checked all the rosters, during the War and after, but he seems to have disappeared just like his daddy.

Mrs. Mundy also helped me to write two letters to Captain Tobin asking after Samuel. They were formal, polite letters with no hint of impropriety. I sent it care of his brother as he had instructed. But I never heard a word in reply. His brother was overseas, you say? My letters must have been lost for sure.

I do not know if Captain Tobin has thought of me at all after that night, but I still have his bottle of eau de cologne. I smell it every night before I go to bed.

Chapter Fifty-four:
Full of Sadness
As Told by Captain James Tobin

I had no knowledge that my brother was overseas. We had not communicated with each other since I left Washington. I visited him before I left for Camp Thomas. We said "goodbye," shook hands, and that was all.

Having received no letters, I concluded that Caroline had never written to me, and was desperate to know the cause of her silence. Every night since our encounter, I have lain awake in bed thinking about the time we spent together and imagining what it would be like to be together again, wondering what had become of her and worrying that she had fallen into dire circumstances. I carry her thimble with me at all times. Perhaps it is the abundance of wine that I have consumed this evening, or your skill in eliciting a confession, or both, but I am not ashamed to tell you, what you have most likely concluded already, that this entire investigation was merely a ploy to discover the explanation for her failure to communicate with me.

I had promised to find her after the War and I truly desire to be with her again. Yet, with all that you have relayed to me about her history, chasing after her seems a fool's errand. Now that civil conventions have returned, lapses in propriety can no longer be justified by war time exigencies. We were in a world of our own making that night; however, it would be extremely difficult under current conditions for us to shut out the world for any sustained period. Can love between two people of such disparate backgrounds survive beyond a night or a week? Would society tolerate such a union? I fear the answers are "no."

What would you do?

Epilogue:
A Letter from the Editor

April 30, 1890

Honorable Mrs. Wheelock G. Veazey
1731 P Street NW
District of Columbia

Dear Madam,
I am delighted that you enjoyed reading my tale and will endeavor to
answer the several questions you put to me.
1). As to the fate of the Elmhurst estate and the families in West
Virginia: I discovered that the terms of Grace Anderson's will, dated
November 19, 1862, dictated that if her son, John Anderson, were to predecease, the estate would become property jointly of her two daughters,
Orpha McClung and Margaret Arbuckle. From May 23, 1862, (the date
of Mr. Anderson's departure from his home), to August 30, 1865 (the most
recent information I was able to obtain at that time), the whereabouts
of Mr. John Anderson could not be confirmed and the house remained
vacant. By order of the Eleventh Circuit Court of Greenbrier County,
West Virginia, dated June 8, 1865, Mr. Anderson was required to present
himself before the court prior to December 31, 1865 or be declared dead in
absentia. Under said conditions and at said date, the property would then
be transferred to Mrs. McClung and Mrs. Arbuckle who intended to sell
the house and land, both preferring their residences in town.

2). *How I originally located Mrs. Anderson: as I mentioned previously, my only clue to discovering where Mrs. Anderson had removed herself to after the war was her skill as a seamstress. My hope was that after leaving Greenbrier County, she had found employment in this capacity. Therefore, I began placing advertisements in local newspapers in nearby towns and cities from Richmond to Baltimore, Lexington to Hagerstown, and areas in between, asking after Mrs. Anderson. I received some extremely interesting replies, but no information on the elusive Mrs. A—. My next course of action was to send inquiries directly to millineries and dressmaker shops as well as seamstresses who worked on private commissions, hoping that someone might have heard by reputation of Mrs. Anderson. In this vain, I had the honor to communicate with Elizabeth Keckley[95], Mrs. Lincoln's former modiste.*

I was occupied thusly for two months when I had a most fortunate encounter. Anna Ella Carroll[96], the distinguished scholar from Maryland who was particularly influential in preventing that state from joining its neighboring states in secession, was speaking at an event I attended. Much fuss was made that evening among the ladies over the dress that Mrs. Caroll was adorned in. I learned from a female acquaintance that the gown had been made in Annapolis and went immediately to my desk to write to the shop where it had been designed and fabricated. Mrs. William Carrington, owner of the millinery, delivered my letter to her employee who created the fine garment, none other than Mrs. Anderson.

3). *What became of Captain Tobin and Mrs. Anderson:*

Three weeks after our visit, Captain Tobin appeared at my office. His spirits were notably uplifted and his grooming significantly improved. We exchanged pleasantries and he presented me with the bottle of port that I have now bestowed upon your husband. Captain Tobin stated that the wine was a parting gift as he intended to leave the city in the spring with plans to travel through Europe and the Orient. After a world tour, he intended to devote himself and his fortune to the study of medicine. In particular, he stated that he was interested in work being done on "germ theory" by a French scientist named Pasteur.

*Shortly after this visit, President Andrew Johnson removed
Ambassador Tobin from his position with the Department of State. I lost
my employment with the government that day as well. However, after
my investigative experiences working for Captain Tobin, I was inclined to
continue in that field of work. Accordingly, I began working as a clerk for
Miss Clara Barton's Missing Soldiers Office[97]. Within two years' time, we
received approximately 63,000 letters requesting assistance and were able to
account for the fates of 22,000 men. In April 1866, while working in this
capacity, I was able to uncover information regarding Samuel Anderson.
His situation had gone unknown to his family since his enlistment. I
immediately wrote to Caroline Anderson to apprise her of his situation.
The letter sent to Mrs. Anderson's home address was returned to me
unopened with no explanation. I made inquiries and received a reply only
from her employer, Mrs. Carrington, who related to me the following:*

I was not well acquainted with my employee. She arrived at
work on time every day and worked hard, but she was quiet and
kept to herself. She never volunteered any personal information
and I was certainly not inclined to ask. All that mattered to me
were her professional qualities. She was an excellent seamstress.
Mrs. Anderson always arrived at work alone and left the same
way except on Friday nights when two women would regularly
pick her up. I believe these women are Jewesses, but I cannot
be certain. I do not know their names as I do not associate with
Jews.

Mrs. Anderson's disappearance was quite mysterious. One
stormy day in March, I noticed a man entering my millinery.
His wool overcoat was clearly army-issued. Although his face
was obscured by a hat and a full, dark beard, Mrs. Anderson
recognized him immediately. She pressed her hand to her
heart as tears streamed down her face. The man seemed tense
and spoke demonstratively. I watched for a while to be certain

that she was in no danger. Propriety, however, required me to remain at a distance, and I was unable to discern more about the man's identity. He presented her with a paper that I judged to be a legal document, and she began to cry heartily. I could not determine if they were tears of sadness or joy.

After presenting her with the news, the man's demeanor seemed to soften, Mrs. Anderson stopped crying, and the two conversed quietly. The sound of my poor cat mewing to be allowed entrance at the back door distracted me. When I turned around again, I discovered that Mrs. Anderson had gathered her belongings and left the shop, presumably with the man, quitting both her position and her residence. She left no forwarding address.

Although I was curious to learn of Mrs. Anderson's fate, a lack of time and resources prevented me from pursuing the investigation. Accordingly, I discovered neither who the unidentified man was nor where Mrs. Anderson removed herself to. Perhaps the dark-bearded man was long-absent Mr. John Anderson, come to claim his wife. Having no access to Confederate records, I was never able to learn more about him. Although highly improbable, he might have survived the War.

The man might also have been Samuel Anderson. He had been living in nearby Baltimore at that time, awaiting his eighteenth birthday and the opportunity to enlist in the newly constituted 7th U.S. Cavalry[98]. Perhaps after some time to reflect on all of Mrs. Anderson's kindnesses, he decided to visit her before heading west.

Or the man could have been someone Mrs. Anderson met during her travels from West Virginia to Maryland. After only one interview with her, I was strangely tempted to return to Annapolis to ask for her hand. A man who had spent a month or so in her company would be even more likely to be besotted.

My hope, however, was that the mystery man was Captain Tobin because the two were clearly in love with each other. Perhaps he had decided to invite her to accompany him on his travels. I was certain that she would readily agree to be his life companion. Maybe they could find happiness in a frontier community in California or Australia where people were less likely to care about one's past.

As before, I look forward to meeting you next month on Decoration Day, and I do hope that we will have an opportunity to discuss your reactions to this tale, as well as your suppositions as to its conclusion.

Yours most sincerely,
Geo. L. Scarborough

TOPICS FROM THE NOVEL FOR DISCUSSION

1. As John Anderson leaves home to join with Confederate forces, he tells his wife, "it's not about a cause any more. It is about honor." How do his reasons for fighting compare to:
   a. His son Samuel's? Sergeant Richter's?
   b. The causes of the Civil War as explained in history books?
   c. Reasons why people join the military today?
2. How has the experience of living in a war zone changed throughout history?
   a. Were civilians safer during the Civil War than they were in ancient times and the Middle Ages?
   b. Were civilians safer during the Civil War than they are today in countries that have experienced civil wars?
3. Sergeant Richter states that he believes that psychological warfare used against civilians is an important component for winning the war. Do you agree?
4. The central theme of the book is the comparative importance of the right to life and liberty. Which is more important?
   a. Is a life without liberty worth living?
   b. Is life worth living without other basic necessities?
   c. What is your definition of liberty and how much liberty does a person need to enjoy life?
5. Who do you believe has returned to Caroline at the end of the book?

    a. Her husband John?

    b. Her stepson Samuel?

    c. Captain James Tobin?

NOTES ON THE TEXT:
WHAT IS TRUE AND WHAT IS A LIE

Lies (based on true stories), is actually based on a real incident. In late June 1864, General David Hunter and his troops arrived in Greenbrier County, VA. Separated from their food supplies, his men had no option but to "forage" to stay alive. Some of these troops arrived at the Elmhurst property in North Caldwell (named after the family that owned the home and not a geographic designation. North Caldwell is actually west of the town of Caldwell) with the intention of burning the house. Although the family had been warned of the danger, matriarch Isabel North Caldwell was extremely ill at the time, and they had been unable to flee. The North Caldwells did, of course, attempt to conceal their valuables, including the silver which was buried below the poultry shed. When the officer in charge at the time was told of Mrs. North Caldwell's inability to leave the house, he ordered his surgeon to examine her to be certain the illness was not feigned. The doctor decreed that she was too ill to be moved; the troops burned the outbuildings, but Elmhurst was spared.

The similar incident depicted in *Lies,* occurs in May 1863, a year before Hunter's men harassed the residents of Elmhurst, and, with the exception of Reverend McElhenney and Dr. William Simpson, the characters in the story are all fictitious. The name "Anderson" was selected for the fictitious family because Captain James Anderson, a recruiting officer for George Washington

241

during the American Revolution, was the original owner of the Elmhurst property. However, Captain Anderson and his family lived in a home across the river from the tavern that was built in 1824 by his son-in-law, Henry B. Hunter. While some similarities exist between the fictional Anderson family and the North Caldwell family, Isabel North Caldwell was thirty-seven years old in 1863 and neither fits the description of Grace nor Caroline. Isabel's husband, James Robinson Caldwell was forty-three in 1863. They married in 1851 and moved into the Elmhurst house in 1853. The North Caldwells had six children; three girls died of diphtheria in 1861. Isabel died in 1897; James died in 1904.

The name of the character of Hartwell Finney is derived from Hartwell Black, a free inhabitant of Greenbrier County who was listed as seventy years of age in the 1860 census. His speech pattern is derived from an interview of "Reverend Williams" that was conducted by Miriam Logan as part of the Federal Writers' Project of the Works Progress Administration (WPA) to interview surviving ex-slaves during the 1930s. The entire collection of narratives can be found in Rawick, George P. [ed.], *The American Slave: A Composite Autobiography*. Westport, Conn.: Greenwood Press, 1972-79.

Many records exist telling of Reverend McElhenney. I relied heavily on Fry, Rose W., *Recollections of the Rev. John McElhenney D.D.* Richmond, VA: Whittet, Shepperson, Printers, 1893, and Dayton, Ruth Woods, *Greenbrier Pioneers and Their Homes*. Charleston, WV: West Virginia Publishing Company, 1942. Few references exist for Dr. Simpkins aside from mentions in the skeleton story that he tells Sally on page 46-47. The verity of this tale cannot be established. Accordingly, all personality traits assigned to Dr. Simpkins are fictional.

The character of Ephraim Richter was inspired by Milton Cline, the scout with the longest and deepest incursion into

Confederate lines. However, unlike Richter who is tall and dark, Cline was short and red-headed. In addition, although Cline was a sailor, he was never a shipbuilder.

One of the most famous photographs of Civil War scouts is in a collection owned by the Library of Congress. Taken sometime between December 1863 and April 1864, it shows the winter quarters at Brandy Station, following the cavalry battle of the previous June. The photo's caption identifies the center, seated figure as, "Lt. Robert Klein, 3d Indiana Cavalry;" however, it is actually Milton W. Cline. The boy seated to Cline's right is identified as Klein's son. This young man was the inspiration for the character of Samuel. Most of the information about Cline comes from Fischel, Edwin C., *The Secret War for the Union: The Untold Story of Military Intelligence During the Civil War,* New York: Houghton Mifflin Company, 1996.

The regiments and troop movements are as close to plausible as I could make them. The information about the formation and early movements of the Third Indiana Cavalry are taken from Pickerill, William N., History of the Third Indiana Cavalry, Indianapolis, IN: Aetna Printing Co., 1906. In May 1863, the Third Indiana Cavalry was stationed in Virginia at that time along the Rappahannock River. They did fight in all of the battles listed and they did send scouts to watch enemy movement. However, no evidence exists to suggest that they were ever in Greenbrier County, West Virginia. The First New York Cavalry was stationed in the Winchester, Virginia area and scouts were sent to try to find General John D. Imboden. However, no evidence that I uncovered suggested that they were ever in Greenbrier County.

Other "true" historical references in the text are:

1: Wheelock G. Veazey was born in New Hampshire in 1835 and attended Phillips Exeter Academy and Dartmouth College, graduating in 1859. After attending law school, he was admitted to the Vermont Bar in 1860, and began practicing law in Springfield. When the Civil War began, Veazey enlisted as a private, but rose to the rank of colonel of the 16th Vermont Infantry. He led this unit at the Battle of Gettysburg, and in 1891, received the Medal of Honor for his actions during that engagement. In 1863, he left the army and returned to Vermont, settling in Rutland. Veazey resumed the practice of law and was elected to many different prestigious offices including judge of the Supreme Court of Vermont. In 1889, he was appointed by President Benjamin Harrison as a member of the Interstate Commerce Commission, a position he held until resigning, shortly before his death in 1898. The address listed in the letter was Veazy's actual residence in Washington DC during his tenure with the ICC.

Colonel Veazey was active in the Grand Army of the Republic, serving as post commander, Department Commander, Judge Advocate General, and finally as Commander-in-Chief.

2: The Grand Army of the Republic (GAR), was founded in 1866 as a fraternal organization for veterans of the United States armed services who fought for the Union during the Civil War. The GAR held an annual "National Encampment" every year from 1866 to 1949. Its peak membership was over 490,000 in 1890, a high point of commemorative activities. The GAR was disbanded in 1956 after the last member died. In 1883, the Women's Relief Corps was established as an auxiliary to the GAR. Its mission is to perpetuate the memory of the GAR and it still exists today.

3: Pre-phylloxera wine is a term for wine that was produced before the phylloxera epidemic in Europe that began in 1863 and by 1889 had destroyed between two thirds and nine tenths of all European vineyards. Phylloxera is caused by an almost microscopic, pale yellow sap-sucking insect, related to aphids that feed on the roots and leaves of grapevines.

4: **The 16th Regiment, Vermont Volunteer Infantry**, was a nine months' regiment, raised as a result of President Abraham Lincoln's call in August 1862, for additional troops due to the disastrous results of the Peninsula Campaign. It served from October 1862 to August 1863, predominantly in the Defenses of Washington. During the battle of Gettysburg, the 16th Vermont regiment played a pivotal role in the Union repulse of Pickett's Charge. Union General Abner Doubleday, hero of Ft. Sumter and supposed inventor of baseball, was noted to have reacted to the 16th Vermont's actions at Gettysburg by waving his hat and shouting, "Glory to God, Glory to God! See the Vermonters go it!" Benedict, G. G., *Vermont in the Civil War. A History of the part taken by the Vermont Soldiers and Sailors in the War For The Union, 1861-5.* Burlington, VT: The Free Press Association, 1888, p. 478.

5: **Virginia Johnson Pegram**, daughter of General William Ransom Johnson, a successful horse breeder known as the "Turf King," and widow of General James Pegram, a Mexican War hero, ran another noted girls' school with her daughter **Mary Evans Pegram** from 1856 to 1866.

6: Mrs. Pegram's school was located on Franklin Street in Richmond's Linden Row neighborhood. During the Civil War, the girls from Miss Pegram's School would often engage in snowball fights with passing soldiers as Sally describes at the end of the novel.

7: **The Ebbitt House.** In 1856, William E. Ebbitt purchased Frenchman's Hotel located on the southeast corner of F Street NW and 14th Street NW in the city of Washington, D.C. and turned it into a boarding house, that he renamed "Ebbitt House." The hotel and accompanying restaurant went through many iterations over the next 150 years, but still exists as the Old Ebbitt Grill, a popular hangout for many politicians and celebrities.

8: **Decoration Day** is the original name for Memorial Day. The tradition of setting aside a day each year to decorate the graves of

Civil War soldiers with spring flowers began shortly after the war. It became a national holiday on May 30, 1881 when President Garfield celebrated it at Arlington Cemetery. Although I am not certain if bicycle races were being held in Washington DC as early as 1890, a May 29, 1895 article in the *Washington Evening Star,* reveals that bicycle races were held in DC as part of the Decoration Day celebrations. The article did not present the races as inaugural or novel; rather, it was written as if bicycle races were a common occurrence.

9: In addition, the article stated that the 1895 races were sponsored by the **Columbia Athletic Club**. *A History of American Amateur Athletics and Aquatics with the Records* by Frederick William Janssen published in 1888 by the Outing Company Limited of New York, contains a short entry about the Columbia Athletic Club known originally as the Columbia Boat Club. Janssen called it a "crack club" that has, "always been in activity when any rowing was to be done." He further stated that, "although rather quiet just at present," it will, "be working with renewed strength on land and water." Janssen further mentioned the Columbia Athletic Club as one of the founding members of the Amateur Athletic Union of the United States.

10: The *Roster of the Columbia Athletic Club, of Washington D.C.: Correct to June 10, 1889*, contains the name, "**Geo. L. Scarborough**." For his address, the roster lists "Dept. of State."

11: Many accounts tell of the **Battle of Lewisburg**. Much of this description is taken predominantly from Rose Fry's *Recollections.*

12: Sally's behavior watching the troops was inspired by a story told to me by Lewisburg resident Tate Hudson. She related to me that her great grandmother stood at the fence of her family home to watch the Battle of Lewisburg and the girl's father had to pry her off and carry her inside for safety.

13: **Edgar's Battalion,** the Twenty-sixth Battalion Virginia Infantry, is named after George Matthews Edgar. Edgar was born in Union, WV in 1837 and graduated from Virginia Military Institute in 1856. When the Civil War broke out, Edgar was serving in Florida as a sergeant in the US army. Her resigned, returned to Union, and helped organize a company of men. Edgar was wounded and captured at the Battle of Lewisburg, but exchanged later in the fall of 1862. He and his battalion then fought at Hanley Hill, Dry Creek, Droop Mountain, New Market, and Cold Harbor, where he was again wounded and captured but managed to escape. He was captured again at Winchester, Va. in 1864 and exchanged shortly thereafter. In 1867, Edgar married Reverend McElhenney's granddaughter, Rebecca Fry.

14: A **fairy diddle** is an Appalachian term for a small squirrel.

15: Tuckwiller and Honaker are common names in Greenbrier County, but the dispute is entirely fictional.

16: The **bridge** at the Greenbrier River in North Caldwell was owned by Henry Hunter and it was burned by the Confederate soldiers after the Battle of Lewisburg to prevent the Union troops from pursuing them.

17: Unfortunately, this is true. **Free Inhabitants of Color** did have to register at the Greenbrier County courthouse in order to stay in the county.

18: Although the story of **Hartwell**'s childhood and his inheritance is entirely fictional, it is derived from Mary McNeil, a Greenbrier County resident who died in 1845. The terms of her will stated:

My Negro boy John Coalter have his freedom after my
death provided he has attained the age of 21 years. In case
I depart this life before he arrives at that age, he is to serve
until he is 21 and then be free and then to have the other
half of my estate both real and personal and the same shall

be herewith conveyed to him or sold and the proceeds paid over to him by my executor and it is my direction that no part of the property or money that John shall get shall be used by him in purchasing any of his relations either to free them or otherwise.

19: The stories of **Henry Hunter** are taken from Dayton, Ruth Woods *Greenbrier Pioneers and Their Homes.*

20: **Lola Montez** was, as Sally would say, "a fascinating woman." She was born Eliza Rosanna Gilbert in 1821 in Ireland. In 1837, she eloped with Lieutenant Thomas James, but the couple separated five years later, in Calcutta. She then became a professional dancer and adopted the stage name "Lola Montez, the Spanish dancer" in 1843. Lola became famous for her Spider Dance in which she pretended that a spider was on her skirts and she tried to rid herself of the arachnid by shaking and raising them higher than was considered decorous at the time. Rumors even spread that she raised them so high that the audience could see that she wore no undergarments.

In addition to her dancing, Lola became famous for her beauty and quick temper. She became a courtesan and had many rich and famous lovers including Franz Liszt. Her dalliance with Ludwig I of Bavaria resulted in him granting her a large annuity and the title Countess of Landsfeld. After several difficult relationships, she spent the years 1851-1853 in California, performing for the gold miners. In 1858, she published *The Arts of Beauty, or Secrets of a Lady's Toilet.* Many of her beauty secrets are still practiced today while others are quite ridiculous. She was living in Brooklyn, NY when she died in 1861.

21: **Godey's Lady's Book** was known as the "queen of monthlies." It was published by Louis Godey of Philadelphia from 1830–1878 and contained only original work by American authors. Edgar Allan Poe, Nathaniel Hawthorne, Oliver Wendell

Holmes, Washington Irving, and Frances Hodgson Burnett were some of the contributors to the magazine. By 1860, it had a circulation of 150,000. Each issue contained hand-tinted fashion plates, an illustration and pattern with measurements for a garment to be sewn at home, and sheet music for piano, as well as poetry, articles, and engravings created by prominent writers and other artists of the time.

Godey's long-serving editor was Sara Josepha Hale who edited the magazine from 1837 to 1877. Ms. Hale was the author of "Mary Had a Little Lamb," and used editorial space to advocate for the establishment of Thanksgiving as a national holiday (In 1863, President Lincoln declared that the last Thursday of November shall be celebrated as a national day of Thanksgiving). She also created a regular section with the heading "Employment for Women" beginning in 1852.

22: **Panada** is made by covering salt-rising bread with hot milk and then flavoring or "strengthening" it with apple brandy. The amount of brandy added was increased according to one's age. According to Ruth Dayton Woods, Reverend McElhenney was known to relish this dish and, when riding to visit the more remote members of his pastorate, it was the meal he typically requested. Jenny Bardwell, Susan R. Brown, and Patricia L. Kisner write about salt-rising bread in "Keeping the Tradition Alive," Extension Service, West Virginia University, www.wvu.edu/~exten/infores/pubs/.../21.wl.pdf.

> *Salt-rising bread is thought to have originated in the 1830s and 1840s. There are many theories about how salt-rising bread came into existence. One theory is that the pioneer women began making this bread because they could not afford to buy yeast for bread making or perhaps they were too isolated and did not have easy access to yeast. When they didn't have 'already-made yeast,' they made salt-rising*

bread. They stirred together water, a little water-ground cornmeal (ground between stones with waterpower), potatoes, and salt. They set the mixture, uncovered, in a warm place, exposing it to the air until bacteria fell into it and formed gas or caused fermentation. Then they removed the potatoes and used the liquid as leavening for this once-famous bread. Baking powder, the standard ingredient used to get dough to rise, was not developed in this country until the 1850s.

23: The story of Grace and Charles Anderson's courtship is based on the marriage of Isabel North to James Caldwell. Isabel's father, John A. North, was a prominent lawyer in Lewisburg who became Clerk of the Greenbrier District Court of Chancery, and Clerk of the District of Virginia Supreme Court of Appeals. He and his wife Charlotte built a house across the street from the building used by the Supreme Court and lived there from 1821 until the 1830s when they moved to a house on the corner of German and Lafayette Streets. Mr. North purchased Elmhurst for his daughter Isabel when she married. North's first home is now operated as a museum and is the headquarters for the Greenbrier Historical Society. Interestingly, the second home on Lafayette Street (where Orpha and Margaret supposedly grew up), has become quite famous and is often visited by tourists because it is believed to be haunted. According to the local legend, a young lady was sent to live with relatives in Lewisburg in order to separate her from a soldier with whom she had fallen in love. When the soldier attempted to visit her, he was only allowed to speak to her from the corner of the street. Although he paid children to deliver spring flowers to her each day, he was never able to visit again. In despair, the young woman hanged herself in the only closet in the house. Since then, owners of the house report smelling flowers, even in the winter, and seeing a female apparition. One owner grew so tired of hearing the sounds coming from the closet that he boarded it up.

24: Although she was not the first to wear a white dress, **Queen Victoria** is credited as starting the tradition of a white wedding when she married Prince Albert in 1840. Prior to this time, colors were preferred with blue being the most common for the reason Orpha cites. The queen's wore a plain cream-colored gown covered with Honiton lace designed by William Dyce, head of the Government School of Design. The choice was made not only because she wanted to look beautiful, but also because she wanted to help promote Britain's lace industry. She succeeded in both.

25: While many sources recount the fate of **David Creigh**, who is often called "The Greenbrier Martyr," this account is derived chiefly from the application to the National Register of Historic Places through the United States Department of the Interior for Montescena, the Creigh estate. A copy can be found at www.wvculture.org/shpo/nr/pdf/greenbrier/75001888.pdf

26: Although **mourning** traditions existed prior to the Civil War, they became increasingly more important with the tremendous number of lives lost. The practices that Orpha describes became the standard, once again, due to the trend set by Queen Victoria who remained in mourning for the remainder of her life after her beloved husband died in 1859. Many sources exist to describe mourning practices, including: http://www.encyclopediavirginia.org/mourning_during_the_civil_war

27: The story of **Virginia Alderson** can be found in McKinney, Tim, *The Civil War in Greenbrier County, West Virginia*. Charleston, WV: Quarrier Press, 2004. A similar story of a convalescent soldier falling in love with his nurse in Greenbrier County is that of Major D.S. Hounshell and Miss Lou Rodgers, the eighteen year-old beauty who was preparing his food. They married and she joined him in their military campaigns, earning the affectionate nickname, "Little Major." Dayton, *Greenbrier Pioneers and Their Homes,* pp. 233-234.

28: For more information on **Dick Pointer** and the attack on Fort Donnally on May 29, 1778, is see Dayton, *Greenbrier Pioneers and Their Homes*, pp. 274-276.

29: The **fish fry** story is attributed by Ruth Woods Dayton to Dr. Milton Wylie Humphreys. Humphreys was an extraordinary man who was born at Anthony's Creek in 1844 and discovered that he was good at "figgering." He enrolled at Washington College (now Washington and Lee University) in 1861, but left in 1862 when he was of age to serve in the Confederate army. Humphreys enlisted in Bryan's Battery of the 13th Virginia Light Artillery and set a precedent for modern warfare by firing an indirect cannon missile. He wrote about his experiences in a diary and in his book *Military Operations in Fayette County, West Virginia.* After the war, he continued his studies at Washington College, graduating in 1869 with a Masters, and then earned a PhD from the University of Leipzig. He became the first professor of Latin and Greek at Vanderbilt University and the University of Texas at Austin. Humphreys spent the rest of his career at the University of Virginia. He also served as the President of the American Philological Association in 1882-1883.

30: Records of the incident with **Joseph Newton and Tom the slave** can be found at the Greenbrier Historical Society including the sum of money allotted to Reverend McElhenney to investigate and the order for a casket for Tom's body. Whether the casket was built and used is unknown. The story is also recounted by Ruth Woods Dayton.

31: The foiled **slave revolt** of 1861 is recounted in many sources including McKinney, Tim, *The Civil War in Greenbrier County, West Virginia.*

32: **Barbree Allen,** and the other songs listed are popular Appalachian folk songs.

33: **Elmhurst.** The description given is a fairly accurate depiction of the house as it appeared in a photograph of the North Caldwell family taken around 1890, with the exception that the house did have a door leading out to the second story porch.

34-35: The story of **Martin Van Buren**'s visit is taken from Dayton, *Greenbrier Pioneers and Their Homes*. She also tells an amusing story of **Henry Clay**'s visit to the town of Lewisburg. In 1826, was staying at the White Sulphur hotel. When this situation was discovered, a public meeting was held and a committee was formed to invite him to be the guest of the town. Congressman William Smith was designated to supervise the preparations. On the day of Clay's arrival, the town was decorated with flags and bunting, the streets were lined with people, and a bugler sounded when Mr. Clay reached the top of Hardscrabble Hill on the east of town. Mr. Clay was to be entertained in Frazier's Tavern and more than two hundred dinner guests were to accompany him. However, when the time arrived to introduce the special guest, Congressman Smith, who was supposed to have the honor, was nowhere to be found. Evidently, the way the political winds were blowing that morning, he thought it would be a danger to his career to be seen endorsing Mr. Clay. A new toastmaster was chosen and Mr. Clay, gave a long speech that refuted his enemies and spoke of his support for improvements to the Kanawha Turnpike which greatly pleased his audience.

36: Andrew Jackson Downing's ***Cottage Residences,*** was published in 1842, to great acclaim. He is often called the Father of American Landscape Architecture, although some reserve the title for Frederick Law Olmsted (who Captain Tobin references later). Among his most important projects, Downing drew the plan for the Smithsonian Mall in Washington DC. Sadly, Downing died at the age of thirty-six in a boat fire while aboard the steamer *Henry Clay.*

37: **Catharine Beecher** was a writer and lecturer who was as equally well-known to her contemporaries as her sister of Harriet Beecher Stowe, author of *Uncle Tom's Cabin*. She wrote twenty-one published works including her *Domestic Receipt Book*, and helped found five colleges for women. Although she advocated separate spheres of influence for men and women, she believed that women should be well educated and engaged, especially in their role as teachers.

38: **The Virginia House-Wife** by Mary Randolph was published in 1824 and tried to improve women's lives by limiting the time they had to spend in their kitchens. It included many inexpensive ingredients that anyone could purchase and popularized the use of more than forty vegetables. Randolph was a descendent of Pocahontas and was related through marriage to Thomas Jefferson. She was a cousin of Mary Lee Fitzhugh Custis, wife to George Washington Parke Custis, builder of Arlington National cemetery and was the first person recorded to be buried at Arlington.

39: A **drugget** was a rug of coarse fabric that was placed over carpets to protect them from the dirt and wear of everyday life. They were removed when families entertained and wanted their carpets to be seen.

40: **The Workwoman's Guide** by "a Lady," was published in 1838. It contained "instructions in cutting out and completing articles of wearing apparel &c., which are usually made at home; also explanations on upholstery, straw-platting, bonnet-making, knitting, &c." https://archive.org/details/workwomansguide00workgoog

41: Moreen is a strong fabric of wool, wool and cotton, or cotton with a plain glossy or moiré finish.

42: Johan Edvard and his younger brother Carl Frans Lundström started a large-scale industry manufacturing **safety**

matches in Jönköping, Sweden around 1847, but the improved safety match was not introduced until around 1850–55. By 1858, their company produced around 12 million match boxes a year and held a virtual monopoly on match production for many years.

43: Women in the 1860s wore **many layers of clothes** and the process of dressing was extensive. Below are the items women wore in the order that they were layered:

- Chemise—similar to a modern woman's nightgown. They were generally made from cotton.
- Stockings—made of wool, cotton, or silk, worn the knee, and held in place by garters.
- Drawers—shin length underpants usually made from cotton. Often they were split in the crotch to make visits to the outhouse easier. Some women tucked their chemises into their drawers.
- Corset—corsets were used to accentuate the waist and support the breasts. They were stiffened with strips of bone or metal and sometimes tied so tightly that they caused physical harm.
- Shirt
- Hoop
- Dress

For a step-by-step illustration, see http://www.memorialhall. mass.edu/activities/dressup/notflash/1860_woman.html

44: **Charles Frederick Worth** is considered by many to be the Father of Haute couture. An Englishman, he moved to Paris in 1846 at the age of twenty-one to work for a well known Parisian draper. Worth began making clothes for his wife and opened his own dressmaking establishment in 1858.

45: The stylish French **Empress Eugenie,** wife of Napoleon III, patronized him and helped popularize his designs.

46: No proof exists to support the claim that **General**

Stonewall Jackson relished lemons, but it was widely believed at the time.

47: The story of the **andirons** is told by Ruth Woods Dayton in her chapter on Elmhurst.

48: Many sources provide information about the **Richmond Bread Riots**, including "Bread Riot in Richmond, 1863" EyeWitness to History, www.eyewitnesstohistory.com (2009) and the Encyclopedia of Virginia http://www.encyclopediavirginia. org/bread_riot_richmond#start_entry.

The Confederate Receipt Book: A Compilation of over one Hundred Receipts, Adapted to the Times was published by G. W. Gary in 1863 to help women cope with the shortages of supplies. Its introduction states:

> *The accompanying receipts have been compiled and published with a view to present to the public in a form capable of preservation and easy reference many valuable receipts which have appeared in the Southern newspapers since the commencement of the war. With these have been incorporated receipts and hints derived from other sources, all designed to supply useful and economical directions and suggestions in cookery, housewifery, &c., and for the camp. Should the present publication meet with favor, another edition with additional receipts will be published, contributions to which will be thankfully received by THE PUBLISHERS.*

49: The stories of **Reverend McElhenney** are taken from Ruth Woods Dayton, *Greenbrier Pioneers and Their Homes* and Rose W. Fry *Recollections of Rev. John McElhenney.*

50: **Prices** were taken from Varhola, Michael J. *Everyday Life During The Civil War: A Guide for Writers, Students, and Historians.* Cincinnati, OH: Writer's Digest Books, 1999.

51: According to Wiley, Bell I. *The Life of Billy Yank: The Common Soldier of the Union,* New York: The Bobbs-Merrill Company, Inc., 1952, Northern and Southern soldiers had different war cries. "The standard Yankee version was a deeply intoned hurrah or huzza, while the Southern cry was a wild, **piercing yell.**"

52: **General David Hunter** was 62 years old when he took command in Greenbrier County. The Confederate government had declared him a felon for his use of Negro troops and his enfranchisement of blacks in North Carolina. He was known to be stern and severe and to have frequent fits of sudden anger.

53: A letter from **Mrs. Henrietta E. Lee** to General Hunter decrying the burning of her home can be found in Jones, Katharine M. *Heroines of Dixie: Confederate Women Tell Their Story of the War.* New York: The Bobbs-Merrill Company, Inc., 1955. Further information about Hunter and the actions of the First New York Cavalry in Lexington, Virginia can be found in that volume in Cornelia Peake McDonald's account "Hunter Burns the VMI."

54: This information about **recruiting** and the early stages of enlistment is taken from Wiley, Bell I. *The Life of Billy Yank: The Common Soldier of the Union,* and Pickerill, *William N., History of the Third Indiana Cavalry*, Indianapolis, IN: Aetna Printing Co., 1906. The former relies on letters and diaries while the latter is a memoir from a former soldier.

55: **The Greenbrier Hotel** was used as a Confederate hospital during the Civil War. General Hunter issued an order for the hotel and all of its buildings to be burned; however, Captain Henry A. DuPont convinced him to rescind the order. Tim McKinney, *The Civil War in Greenbrier County, West Virginia.*

56: **Thaddeus Stevens** was a member of the US House of Representatives from Pennsylvania and one of the most active and vocal leaders of the abolitionists in Congress who became known as the Radical Republicans. After the Civil War, he championed the idea of giving the freedmen forty acres and a mule.

57: *The Horrors of the Black Death* is fictional. I know of no book by that title.

58: **Rag dolls** and other similar items were used to smuggle messages and medical supplies. Another fascinating toy that originated at this time is the topsy-turvy doll. These are cloth dolls where two opposing figures are fused at the hips with clothing that flips over and hides one head at a time. During the Civil War period, these dolls featured both a white face and a brown or black-faced character. Historians are not certain as to the purpose of these dolls. Some speculate that Harriet Beecher Stowe chose the name for her character Topsy in *Uncle Tom's Cabin* from the doll.

59: **Philomela** is a Greek Myth and the inspiration behind William Shakespeare's *Titus Andronicus*.

60: **Camp Thomas** was a US Regular Army training camp used to organize and train infantry.

61: When the Civil War began, medical knowledge still centered on Humorism, the Ancient Greek idea of bringing the four humors of the body, blood, yellow bile, black bile, and phlegm, into balance. The practice of **"Heroic Medicine"** included bloodletting, purging, sweating, and blistering. Doctors had no knowledge of germ theory or antiseptics. As a result, for every Civil War soldier that died of an injury or gunshot wound, more than two died from dysentery, diarrhea or other infectious diseases. One of the positive outcomes of the War was that it helped to modernize medicine: the techniques that were developed to treat the sick and wounded soldiers led to many advances.

62: **Frederick Law Olmsted** began his career as a journalist. From 1852-1857, he was commissioned by *The New York Daily*

Times, which became *The New York Times,* to write about the slave economy. His dispatches were published in a three-volume work was a scathing indictment of the system. In 1858, Olmsted won a design contest to improve New York City's Central Park and began overseeing the construction of it that same year. He took leave from this position in 1861 to serve as Executive Secretary for the US Sanitary Commission. Olmsted also raised three Colored regiments from New York City and organized a fair that grossed one million dollars for the US Sanitary Commission.

63: **The Crimean War** was fought from 1853-1856 along the Black Sea between Britain, France, and the Ottoman Empire against Russia. One of the most notable features of the war was the improvements made in the treatment of the wounded, especially the professionalism of the nurses led by Florence Nightingale.

64: **Dr. Jonathan Letterman** is known as "The Father of Battlefield Medicine." In 1849, he became an assistant surgeon in the Army Medical Department. When the War broke out, he was first assigned to the Army of the Potomac and in 1862, was named medical director for the Department of West Virginia. Later that year, he was appointed to the rank of Major and named medical director for the Army of the Potomac. In this capacity, he designed a system of forward first aid stations where principles of triage were introduced. He organized the intake system, field hospitals, the distribution of supplies, and the ambulance corps. Letterman resigned his commission in 1864 and moved to San Francisco. The army hospital at the Presidio is named for him.

65: **"Before Sumter"** is a reference to the firing on Fort Sumter in April, 1861, which is considered the beginning of the Civil War.

66: A **haversack** was actually a small envelope-style shoulder bag that soldiers carried a soldiers rations. It was often called a "bread bag." According to Bell Wiley's *The Life of Billy Yank,* a soldier would have been issued a haversack, canteen, blanket, and knapsack. The knapsack would have held such items as "underclothes, stationery, photographs, toothbrush, razor, soap, books, letters, and a mending kit known as a 'housewife.' Mess equipment, comprising a metal plate, knife, fork, spoon and cup —and sometimes a light skillet—was usually divided between knapsack and hooks attached to the belt." However, Wiley explains that as the war progressed, soldiers reduced the loads that they had to carry. The first item to be discarded was the knapsack. Soldiers wrapped their personal belongings in their blanket. As a wealthy man, Captain Tobin has a well-made haversack that holds his personal items and food.

67: Information about the occupations of **free inhabitants of color** in Greenbrier County were compiled by Carol L. Haynes from census data and individual researchers and can be found at http://www.wvgenweb.org/greenbrier/aa/free.htm.

68: More information about **rape** can be found in Murphy, Kate, *I Had Rather Die: Rape in the Civil War.* Batesville, Virginia: Coachlight Press, 2014.

69: "**Rab and his Friends**" is a short story by Scottish writer Dr. John Brown about an old, grey, brindled mastiff that was published in 1859 and was popular among adults. It was often published as a single volume with illustrations.

70: A **pit school** was a secret school for African American children in the antebellum South where education was prohibited. Classes were often held at night in pits that could be covered and hidden.

71: **4711 Eau de Cologne** was created in the late 18th century in Cologne, Germany. The name is derived from the street address where Wilhelm Mulhens operated a small factory to produce the fragrance. Although the original label was brown, I described it with its modern signature blue and gold label.

72: According the Bell Wiley's *The Life of Billy Yank* many letters written by Union soldiers stationed in the south mentioned Southern women using **tobacco products**, most notably snuff. Even the children were said to be addicted.

73: In order to outfit the steamboats that were being built in New Albany with engines, boilers, and other types of machinery, the city became a center for iron works. The **Phoenix Foundry** was established in 1825 under the name Morton & Cox Foundry. It was the first in the city and at its height in the 1840s and 1850s, it employed 150 men. Although the Civil War brought an end to boat building in New Albany, the city continued as a center for rolling mills and iron works until the Great Depression of the 1930s.

74: The historical novel *Ivanhoe* is Sir Walter Scott's most famous work. Published in 1820, it tells the story of Wilfred of Ivanhoe, a disinherited Medieval knight who struggles to restore himself to favor with his father, win the love of the fair lady Rowena, and protect the crown of King Richard the Lion-hearted from his usurping brother Prince John. In his quest, Ivanhoe must fight in a tournament, siege a castle, and grapple with his feelings for the beautiful Rebecca, daughter of Isaac the Jew. Ivanhoe receives assistance along the way from the famous outlaw Robin Hood.

75: According to Wiley's *The Life of Billy Yank,* **reading** was an important source of relaxation and entertainment for the Union soldiers. A high degree of literacy existed among the ranks and reading material was abundant: everything from newspapers to dime novels to high fiction from authors such as Victor Hugo, John Milton, William Shakespeare, and Sir Walter Scott. Through a process of competitive bidding, General Hooker awarded John M. Lamb a contract for $53.20 a day to supply newspapers to the army of the Potomac and Lamb provided newspapers to other commands at five cents a copy. The Christian Commission arranged for publishers to ship magazines to the Army of the Cumberland and established loan libraries in hospitals.

76: The **log and chain** was a common punishment for runaway slaves. One man who suffered this fate in Greenville, Mississippi was William Massey who later became a minister and educator. Massey recounted how "a log and chain was placed upon my legs and I was forced to drag them around. During this sad experience of 1859, I professed a hope in Christ and my master licensed me to preach."

77: The slave auction depicted here is fictional. The **Town Clock Church**, now the Second Baptist Church of New Albany, Indiana, was a station on the Underground Railroad.

78: **"Powder Monkey"** is a term coined in the Seventeenth Century to describe the boys between the ages of twelve and fourteen who served in the navy and delivered stores of gunpowder from the magazine in the ships hold to the artillery pieces.

79: **The Emancipation Proclamation** was issued by President Abraham Lincoln on January 1, 1863, five months before the incident described in *Lies*.

80: **Hardtack** is a type of biscuit made from flour, water, and salt. It is inexpensive and long-lasting. Variations of hardtack have been a military staple since Ancient Egypt. To eat it, the hardtack must be softened in a liquid. During the Civil War, soldiers dunked it in coffee or mashed it up and used the meal to make a pancake. If supplies allowed, they would also add sugar and whiskey to the mash to create a pudding-like desert.

81: **Nicknames** were commonly used by the soldiers, everything from "Fox" to "Piss-ant."

82: The story that Walker tells Orpha and Margaret about volunteering is taken from an interview that Arch Rowand gave to *Harper's*. Rowand was in the First West Virginia Cavalry when his captain asked for volunteers. He and his friend Ike Harris both stepped forward. After they were taken to headquarters and given Confederate uniforms to wear, Rowan said, "we wished we had not come," but they, "hadn't the face to back down." Later, they were assigned to General Phillip Sheridan and became known as "**Jessie Scouts.**" http://www.jessiescouts.com/Jessie%20 Scouts%20Home.html

83: **Sutlers** were civilian merchants who sold provisions to the soldiers.

84: Although her two brothers fought for the North, **Nancy Hart** became a spy for the Confederacy, joining Perry Conley and his Moccasin Rangers. She trained as a nurse and used this cover to garner information about Union troop movement for Stonewall Jackson. The story of her escape is documented as being true.

85: **Euchre** is a trick-taking card game that was extremely popular at this time.

86: **Typhus** is a disease spread by parasites such as fleas and ticks that begins with flu-like symptoms, progresses to a rash, and then inflammation of the brain. If left untreated, it causes death. Outbreaks of typhus were common in the nineteenth century.

87: **Aura Lee** is an American folk song. Elvis Presley used the melody for his hit song, "Love Me Tender."

88: **The Fireman's Polka** was a popular dance tune at the time.

89: The idea for **Frank's death** came from a story about HR Hodson during the Battle of Lewisburg. A member of Edgar's Battalion, Hodson was stationed behind a rail fence. Not knowing that a comrade of his had already loaded his gun, Hodson loaded it again. As soon as he caught sight of the Union troops, he fired. The recoil from the shot knocked him unconscious. When he came to, his comrades were gone. He tried to run away, but he was captured and imprisoned in a store on Washington Street.

The next morning, a Federal officer asked him, "What kind of powder do you fellows use now?" Hodson replied, "Why do you ask?" "Because yesterday, just as we reached the church, one shot was fired and I can swear that it was but one shot, but it killed two men and wounded a third." Hodson wanted to add that, "It nearly killed a fourth, namely me," but he thought it best not to reply.

90: The **lullaby** that Scant is singing is the Scottish folk song "Castles in the Sky."

91: The first professional tattoo artist in the US was German immigrant **Martin Hildebrandt** who tattooed both Union and Confederate soldiers.

92: On May 22 and 23, 1865, exactly 2 years after the fictitious incident in this book, over 145,000 surviving Union soldiers paraded down Pennsylvania Avenue in Washington DC in what was called the **Grand Review of the Armies**.

93: Many abolitionists like the Radical Republican Thaddeus Stevens understood that without a means of support, the former slaves were getting, "Nothin' but freedom." Accordingly, Stevens proposed giving the freedmen **forty acres and a mule**.

94: The First New York Cavalry was mustered into the United States service between July 16 and August 31, 1861. From August 1863 to August 1864, they served with the Army of West Virginia and fought in West Virginia, Pennsylvania, Maryland, and Virginia. Although I did not locate any evidence to support their being in Greenbrier County, passing through the area on their way to Maryland was not out of the realm of possibility. Interestingly, in a report filed by Colonel James A. Galligher, Thirteenth Pennsylvania Cavalry, about a scouting mission he undertook from Winchester, VA, to Hampshire County, WV, in May 1863, Galligher comments, "My duty will not allow me to close this report without mention of the conduct of the First New York Cavalry. All my attempts to keep them in order were ineffectual, and the regiment seemed entirely undisciplined, and beyond the control of its own officers. At no time was more than half the regiment together; but they straggled in all directions, and I am informed stole about 15 horses, which were taken with them, and for which the various [owners] are now demanding restitution." http://www.wvculture.org/history/sesquicentennial/18630504b.html

95: **Elizabeth Keckley** was a former slave who became Mary Todd Lincoln's seamstress and confidante.

96: Anna Ella Carroll was a pamphleteer and lecturer who worked with the Lincoln cabinet on issues pertaining to emancipation. Like many abolitionists, she favored colonization, sending former slaves out of the United States to establish colonies in the Caribbean.

97: In addition to her pioneering work as a nurse during the war, **Clara Barton** also established the Office of Missing Soldiers after the war in Washington DC to help families receive information about their loved ones. Her work in this regard had been long forgotten when a government worker stumbled upon artifacts in the building that was slated for destruction. Fortunately, the building and its collections were saved and is in the process of being restored as a museum.

98: Samuel joins the **7th Cavalry,** the ill-fated regiment led by Civil War hero Lieutenant Colonel George Custer that was defeated by the Lakota at the Battle of Little Big Horn.

CPSIA information can be obtained
at www.ICGtesting.com
Printed in the USA
LVOW08s0117050817
543768LV00009B/88/P

9 781942 294092